Fake Dates
AND
Mooncakes

Fake Dates AND Mooncakes

SHER LEE

UNDERLINED

Text copyright © 2023 by Sher Lee
Cover art copyright © 2023 by Myriam Strasbourg

GetUnderlined.com

Educators and librarians, for a variety of teaching tools, visit us at RHTeachersLibrarians.com

Library of Congress Cataloging-in-Publication Data is available upon request.
ISBN 978-0-593-56995-5 (pbk.) — ISBN 978-0-593-56996-2 (ebook)

The text of this book is set in 10-point Dante eText.
Interior design by Ken Crossland

Printed in the United States of America
1st Printing
First Edition

To Mum and Dad,
for always believing

Chapter 1

Something's burning. Aunt Jade says if the smoke's white, it's all good. But if the smoke is yellow, I'm in trouble. Which means I have to decide whether I should save the fried radish and egg pancake I forgot to flip or the five sticks of pork satay blackening on the grill.

As the charred scent wafts through the kitchen, I dive for the sticks of skewered pork cubes. The fat on the meat burns with a ton of smoke, and if the fire alarm goes off and the sprinklers kick in, we're all screwed.

Megan snatches the pan with the sizzling pancake off the fire. She shoots me a look. "Dylan, weren't you supposed to be watching the chye tow kuay?"

"*T*-minus three on order number thirty-eight, sixteen xiao long bao!" Tim calls through the serving window. He's eleven, so he's not allowed into the war zone, but he's handling the counter like a boss, taking orders online and from walk-ins. Tim wrote an algorithm to crunch data and determine *T*, the time hangry customers detonate and cancel their orders. "And Auntie Heng's still waiting for her Hokkien prawn mee!"

"I'm on the xiao long bao!" I snatch the cover off the steamer basket and carefully scoop the soup dumplings into a box lined with waxed paper. Like an unstable element, a xiao long bao has a core of minced pork surrounded by a volatile mixture of soup and wrapped inside a thin layer of dough. If the dough breaks, the soup will leak out. One of us will still eat the ruined dumpling, but we should be selling food, not putting it into our stomachs.

Chinese people believe names have a powerful effect on how something or someone will turn out, which is why most restaurants are called some variation of *Happy, Lucky,* or *Golden.* Something serene, positive . . . nonviolent. When Aunt Jade set up her Singaporean Chinese takeout here in Brooklyn, New York, she should've known better than to call it Wok Warriors.

But maybe there's more truth to our takeout's name than meets the eye. Aunt Jade's a warrior at the stove, tuned out to the chaos and completely focused on conquering her signature stir-fried egg fried rice. The cast-iron wok can burn as hot as the sun, but she doesn't flinch as flames roar up around it. She grips the handle and uses the curved side of the wok to flip the fried rice into the air. Tossing the food nonstop is the secret to capturing the elusive wok hei—the "breath of the wok," a deliciously smoky, flame-singed aroma that lingers on your tongue.

Tim sticks his head through the window again. "Chung called—he's got a flat tire! What should we do about these orders that're ready to go?"

Shit. Our delivery radius in Brooklyn covers Sunset Park and Bay Ridge, and we usually have two guys on motorbikes handling deliveries. But Uncle Bo's sick—we call anyone around our parents' age Uncle or Auntie, though we aren't related—so Chung's flying solo tonight. It's Labor Day weekend, and we're slammed with orders.

I look at Aunt Jade and my cousins. Aunt Jade has a splash of soy sauce on her sleeve. Megan's using a pizza wheel instead of a knife to chop spring onions more quickly. Tim's frowning as he checks the timestamp on five orders waiting to be delivered.

There's a Cantonese phrase Aunt Jade likes to use: "Sup gor cha wu, gau gor goi." Ten teapots, but only nine lids to cover them.

"I'll do it." I yank off my apron and hang it up. "I've got my bike."

We try not to stack more than three orders in each run so the food won't arrive cold, but we don't have a choice. Tim and I load the boxes of food into a gigantic warmer bag, which is so bulky and full it threatens to throw off the balance of my bike. Hopefully I won't wobble into a dumpster or clip one of the cars double-parked along the avenues. Which will give our takeout's name a whole new meaning, since I'll have to wok back. Megan hates my bad puns.

I strap my helmet on and ride along the side of the road, avoiding puddles in gutters clogged with litter and dead leaves. This is the first weekend of September, and even after the sun has gone down, the city's still a giant oven. A thunderstorm drenched the streets earlier, and now the air is not only hot but also unbearably humid. Before I arrive at the first destination, my T-shirt's soaked with sweat.

I make four deliveries, apologizing for the delay each time. My last stop is a Bay Ridge condo on 74th Street. I enter the lobby and show the doorman the slip Tim always staples neatly onto the corner of the paper bag. The order's for "Adrian R." I hope he'll tell me to leave the food at the front desk so I can get out of here.

The doorman picks up the phone and dials. "Good evening, Mr. Rogers? There's a rider with a meal delivery for you. Certainly, I'll send him right up."

Tonight's really not my night.

I'm headed to the penthouse. When the elevator opens, a guy in his late teens stands in the doorway. He's wearing an oversized Fendi T-shirt over his shorts. With his platinum-blond hair and hollow cheekbones, he could be on the runway at New York Fashion Week. But he's not my type, especially when he's glaring at me like I'm a piece of gum stuck to the sole of his calfskin loafers.

"Adrian R.?" I ask, walking briskly toward him.

"About time," Adrian snaps. "I don't care how good your fried rice is, it shouldn't take over an hour to get here. People need to eat, you know."

My lips are parched from thirst. My fingers are raw from shredding ginger. My feet are sore from rushing around the kitchen and pedaling my bike faster than ever. But sure. People need to eat.

"Sorry for the long wait." I hand him the paper bag. Over his shoulder is a stunning view of the Brooklyn skyline through the floor-to-ceiling windows. "Enjoy the food."

I'm about five feet to the elevator when an outburst makes me spin around.

"What the hell is this?" Adrian holds up the box of fried rice, his face contorted with disgust. "This isn't what I ordered!"

I warily retrace my steps. Tim rarely messes up the instructions. "Ten sticks of pork satay and two boxes of egg fried rice with shrimp?"

"AND NO SPRING ONIONS!" Adrian rips the slip from the bag and thrusts the piece of paper in my face. "The note is right here! So why is my dinner covered with clumps of gross green stuff?"

Tim even highlighted the special instructions in yellow. But in the chaos, we all missed it. The spring onions are sprinkled on top and can be scraped off. But I get the feeling that suggestion may make our angry customer go nuclear.

"I'm sorry, this is our fault," I say. "Your food was paid for on-line, and the refund will go back to the credit card you—"

"I don't want a refund. I want what I ORDERED!" Adrian explodes. Road rage is bad, but food delivery rage is on a whole other level. "Am I supposed to be happy to have MY OWN money returned for dinner I PAID FOR but didn't GET after waiting for over AN HOUR? What kind of moron do you think I am?"

"Come on, baby." Another male voice drifts from inside. "Let's order pizza, okay?"

The guy who comes into view makes my train of thought jump the tracks. He's around my age and looks half Asian, half white. He's wearing nothing but boxer briefs—which means Adrian's parents probably aren't home and the two of them have the entire condo to themselves. And all I can think is, why is Adrian having a meltdown at the poor delivery guy when he could be, I don't know, licking whipped cream off those abs for dinner and dessert?

"Stay out of this, Theo. I'm handling it." Adrian glowers at me. "What if I'm fatally allergic to spring onions? And all you can say is sorry? Is your chef blind or illiterate?"

Blood rushes to my brain. Aunt Jade works six days a week from dawn to midnight. She never gets to let her hair down—literally, since she's always wearing a chef's hairnet, doing the kind of backbreaking work I'm pretty sure this guy has never done in his life.

"You have every reason to be upset that your food wasn't prepared the way you wanted," I retort. "But you have no right to insult the chef, who happens to be my aunt."

"I honestly don't care." Adrian points a finger in my face. "You know what? Since you're not even remorseful, I want compensation."

I blink. "You didn't eat the food. And we're giving you a full refund—"

"I want compensation for the emotional distress you've caused. Punitive damages are a thing. My dad's a senior partner at his law firm."

I bite on my lip, reining in my anger. Threatening legal action is nuts, but if he's allergic, we could've made him sick. Food preparation is a responsibility, and we screwed up this time.

Because we ran late on this batch of deliveries, I ended up getting more frowns than tips this evening. I dig into my pocket and pull out a few crumpled fives. Guess Clover won't be getting her favorite bacon dog treats this week.

"I'm sorry, this is all I've got on me," I say. "If you want more, you'll have to call the shop and talk to my aunt—"

"Adrian, stop it. I mean that."

The guy he called Theo comes to the door. His brown hair is short on the sides and sticking up in wet spikes on top. His boxer briefs have ARMANI on the waistband. I always wonder why people bother splurging on branded underwear practically no one else gets to see. Maybe it's for times like this, when the delivery guy has had a tough night and could use a pick-me-up. Okay,

6

Dylan. Stop staring. You don't need to give his boyfriend another reason to murder you.

"Fine, whatever," Adrian says to Theo before narrowing his eyes at me. "I'm never ordering from you again. And I'll be leaving one-star ratings on all the review sites, telling everyone how your food could've KILLED me."

He shoves the box of fried rice into my hands and slams the door in my face.

I stand there, stunned, before I walk away. As I exit the building, Chung texts that he's fixed his flat tire and he can take care of the rest of tonight's deliveries.

Stifling convections of heat and exhaust fill the air as I sit on the curb next to my chained bike. My stomach lets out a growl, and I open the takeout box. They say culinary masters dish out fried rice with a bit of egg stuck to every grain. I'm probably biased, but I bet Aunt Jade could give them a run for their money. I take the plastic spoon and shovel the fried rice into my mouth. Even though the food has gone cold, it still tastes like the best thing ever after this shift from hell.

Chapter 2

"Hell definitely has something to do with that," Megan says as we clean up the kitchen after closing. "They don't call it the Hungry Ghost Month for nothing."

During the seventh lunar month—which begins in either late August or early September—Buddhists and Taoists believe the gates of hell open and ghosts of the deceased roam free in our world. Those who are superstitious don't stay out after dark or go swimming, afraid drowned spirits might come for them. Mom never believed in these traditions, and neither do I. But this year, Por Por and Gong Gong, my grandmother and grandfather back in Singapore, will perform rituals for her for the first time—putting out food on their altar and burning joss sticks and paper money.

"Well, the hungry guy on my last delivery nearly bit my head off because his fried rice had spring onions," I tell Megan. "Said I could've poisoned him and threatened to make us pay for emotional damages."

"Seriously? What a jerk."

I pour leftover Chinese tea onto the greasy worktable, which does the job getting out the oil and is more environmentally friendly than cleaning chemicals. Same with the grill, which Megan's cleaning with a leftover cut onion. The enzymes in the onion loosen the grime and grit much better than wire brushes, especially when their bristles get stuck between the grates.

I sigh. "He's going to tank our review rating. Probably get a bunch of his rich friends to pile on too. But he backed down when his boyfriend stepped in."

Athletic guys are my kryptonite, although I'm not exactly sporty—I get most of my cardio rushing around the kitchen, saving food from getting overcooked.

"How did you know he's his boyfriend?" Megan asks.

"Uh, it was pretty obvious. The boyfriend was half naked. He was lean and super toned, and his lower abs had this perfect V-cut—"

Tim, who's tallying receipts at the serving window, crinkles his nose. "Uh, Dylan, that's kind of TMI."

"What's kind of TMI?" Aunt Jade comes into the kitchen.

"Dylan got chewed out on a delivery," Megan tells her. "But all he can do is talk about the customer's hot boyfriend like he's a piece of steak."

"I did not!"

"Your words, Dyl. Lean, toned, perfect cut . . . done just the way you like it."

"Ugh, don't say that. It sounds so demeaning."

Megan smirks. "Don't worry. We're all shallow sometimes."

Megan's sixteen, a year younger than me. Mom and Aunt Jade were only a year apart too. Mom and Dad met at NYU and continued working in the city. After they divorced, Dad left to start his own business in Shanghai. Aunt Jade went to culinary school in Hong Kong, where she met Megan and Tim's dad. When they split up, Aunt Jade moved here with Megan and Tim.

Aunt Jade's dream is to have her own dine-in restaurant serving authentic Singaporean Chinese food. This little takeout is all she has for now. Sunset Park is home to Brooklyn's Chinatown, but the rent on Eighth Avenue is way too expensive. Since we're takeout and delivery only, we're tucked away in a quieter spot near the parkway, sandwiched between a laundromat and a comic-book store. This crazy, chaotic kitchen . . . it's home. Literally. We live in a small two-bedroom apartment on the second floor, which is connected to the shop by a flight of stairs behind the counter. I share a room with Tim, and Megan shares with Aunt Jade.

Tim goes to count the cash in the register and Aunt Jade heads out the back door lugging two bags of trash.

Megan nudges me. "Have you been bringing in the mail every day for the past week?"

I shake my head. "I thought you were the one stalking the mailbox for your Blackpink merch."

Megan sighs. "Not again."

Aunt Jade intercepts the mail only when there's a letter she doesn't want us to see . . . such as overdue notices on our rent. She never says anything, but we know money's tight. Suppliers are giving shorter credit. The cost of ingredients has gone up. Raising our prices is difficult to do because of stiff competition. Tim borrowed a violin from the music school after the wood on his old one cracked, and Megan stopped asking for a new phone and fixed her screen with clear tape.

"You're always watching TikTok," I tell her. "Can you make a funny clip about Wok Warriors that'll get a gazillion views?"

"If going viral was so easy, don't you think I'd have done it already?" Megan scrubs a wok with a special scouring brush. The cast-iron woks we use are handmade by a Chinese ironsmith in Shandong with a two-year waitlist. "I've been ramping up our social media presence, but people have the attention span of goldfish—"

Footsteps approach outside, and we break off as Aunt Jade comes back in. She's too deep in thought to have overheard us talking. Megan and I exchange glances.

I head outside to bring in our standing signboard advertising our weekly specials. This week, the deal is $5.95 for eight xiao long bao. A gust sends a flurry of dead leaves swirling. It's like the sound of washing rice, uncooked grains swirling inside a pot. A flyer taped to our shop window rustles in the wind, catching my attention: MID-AUTUMN FESTIVAL MOONCAKE-MAKING CONTEST: THE NEW GENERATION.

The Mid-Autumn Festival is the second biggest celebration after the Lunar New Year. It's on the fifteenth day of the eighth lunar month, which corresponds to late September or early October—this year, it's at the end of September. All the China-towns in New York City will be decked in lanterns, and in Sunset Park, the celebrations on Eighth Avenue will stretch from 50th to 66th Streets. Thousands will show up to watch performances, visit street bazaars, and of course, eat delicious mooncakes.

Mom was the one who saw this flyer last year, but by then, the registration deadline had passed. The contest is targeted at teen bakers—full-time students between sixteen and nineteen. Each can be accompanied by a sous-chef of any age, such as a sibling, grandparent, parent, or friend. Eight pairs will be chosen for the contest.

"Let's enter the contest together next year," Mom had said. "When I was little, I used to help your Por Por make her special snow-skin mooncakes. They were the most beautiful shade of blue. She learned the recipe from her grandmother." She'd grinned. "You and me, we'll show them how it's done."

I pick up the flyer. Something tugs inside my chest like a thread pulled too tightly. This time last year, she hadn't discovered the lump yet. Suddenly my throat is tight, and I feel as if sand's gotten in my eyes. Grief has a way of sneaking up on you when you're least expecting it. A song, a phrase, a scent . . . then you're falling into an empty space inside that you thought you'd patched. That you thought could bear the weight.

I force my attention back to the contest. It will be held at the culinary studio of Lawrence Lim, a celebrity chef from Malaysia who now lives in Manhattan. His show, *Off the Eaten Path*, highlights culturally diverse food places all over New York City. It's one of the highest rated programs on network TV and has spun off a bestselling cookbook, culinary classes, and a range of ready-to-cook premix spice pastes, which have been flying off the grocery store shelves. (Even Aunt Jade agrees the sayur lodeh gravy—an Indonesian-style mixed vegetable dish stewed in coconut curry—is the closest to the real thing you can get out of a box.)

The winner of the mooncake contest will not only get to join Lawrence on an upcoming episode of his show, but also choose the food spot to be featured.

Excitement rushes through me. For most contestants, appearing on the show with Lawrence would be thrilling enough—but for me, getting Wok Warriors on *Off the Eaten Path* is the main prize.

Mom used to say Mid-Autumn is a time for family. For re-union. This will be the first year she won't be with us at the fes-tival. Joining the contest is the perfect way to remember her and give our takeout the big break we've been looking for. All I need to do is make the winning mooncake with a recipe that's been passed down for generations.

I bring the flyer inside and lock the doors behind me. We had a break-in a few months ago—they smashed the register and took five hundred dollars. Chung helped Aunt Jade install an alarm sys-tem and put a motion-activated chime on the door. The four of us live here with my dog, Clover the corgi. She's fierce, but she's not a guard dog. The thought of someone breaking in and com-ing upstairs while we're asleep . . . it's scarier than ghosts. Even hungry ones.

Chapter 3

It's Sunday morning. We don't open for another hour, but the heat's so unbearable I wedge the shop door open to let in a breeze. Most Chinese takeouts are painted red, an auspicious color. But Aunt Jade chose green, which is also lucky and stands out.

There's a small ledge and a few wooden stools in the front of the shop for people waiting for their orders. A white porcelain fortune cat sits on the counter next to the register, its right paw waving rhythmically to welcome customers and bring good luck. A dive bar used to occupy this space, and Aunt Jade couldn't afford renovations beyond the kitchen. So the interior of our Chinese takeout looks like a pub, with exposed ceiling beams and wood panels on the brick walls. Customers sometimes point out the odd décor, but the good food is what keeps them coming back.

I take Megan's Hello Kitty apron off a hook on the wall. My plain white one's in the wash, and I don't want to get flour all over my clean T-shirt. I push my bangs aside with the back of my hand. I need a haircut. This summer, Megan insisted I try the two-block hairstyle Korean stars love—long on top with a sharp, textured cut that can be worn in different ways. She went with me to a hair salon in Chinatown and even showed the hairstylist examples of what she was envisioning: "Give him heartthrob vibes."

I didn't want anything too edgy. I'm not in a boy band, and I don't have time to blow-dry or flat-iron my hair every morning. Besides, what's the point when the temperature outside is going to be over ninety degrees?

We settled on an undercut with medium length on top, which could be styled back with wax or left down as bangs. It turned out nicer than I expected. Even Megan was pleased.

"Your girlfriend?" the hairstylist asked.

I laughed. "My cousin."

Megan's sitting at the serving window, plucking the heads and tails off bean sprouts. Her earbuds are plugged in, and she's watching the new Blackpink music video on her phone. Aunt Jade's gone to the store to pick up some vegetables that didn't come in this morning's shipment from our supplier. Tim's at the counter, buried in a secondhand math textbook. Clover's running around, alternating between chasing her favorite spiky rubber ball and attacking the laces of my sneakers.

I sit at the small indoor pub-style table near the counter, where I've laid out ingredients for making xiao long bao. First, roll the dough into a long, skinny snake and pinch out little chunks. Flatten them into circles with the roller and scoop a ball of minced pork that's been frozen overnight. Other Chinese takeouts sell them with fillings such as crab meat, scallops, and shrimp. But since Singaporean Chinese dishes are our specialty, we're sticking to the signature pork filling.

The chime on the door dings. Clover barks.

I look up. "Sorry, but we're—"

I break off. The hot boyfriend from last night is standing in the doorway.

"Uh, hi." Theo gives me a tentative smile. He's dressed in jeans and a black T-shirt with a logo I don't recognize, which probably means it's ridiculously expensive. His hair is tousled just enough to make it seem as if he rolled out of bed like this. "I'm not sure if you remember me from your delivery last night—"

"I remember," I blurt out.

Megan raises her eyes from her K-pop video. Clover moves forward, baring her teeth.

"Clover!" I quickly grab her collar. She hates strangers, and she'll growl at anyone she doesn't know. "Sorry, she's a rescue, and she spooks easily. I've been training her not to. Hang on, let me try something."

I point my hand at Theo, keeping it extended. I step closer to him and touch his shoulder—the sign for a friendly stranger I've been teaching Clover to recognize. It worked with a couple of regulars at the dog park, but this is the first time I'm testing it out on someone she's never seen before.

I suddenly realize I'm touching Theo. I expect him to move away, but he doesn't.

Clover eyes him balefully, but she's stopped growling. She turns to me for confirmation.

"Good girl," I tell her. "Very good. Stay."

Tim looks at Theo. "Your friend's the guy who left one-star ratings on Yelp and a bunch of other review sites under the username ALLERGIC-TO-DUMBASSES?"

"Oh God. He did that? I made him swear not to." Theo sounds

thoroughly abashed. "I came here to apologize for what happened."

"It was our mistake," I say. "I made sure the refund went through."

Theo takes some cash out of his wallet. "Here. Consider it a tip."

I stare at the hundred-dollar note. "Uh, did you mean to take out a ten?"

Theo chuckles. "No, I didn't."

"What's that for?" Megan cuts in. "A lap dance?"

Theo's head whips in her direction. She strides over from the serving window and glowers at him. "What's your name?"

Theo appears caught off guard by her hostility. "Theo Somers."

Megan crosses her arms. "How'd you get a last name like that? You don't look white."

"My dad's white, and my mom's family's from Hong Kong—"

"Well, you don't seem to realize that tipping is a huge insult in Chinese culture," Megan cuts him off. "Try this in China and the waitress will chase after you, return your money, and glare at you like you're panda shit."

I scrunch my nose. Megan doesn't do subtlety.

Theo's expression falls. "I'm sorry, I didn't know—"

"Let me get this straight," Megan interrupts again. "First you let your boyfriend go ballistic on my cousin because of the spring onions in his fried rice. And now you're trying to make up for it by throwing money at him, as if he needs your charity to get by?"

The whirring of the ceiling fan is deafening in the abrupt silence. Theo looks like he just swallowed some noodles that were left in the fridge too long but is trying his best not to show it.

Megan bursts out laughing.

"Damn, your face! That was priceless. I wish I'd caught it on camera." She shoves Theo on the arm. "We're in Brooklyn, not Beijing! Hell yeah, we love good tippers! The tip jar's right there by the register!"

Theo can't hide his relief. Neither can I.

Megan grins at Theo like he's just passed some kind of test. "Since you're here, want something to eat?"

"Our weekly special is xiao long bao," Tim says. "They're five ninety-five for eight, so a hundred dollars gets you a hundred and thirty-four of them." He doesn't need to touch the calculator.

Theo gestures at the xiao long bao on the tray in front of me. "You made these?"

"Fresh every day. My aunt would never let us get away with serving ready-made frozen ones. Want to try eight for now?"

"Sure," Theo replies. "Especially since you made them."

I can't help but smile.

"Right, eight xiao long bao coming up." Megan takes the hundred-dollar note out of Theo's hand. "The change will pay for sushi on my mom's day off."

"Hang on, I thought I was getting a lap dance?" Theo deadpans.

My heart jumps into my throat, and I almost choke on it.

Megan winks at me and points a finger at Theo. "I like this guy." She grabs the tray of dumplings. "I'll go fire up the steamer. You boys stay here and chat, m'kay?"

My face burns as Megan disappears into the kitchen. My cousins letting slip that I talked about Theo after last night's delivery is more mortifying than the Hello Kitty apron I'm still wearing. I quickly take it off.

"I'm sorry, Megan loves messing around," I say. "I swear, I had no idea she was going to give you such a hard time."

"After what happened with Adrian, don't worry about it," Theo replies.

I shake my head. "She's right, though. The reason the wait-staff in China are insulted by tips is because they believe good service is part of their job. But we totally messed up your boyfriend's dinner."

I'm hoping Theo will say *"he's not my boyfriend"* and offer a perfectly reasonable explanation as to why they were getting cozy in Adrian's condo. Or why he called him *baby*.

But he doesn't. Instead, he walks to the wall next to the counter, which is covered with photos in mismatched frames. A few pictures are of Aunt Jade with Hong Kong celebs who visited the restaurants where she worked, but the rest are of family. Aunt Jade and Mom when they were kids, with Por Por and Gong Gong. Six-year-old Megan, showing the gap left by her two missing front teeth as she carries baby Tim in front of his first birthday cake. Megan, Tim, and me at the Prospect Park Zoo a couple of years ago, feeding an alpaca.

"This is in Singapore, right?" Theo points at the most recent photo with all five of us: Mom, Aunt Jade, Megan, Tim, and me. The iconic Marina Bay Sands is in the background, its three towers topped by a sky garden that looks like a giant moored ship.

"Yeah. We went last December to visit my grandparents." Tim's in that gawky, skinny phase, which made Por Por fret he's too thin. Megan's tall and long-limbed, posing with a sultry expression she picked up from her K-pop idols. Aunt Jade's wavy hair, liberated from its usual hairnet, flows in the wind. The brim 's hat casts a shadow across her pale face. Her hair had growing, but she didn't want to attract stares. She's got her sunglasses on—the chemo made her extra photosensitive.

"Were you born there?" Theo asks.

"No, but my mom and aunt were." I point at a photo of Mom and Aunt Jade in their late teens in Tokyo Disneyland. "This was their first vacation together, just the two of them."

Theo turns to me. "Do you go to school around here?"

"Sunset Park High." It's a few blocks from here, and Megan goes there too. "I'm starting senior year next week. What about you?"

"Senior year, too, at Bay Ridge Prep. It's not far from where I live."

Funny how he says this like he's attending a private school that costs fifty thousand a year only because it's down the road from his house. Bay Ridge is in our delivery radius, and whenever I ride past the school, I can't help glancing at the rich kids hanging out on the front steps. With their draped sweaters and rolled-up sleeves, they'd be perfectly at home on any Ivy League campus. Theo is no exception.

"Nice shirt, by the way," Theo adds.

My T-shirt says MILL COTTON, NOT PUPPIES. It's from the adoption drive the animal clinic holds every summer. Even though Mom wasn't around, I still volunteered this year.

"That's where we got Clover." I pull a stool over to the small table by the counter. "Why don't you take a seat while I go check on the dumplings?"

When I walk into the kitchen, Megan's at the steamer—a metal stovetop with boiling water underneath. Steam shoots through the holes like geysers.

20

"You're right, Dyl," she says. "He's hot."

"Shhh! He's just outside the door. He can hear you!"

"What are you doing in here anyway?" She puts eight dumplings onto a cotton cloth inside a large bamboo basket. "I gave you two the perfect opportunity for some one-on-one time."

"I'm not sure what to talk to him about. I don't want to babble like an idiot."

"You could ask about his underwear size. He looks like a medium to me." She smirks. "It's a little hard to tell with his pants on."

"Meg, I swear, if you weren't holding the dumplings, I'd kill you."

Megan cackles as she sets the bamboo basket on the steamer. The steam from the holes on the stovetop goes through the perforated base and cooks the food. Aunt Jade told us that when she worked in a dim sum restaurant, she had to manage at least five baskets on the steamer, each with different cooking times.

Ten minutes later, I emerge from the kitchen with a covered basket. Theo's at the counter with Tim, examining the strings on the violin Tim borrowed from his music school. Tim's telling him something about the pegs slipping. I'm surprised they're chatting. Tim's an introverted kid, and he doesn't open up to strangers unless they talk to him about math or music.

"Thanks for the tip, I'll try that," Tim says. He tucks his violin under his arm and disappears upstairs with Clover.

Theo comes to the table, and I set the basket in front of him. When I lift the cover, a dramatic *whoosh* of steam fills the air between us.

"Smells delicious." He leans forward, peering at the eight dumplings inside. "My mom said there's an art to eating xiao long bao. If it's too hot, the soup inside will scald your tongue. But if you let it get cold, the outer layer of dough will dry out and break when you try to pick it up."

"That's solid advice." I give him a flat spoon, a pair of chopsticks, and a sauce plate of black vinegar and sliced fresh ginger. "Dig in when you're ready."

"I have a question." Theo waves at the xiao long bao ingredients spread out on my side of the table. "I've eaten a ton of these before, but I still have no idea how you get the soup inside the dumpling."

I sit down across from him. "Well, first we boil pork bones with meat, strain the soup, and stick it into the fridge. When the chilled soup becomes gelatinous, we add minced pork and wrap the mixture inside the dumpling. When the dumplings are on the steamer, the heat melts the gelatin back into soup."

"Brilliant." The sunlight coming through the window turns Theo's hair a lighter shade of brown. "How do you seal the dumpling with all the little folds on top?"

"Ah, that's the trickiest part," I say. "I ruined dozens of them before I got the technique right. The secret is to pinch the edges together before pleating the folds and twisting them into a knot. Chefs at Michelin-starred restaurants only serve dumplings with exactly eighteen folds."

"That's wild, considering how small they are." Theo takes the chopsticks. "Now I'm going to savor each xiao long bao more after finding out how much work goes into making them."

He picks up a dumpling without breaking the dough. Pretty impressive. He's holding the chopsticks the right way too. His mom taught him well. He dips the dumpling into the sauce plate of vinegar and fresh ginger, puts it on the spoon, and bites into the folds on top to let out some of the steam before eating the whole thing.

"Mmm, this tastes fantastic," he says, chewing. "The dough's soft, and the minced meat and soup inside are full of flavor. I love it."

"We should get you to say that on a commercial for us," I joke.

He grins. "Let me know which network you want, and I'll make a few calls."

It's hard to tell if he's serious. I can't imagine Aunt Jade's face if a film crew showed up at the takeout. "Uh, I was just kidding. We couldn't afford an ad."

There's a short window of time to eat the dumplings before they become cold. I can't take my eyes off Theo as he wolfs them down one after another. I feel like a xiao long bao on the steamer—each time he licks his lips, I melt a little more inside.

Just my luck that when I *finally* run into someone who's my type, he's hanging out in a penthouse with his boyfriend the first time we meet.

"What's this?" Theo asks.

I follow his gaze to the flyer for the mooncake contest. I stuck it on the pin board to remind myself to talk to Aunt Jade about joining.

"Oh, it's a mooncake-making contest for aspiring teen bakers organized by celebrity chef Lawrence Lim." I take the flyer off the board. "Each contestant can apply with a partner, and they'll pick eight pairs. The mooncakes will be judged during the Mid-Autumn Festival, and the winner will be featured on an episode of his foodie show, *Off the Eaten Path*."

"Cool, I've seen that show a couple of times," Theo says. "I

23

went to try one of the Vietnamese restaurants he recommended. But when I got there, the queue was halfway around the block. So, he's sponsoring the mooncake contest?"

"Yeah. The Mid-Autumn celebrations are a pretty big deal in Singapore and Malaysia—that's where he grew up."

Theo looks at the entry form, where I've filled out my name and Aunt Jade's. "What kind of mooncake will you be making?"

"My grandma has this special blue snow-skin mooncake recipe that's been in our family for generations," I reply.

"What does that taste like? Blueberry flavored?"

"I haven't tried one before," I confess. "Mooncakes are only made during the Mid-Autumn Festival, and we usually visit my grandparents during the summer or over Christmas break. But my mom said the blue coloring comes from tea made with the butterfly pea plant."

My biggest regret is not asking Mom more about Por Por's mooncakes when she talked about joining the contest last year. I just assumed I had more time to find out.

"So, there's something else I've been wondering. . . ." Theo sets down his chopsticks. "Why don't you guys partner with Uber Eats or any of the food delivery companies in the city instead of doing everything on your own?"

I raise a brow. "Having me deliver your meal was that bad, huh?"

He laughs. "No, that's not what I meant at all. I just remember Adrian complaining about having to order online directly from the takeout instead of through an app. Seems easier to outsource the deliveries so you and your aunt can focus on what you guys are good at without worrying about who's sending the food out."

"That's true, but these companies take about one-third of

each order in commissions, which is pretty steep for smaller businesses like ours," I tell him. "My aunt partnered with a couple of them when she first started out, but after a year, she decided she'd rather have our own delivery people. She's known Chung, our main guy, since her days working in Hong Kong—he was the only plumber who showed up when she had a burst pipe emergency during her shift at a restaurant. She helped him apply for a work visa and gave him this gig. And Uncle Bo lost his job after falling from a ladder. He's been out sick, which is why I did the delivery run for him last night."

"I love your aunt's business ethic," Theo replies. "Helping her friends is more meaningful than cutting costs by working with a big, impersonal company."

I'm surprised he shares the same point of view as Aunt Jade. "Yeah. She's the kind of person who's always looking out for other people."

"So does her nephew. You stepped up and helped out with deliveries." Theo meets my gaze. "And for the record . . . having you send over the meal was a stroke of luck." He waves his hand at the empty bamboo basket. "Otherwise, I would never have gotten a chance to try these insanely delicious handmade xiao long bao."

I blush. Where's a quip when I need one?

Theo gets to his feet and checks the time on his iPhone—the latest one. "Sorry, I've got to run. My coach will kill me if I'm late for tennis practice again."

He totally has the physique of a tennis player. Aunt Jade is the resident tennis fan, but I should start following the sport for . . . reasons.

"Yeah, sure." I walk him to the door. "Thanks for stopping by."

"Thanks for the delicious food," he says.

25

"Could you put that in writing?" I ask. "Our online reviews sure could use the boost."

"Definitely." He winks. "Wok Warriors has another satisfied customer."

The chime sounds as he leaves. As Theo heads down the street, Aunt Jade walks toward the shop from the other direction, her arms full of groceries. They pass each other, and Theo disappears around the corner.

Megan bursts out of the kitchen, cawing with delight. "That was *epic*."

The chime dings again as I open the door for Aunt Jade. She catches Megan's expression. "What's going on?"

"Remember the cute guy from Dylan's delivery last night?" Megan tells her. "He was just here. He came to apologize for his friend. He gave Dylan a hundred-dollar tip, and they had an impromptu date."

"What? That wasn't a date." I take the groceries from Aunt Jade. "He ordered food and paid for it."

"Yeah, well, I don't see you making heart-eyes at other customers."

"I did not make heart-eyes! Were you spying on us?"

"Of course. You looked like you wanted to eat him with a spoon." Megan smirks. "When's he coming back?"

Theo said Wok Warriors has another *satisfied* customer. Not *repeat*. Might be semantics, but I have a feeling he wouldn't want his boyfriend ALLERGIC-TO-DUMBASSES knowing he's eaten at our takeout. He didn't even ask for my number.

I shake my head. "He was just being polite."

As Megan and Tim bring the groceries into the kitchen, Aunt Jade notices the flyer on the small table. "What've you got there?"

26

"This is for the mooncake-making contest Mom wanted to join last year." I show her the entry form. "I thought you and I could do it instead. We could make Por Por's blue snow-skin mooncake, like Mom wanted."

"That's a great idea." Aunt Jade chews on her lip. "There's just one tiny problem. I don't have the recipe."

I blink. "What?"

"Your mom enjoyed baking, but I was keener on cooking. Your Por Por had a notebook with all her secret recipes, but after her dementia set in, she couldn't remember where she put it." Aunt Jade sighs. "Your mom knew the recipe, but with everything going on, I didn't think of asking her to write it down for me."

This is going to be more difficult than I thought. Trying to piece together a forgotten recipe for a dessert I've never tasted doesn't seem like a winning combination.

"We should definitely do this contest together, though," Aunt Jade adds. "Especially since it's something your mom wanted. We'll get to work on my day off and reconstruct them as best we can, okay?" She puts a hand on my arm. "Don't worry, we'll bring Por Por's mooncakes back to life again."

Chapter 4

At the end of the first day of school, I meet Megan on the sidewalk. She just cut her bangs short to look like Lisa from Blackpink. I catch a couple of boys stealing glances.

"What's up?" I ask. "Why can't we talk at home?"

"Because I snooped around Mom's room and found the letter she didn't want us to see at the bottom of her nightstand drawer." Megan's expression turns grim. "It's a notice to vacate."

My heart plummets. "Shit. How many months of rent do we owe?"

"Not sure. I had to speed-read and get out of there before she caught me. But the last paragraph said that if we can put together five grand by the end of the week, they'll give us extra time to work out a payment plan for the rest."

"If not?"

"They'll start eviction proceedings."

I run my hands through my hair. "Damn." Now I feel bad about asking Aunt Jade to be my sous-chef for the mooncake contest. She has so much weighing on her mind, and she still said yes.

The low, powerful hum of a sports car engine makes everyone

turn. A black Ferrari convertible pulls up by the curb with a short screech of tires. A murmur rises from the kids around us. Less than a handful of teachers and students drive to school—nearly everyone walks, cycles, or takes the bus or subway.

The Ferrari's metallic roof is up, and the windshield reflects the glare of the afternoon sun. I can't see who's in the driver's seat.

The door swings open, and Theo steps out.

My breath catches in my throat as he walks toward Megan and me. His navy polo shirt has the Bay Ridge Prep crest. "Hey."

"Uh, hi." I clear my throat. "What are you doing here?"

Megan gives me a Cheshire cat grin. "Oh, did I forget to tell you? Theo called the shop yesterday when you were out. We swapped numbers, and I gave him yours too." She turns to Theo. "So, you were saying something about going to Chinatown to check out mooncakes?"

"Yeah, Dylan was telling me the other day that he's planning to make your grandma's mooncakes for a contest." Theo looks at me. "Bakeries in Chinatown have started selling them ahead of the Mid-Autumn Festival, so I thought we could check them out together."

My heart skips a beat. I can feel my schoolmates watching us. I still can't believe Theo showed up. I never expected to see him again.

"Unless . . . you already have plans?" Theo prompts, probably because I'm staring at him like a newborn donkey.

"I don't," I blurt out.

"Yeah, he does nothing after school except watch TikTok animal videos and drool over cute Chinese actors on Weibo," Megan pipes up.

I shoot her a pointed look. Theo smiles.

"I skipped lunch, so I'm starving," he says. "We can grab a bite along the way."

Megan winks at me. "You boys have fun!"

Eighth Avenue is just a few blocks south. Theo leaves his car parked in front of my school, and we start walking. My pulse is still fluttering, and my palms are a little sweaty. Is this a date? Of course not. We're just two guys going to browse mooncakes in Chinatown. Completely platonic.

We pass boutiques touting knockoff designer T-shirts and 99-cent shops with tacky souvenirs. Signs are in Chinese first, English second. Fruit stalls spill onto the pavement, where cartons of pomelos are stacked like Jenga towers. They're in season for the Mid-Autumn Festival. Elderly ladies trawl the mom-and-pop markets selling specialty food from China, such as sea cucumbers and reishi mushrooms. Their bulky trolley bags on wheels trail behind them, waiting to trip you up.

A motorbike appears from a narrow back alley ahead and swerves onto the road in front of Theo.

"Watch out!" I grab Theo's arm, pulling him out of the way just in time.

His shoulder bumps into my chest, and his hand closes around my arm to steady himself. His fingers send a jolt across my skin, like static electricity.

"Nei mou ngaan tai ah?" the guy on the bike yells as he whizzes past us.

Theo lets go. "Thanks. Pretty sure he wasn't telling me to be more careful in Mandarin."

More along the lines of *Don't you have eyes?* "He was speaking Cantonese, actually."

"Oops. I can't even tell the difference." Theo sounds wry. "I wish I could understand a few words. My grandparents emigrated from Hong Kong when my mom was two. They live in San Francisco, so I don't see them often."

"My mom taught me both dialects," I say. "But shopkeepers can still tell from my accent I was raised here."

The food stalls are bustling, serving a brisk crowd in the middle of the afternoon. People eat at rickety tables lining the street. Theo points at the whole roasted ducks and crispy-skinned chickens hanging by their necks in the stall window.

"I love street food, but my dad can't stand that their heads are still on," Theo says. "The eyes freak him out. As if he didn't know they had eyes before they ended up on his plate."

We find a table on the sidewalk. Theo buys roasted duck and soy sauce chicken on a plate of rice, while I join the queue at a mixed-rice stall. It's the ultimate working-class Chinese meal—in Singapore, it's called jaap jaap faan, which literally means "point point rice." People order by pointing at the meat or veggie dishes they want. Every now and then, you'll hear a burst of dismay when the stallholder scoops the wrong dish. "No, Auntie, wrong! Not that one lah!"

I come back with a plate of sweet-and-sour pork, sliced beef with bitter melon, and steamed egg heaped over a bed of white rice. As we dig in, I put some beef slices on Theo's plate, and he gives me a few pieces of duck and chicken. Sharing food with friends is common in Chinese culture, but doing it with Theo feels more intimate than it should.

"Turns out, making mooncakes is going to be a little more complicated than I expected," I tell him. "Aunt Jade didn't learn

31

the recipe from my grandma before she got dementia, and we have no written copies. We'll just have to work harder to re-create her blue snow-skin mooncake."

Theo tilts his head. "If you don't mind me asking: Why are you entering the contest with your aunt instead of your mom?"

My fingers curl around my fork and spoon. I force a steady tone. "My mom passed away earlier this year."

There's a beat of silence.

"I'm so sorry." Theo's tone is sober. "Do you want to talk about it?"

I shrug. Everything happened so fast, it almost didn't seem real. "One month we were eating mooncakes at the festival, and the next we were in the hospital planning chemo cycles and ask-ing the doctors if she'd be well enough to fly back to Singapore to see my grandparents."

"Wow, that's a long flight. Did she get to go?"

"We shelled out for Singapore Airlines tickets—the only non-stop flight from JFK. It was eighteen hours, but my mom was really upbeat. She said she was tired of being stuck in the hospi-tal." I muster a strained smile. "As it turned out, when we went to the beach the morning after we landed, Tim stepped on a sea urchin. We ended up in the ER for the rest of the day."

"What about your dad?"

"He moved to Shanghai after he and my mom divorced." My dad and I aren't close—I guess I resented how unhappy he made Mom when they were together. "My mom and I used to live a couple of blocks from the takeout, and I'd spend weekends and summers helping out."

After losing Mom, the takeout became the closest thing to home—and I can't imagine losing that too.

Theo is quiet for a moment. "I was five when my mom died," he says. I stare at him in disbelief. "Another driver had a heart attack and hit her car. She went into a coma and never woke up."

"Oh God, that's terrible." Theo has mentioned his mom a couple of times, but I never got the impression that she wasn't around any longer. "I'm sorry. So it's just you and your dad now?"

"You could say that." Something flickers in Theo's eyes. "The other day, when you talked about making your grandma's mooncakes, I realized how little I know about my mom's culture. I've only eaten mooncakes a handful of times, and I thought this could be a good chance for me to reconnect with my heritage."

This is the first personal thing he's shared with me. "So that's why you suggested coming to Chinatown to check them out together?"

The corners of Theo's eyes pinch in an adorable way. "One of the reasons, yeah."

At least I can blame the flush that rises around my neck on the sweltering weather. Beads of sweat dapple Theo's forehead. He's a long way from the air-conditioned lounges in private clubs he's probably used to dining in, but he doesn't appear to mind.

"So, you seeing anyone?" he asks casually.

His question catches me off guard. *I'm on the lookout*—too thirsty. *I'm between boyfriends*—not even true since I haven't had one before. There was Simon, a guy I met while walking Clover. We hung out a few times, and I thought we were vibing . . . until he showed up at the dog park with his new girlfriend.

"Um, no, not right now." I try not to sound as awkward as I feel. "What about you and Adrian? Did you guys meet at school?"

"Our moms were best friends, so we've known each other

since we were little," he replies. "He's not my boyfriend, by the way."

I don't believe it. "Really? Because when I delivered his order, you were, uh, in your underwear. And you called him"—I suppress a gag—"*baby.*"

Theo breaks into a grin. "Yeah, you can say he's the first guy I dated. I'm talking about playdates when we were kids. I wouldn't call the stuff we did during freshman year dating as much as, well, experimenting."

My stomach twists.

"But we both agreed messing around wasn't worth ruining our friendship," Theo continues. "The other night, you heard me call him BB, not baby. Bumblebee was his favorite Transformer when he was little, which was how he got the nickname."

I exhale in a rush. "So . . . you're not seeing anyone?"

His eyes meet mine. "Nope."

It feels like my heart has sprouted wings. For once, the guy I have a crush on isn't either terminally straight or already taken.

After our meal, we wander through Chinatown, stopping at different Asian-owned bakeries. Most bakeries in this neighborhood are old-fashioned, with narrow aisles and shelves crowded with rows of buns that have a variety of fillings—sweet red bean, salted egg custard, or savory roast meat. The buns don't have any description cards, but the regulars can recognize them. People line up with a tray and a pair of tongs in hand, trying to grab the biggest piece of their favorites without earning a glower from other customers for taking too long.

"You can tell the baked mooncakes by their brown skin," I explain to Theo. The bakeries have cut their mooncakes into small pieces for customers to try. "The traditional fillings are lotus paste, red bean, or black sesame. Snow-skin mooncakes, on the other hand, don't need to be baked but must be kept frozen. They come in all kinds of fusion flavors, such as mango-pomelo or matcha-azuki."

"I sampled so many mooncakes, I'm going to get a stomachache later," Theo says after we leave the fifth bakery.

"You know, I got an idea from the bakery that replaced the salted egg yolk with a peanut butter and chocolate core," I reply. "I still want to try to re-create my grandma's blue snow-skin mooncake recipe, but since my mom didn't like the yolk in the center, I'll use something else. Maybe a white chocolate truffle core? That was her favorite."

"We should give it a catchy name," Theo says. "Extra points for a mooncake pun."

"Mooncake It Till You Make It?" I joke.

"You Had Me at Mooncake?" Theo suggests.

"Once in a Blue Mooncake?" I venture.

He snaps his fingers. "We have a winner. I love that."

It's past five by the time we start walking back to my school, where Theo's car is parked. Along the way, we pass a vacant two-story building, and I halt in front of the For Rent sign.

"This is Aunt Jade's dream spot for her future restaurant," I tell Theo. "If she won the lottery or something, she'd snap it up in a heartbeat."

"You mean for the takeout?" Theo asks.

I shake my head. "She's always wanted to have her own dine-in place serving authentic Singaporean cuisine. This location has great visibility and a parking lot across the street. Locals can try

Singapore's most famous dishes from halfway around the world, and Singaporeans living in New York City can enjoy their favorite comfort foods right here."

Theo goes up to the front doors, which are boarded up and chained shut. He peers through a gap between the boards. "Did another restaurant operate here before?"

"A bistro. Which means the shop already has the basic setup for a commercial kitchen. We could save money on renovations and cut down a bunch of work when we're getting licenses and inspections." I point to the upper level. "The best part is, there's a residential unit on the second floor. We could live upstairs like we do now at the takeout."

"Sounds like you've got everything figured out," Theo says. "When can I make a reservation? I'd like a table for two."

A pang hits me. He's kidding, but his words are another reminder of how unattainable Aunt Jade's dream is right now. We're already struggling not to get kicked out of our current place. Affording this building is nothing more than an impossible hope.

"Like I said, we'd have to win the lottery." I try to shrug off the topic, but my shoulders feel heavy. "I'd be happy enough to find an angel investor or a nonprofit that'll give a small, family-owned business a five-grand grant, like, tomorrow. Something legit, I mean. Not a loan shark who'll take our kidneys if we don't pay up in time."

Theo raises a brow. "Five grand? Why do you need that specific amount so soon?"

"Uh, the takeout got hit with some unexpected expenses." I don't want to tell him about the eviction notice. Aunt Jade's not even aware that Megan and I know. "My mom left me a small inheritance, which is being held until I turn eighteen. I've told my aunt a million times to use the money to pay off urgent bills, but she won't touch a single dollar. I'm one hundred percent sure if my mom were here, she would've lent her the entire amount, interest-free."

Theo's voice goes quiet. "Your mom and your aunt must've been really close."

I can't keep the frustration and helplessness out of my tone. "Aunt Jade's always caring for everyone else—but who's going to look out for her? My mom used to, even though she was a year younger. But she's gone. She would've wanted me to take her place as someone who my aunt can lean on, but I just . . . don't know how to." A prickle stings my eyes—I quickly avert my gaze and force a laugh. "Sorry, you signed up for a mooncake tour, not to be my therapist."

Theo doesn't miss a beat. "First consultation's free of charge."

I manage a chuckle. "Good, because I'm a little short on cash."

Theo's expression turns serious. "Honestly, Dylan, I can tell you're doing the best you can. You're helping your aunt with food prep, cooking, and delivery runs when she's shorthanded." He puts his hand on my shoulder, sending a startling rush of warmth through me. "Your mom would've been proud of you for busting your ass to keep the takeout going."

For a wild moment, I want to put my hand over his. But we barely know each other. I'm not even sure why he wanted to hang out with me today. I have no idea if this means anything . . . and I don't want to mess it up.

"Thanks," I say. "That means a lot."

Theo takes his hand away. The evening sun is warm on the

back of my neck as we resume walking. A girl on a scooter rides toward us. Theo moves closer to me to let her pass, and his arm brushes mine.

When we reach his car, I turn to him. "I had a great—"

"*It's me, pick up the phone!*" comes a familiar voice in a singsong tone, startling us both.

Theo swears and answers the call. "Adrian, I told you not to mess with my ringtones."

My heart sinks. Adrian continues yapping on the other end of the line, and Theo rolls his eyes.

"Chill, I'm on my way, okay? They'll hold the reservation for fifteen minutes. Whatever you do, don't freak out on them. If you piss them off, they definitely won't let us have the counter seats."

He hangs up.

"You have dinner plans with Adrian?" I ask.

"Yeah, he's been talking nonstop about this new omakase place in Midtown." Theo taps rapidly on his phone. "The best seats are at the counter, where you can watch the head chef prepare your food. He tracked me on Find My Friends, and now he's mad that I'm nowhere close by." He looks up. "Sorry. You were saying something?"

"Oh. Nothing important."

He pockets his phone. "Can I give you a ride home?"

I shake my head. "The takeout's just a few blocks away, and you're headed the opposite direction. Don't want to keep Adrian waiting."

He shrugs. "He can wait. It's not a date."

"It's fine, really," I lie. "I need to pick up some groceries from the store along the way."

Theo leans against the side of his car. "Maybe we can hang out again sometime."

"Yeah, sure." I keep my tone light. "You know where I go to school. And where I live. Wait, I didn't mean to make you sound like a stalker. . . ."

Theo's mouth twitches with amusement. "I get what you mean."

I stand on the sidewalk as Theo drives off, catching the green light. Wouldn't want him to be late for his not-date with his not-boyfriend.

Maybe I'm reading Theo wrong, the way I did with Simon from the dog park. Theo's interested in guys, but that doesn't mean he likes *me*. He didn't hide the fact that he and Adrian hooked up in the past, and they still seem pretty tight. Who's to say history won't repeat itself?

The glimmer of disappointment I thought I saw in Theo's eyes when I declined his ride was probably my imagination—but as I start walking home, the deflated feeling inside my chest is entirely real.

Chapter 5

I t's Friday afternoon—thank God the weekend's almost here because I have a ton of reading to do. I'm taking four AP classes this year—if I don't get at least a 3.5 GPA, I can forget about a college scholarship. I'm a B-plus-average student, so I've got to work harder to keep up.

Megan's in her room, watching a YouTube tutorial on how to dye her hair two different shades, the latest trend among K-pop stars. I lie on the living room couch and throw Clover's favorite spiky ball around, letting it bounce off the walls. She goes wild chasing it, her short tail wagging. Corgis were bred as cattle-herding dogs, but the only creatures Clover herds around here are my cousins and me.

A loud crash echoes downstairs, followed by Aunt Jade swearing. I bolt upright, and Megan rushes out of her room with half of her hair clipped up.

"Mom? Are you okay?" Megan yells as we barrel down the stairs.

"Sorry, kids, I'm fine." Aunt Jade is standing at the counter, coins and bills around her feet from the tip jar she knocked over with her handbag. Her face is pale as she grips an envelope. "I'm such a klutz—"

I lead her to a wooden stool. "What happened?"

She hands over a piece of paper. My heart thuds. It must be the final eviction notice—

Dear Ms. Jade Wong,

Congratulations! As the owner of Wok Warriors, you have been awarded the Revolc Foundation's inaugural Small Business Grant, an initiative to support experienced industry professionals running family-owned businesses. The Revolc Foundation, based in Brooklyn, New York, is a nonprofit organization privately funded by anonymous donors.

Please find enclosed a cashier's check in the amount of Five Thousand U.S. Dollars ($5,000). . . .

"I was so shocked when I saw the amount that I knocked over the tip jar." Aunt Jade lets out a wobbly laugh. "Your Por Por would say that dropping money all over the floor is a bad sign, but I'd say it's a good one."

"Is this for real?" Megan holds the check with Aunt Jade's name to the light as if she can spot a fake. "Is it some kind of scam?"

"Do you think they could've made a mistake?" Aunt Jade says. "I don't remember applying for any grants—"

Oh. My. God. I remember talking about one. Specifically, a nonprofit willing to give a small, family-owned business five grand. The exact amount Aunt Jade received.

"Let's go to the bank right now." Megan takes her mom's arm

and pulls her to the door. "We can make sure the money's legit and cash it out before anyone has a chance to change their mind. Dylan, you coming?"

"No. I, uh, need to use the bathroom," I lie. "You guys go ahead. Tell me what the bank says when you get back."

I wait until Aunt Jade and Megan—her hair still half dyed and clipped on top of her head—disappear from view. They took the letter but left the envelope behind. The Revolc Foundation's return address is in Brooklyn. Bay Ridge, to be exact.

Damn. I should be relieved, thankful . . . but owing Theo this much makes me uneasy. Unsettled. Borrowing money from him wasn't an option—we just met!—but now this "grant" is more than a loan. It's an outright handout. And I can't exactly return it, since Aunt Jade and Megan are headed to the bank to cash the check. On the other hand, this money can help to keep the lights on long enough to give me a shot at winning us a spot on *Off the Eaten Path* and bringing some real publicity to the takeout.

My bike is chained to a lamppost, and I unlock it and don my helmet. I ride through the streets from Sunset Park into neighboring Bay Ridge, finally halting in front of a sprawling mansion surrounded by high walls. I take out the crumpled envelope and double-check the address. The brass lettering on the pillar next to the massive wrought-iron gate tells me I'm at the right place.

I chain my bike to the lamppost on the sidewalk—a habit ever since I rode up a driveway on a delivery and got yelled at for nearly clipping the side mirror of some rich guy's Bentley—and press the intercom buzzer.

A male voice with a crisp British accent comes through the speaker. "Somers residence. How may I help you?"

"I'm here to see Theo," I reply.

"Is Mr. Somers expecting you?"

I roll my eyes. "No, but you can tell him Dylan wants to talk."

A few minutes drag by. I stand there, sweat trickling down the back of my neck from the long bike ride. Just when I'm starting to think Theo isn't interested in entertaining my unannounced visit, the gate rolls open, grating smoothly on metal tracks.

I step inside. In a place as crowded as Brooklyn, it's like going through a portal into another world. The whole place is bigger than my school compound. Water cascades from a black stone fountain in the courtyard, filling the air with calming splashes. The Ferrari is parked next to a silver Porsche. I wonder what they have around back. Maybe a helicopter pad.

I walk up the long driveway toward the mansion. The exterior has earthy tones of terra-cotta and whitewashed stone, like one of those luxury Mediterranean destinations in travel magazines, except it's not perched on a cliff in Tuscany or something.

Two bonsai trees stand on either side of the front door. People who believe in feng shui are divided on whether bonsai is good or bad. Some say it bestows peace and good fortune, while others think it brings bad luck because its growth has been stunted. Pruning bonsai is supposed to be an art form, but I can't help feeling sorry for the plant, squashed into a too-small pot and pruned until it's given up trying to grow taller than three feet.

The front door opens before I can knock. A distinguished-looking man in his forties wearing a pressed white shirt with a gray vest and a black suit jacket appears. He eyes my faded jeans and the frayed laces on my beat-up Converse sneakers before he stands aside unsmilingly. I self-consciously scuff my soles on the doormat before going inside.

The entranceway is huge. Its sky-lit ceiling is at least three stories high. There's so much space—beautiful, empty space. A curved marble staircase leads to the floor above, and a blur of movement near the top catches my eye.

Theo's coming down the stairs. More accurately, sliding down the wide banister with a combination of boyish glee and ridiculous grace. He sticks the landing perfectly on the carpet in front of us and smiles. "Hey, you."

The man in the suit sighs. "Theo, I must ask you, again, to refrain from sliding down the banister."

"Why? I doubt my dad cares about that rule. He doesn't live here anymore."

"It has less to do with your father's rules than the fact that you might fall over and hurt yourself. We have a fully functional elevator."

"I know, Bernard, but taking the stairs is good for the heart." Theo gives him a maddening grin before turning to me. "Come on, let's talk in my room."

I follow him up the marble steps. Natural light streams through the arched windows and takes the edge off the stillness, illuminating and shaping it into something more picturesque. On the wall of a long hallway is a framed portrait of an Asian woman in her twenties wearing a stunning black-and-red cheongsam. A white man dressed in a tux has an arm around her waist. His smile is restrained, and the side part of his blond hair is so straight, it's as if it were made with a razor instead of a comb. The young woman's expression is softer, warmer, livelier, like the curls of dark hair on her shoulders. In her arms is a toddler in a bow-tie-and-suspenders outfit. His wide grin lights up the entire picture.

We enter Theo's room, which is the size of our entire apartment above the takeout. The first thing that strikes me is how spotless everything is. No stickers on the closet doors. No picture frames on the nightstand. There isn't any mess on the floor. Everything is neat and perfect and empty. A ghost might as well be living here instead of a teenage boy.

"So where does your dad live?" I ask.

"He remarried last year and moved into his dream home on Long Island," Theo replies. "Moshe Safdie was his architect. He's the guy who designed Marina Bay Sands and Jewel Changi Airport in Singapore."

Wow. Marina Bay Sands is an iconic part of Singapore's skyline. Jewel, right next to the airport, is a huge mall with the world's tallest indoor waterfall in a dome of glass and steel. Mom loved the gardens on every level. Exactly how rich is Theo's dad to afford the same architect who built these award-winning international monuments?

"Does your dad own an offshore bank or an oil rig?" I say, only half joking.

"Semiconductors." Theo doesn't laugh. "So, what's up?"

"I think you know." I hold up the envelope. "The address led me here."

"Oh, yes. The Revolc Foundation is affiliated with my family."

"I Googled it. There's no record of such a nonprofit."

Theo shrugs. "They try to keep a low profile. You were looking for a company that gives grants to small businesses, which is what the Revolc Foundation was set up to do—"

"You knew my aunt wouldn't accept money from you, so you invented a bogus grant and sent her a check for *five thousand dollars*?" I take a deliberate step forward. "She may be cool and open-minded, but she still holds to some traditional Chinese values, like not accepting anyone's charity—"

"Which is precisely why I made sure the grant came through the Revolc Foundation."

"Right. That's Clover spelled backward. Appropriately named after my dog, who, like me, knows better than to trust strangers."

Theo's expression turns wry. "I had a feeling that was a little too on the nose. You said you were worried about who would look out for your aunt when she needed help—"

"I was talking about *me*," I cut in. "We've only known each other a few days. Why would you do all of this for my family?"

A shadow darts across Theo's face, but I blink, and it's gone.

"Listen, you don't trust me," he says. "I get that. But I want to help. I wish you'd believe that."

"My mom told me not to take favors because I'll never know when they'll be called in." I meet his gaze. "Five grand is too much. I can only accept it if you let me pay you back. When I turn eighteen in January, I'll get the money my mom left for me—"

"If your aunt refuses to borrow from your inheritance, there's no way I'm taking a cent." Theo suddenly has a gleam in his eye. "Hey, this wouldn't count as a favor if you help me out with something I need, right?"

I frown. "What do you mean?"

He picks up a gold foil–stamped invitation printed on thick card stock and gives it to me. The glitter rubs off onto my fingertips.

Mr. and Mrs. Jefferson Wallace Leyland-Somers

&

Mr. and Mrs. Miguel Paulo Sanchez

request the pleasure of your company

Mr. Theodore Somers & Guest

at the marriage of their children

NORA CLAIRE

&

ANGELO JUAN

"My cousin on my father's side is getting married in the Hamptons next weekend," Theo says. "I need a plus-one."

"And?"

"And . . . what are you doing next weekend?"

"Wait—you want *me* to go with you? As your *date*?"

"My relatives are always trying to set me up," he replies. "If I show up at this wedding alone, I'll have blind dates lined up for the rest of the year. If you want to return the favor, you can be my fake boyfriend."

My mind is racing. "Your relatives know you're gay?"

Theo nods. "Don't worry, they're cool. They saw Adrian and me kissing under the mistletoe a couple of years ago, which is when I came out to them."

I bristle a little. "Then why aren't you bringing Adrian as your date?"

"He'll be in California with his parents for some wine-tasting event." Theo's watching my reaction while betraying none of his own. "But if you think you're going to feel too weird, forget it. I don't want you to agree to anything you're uncomfortable with."

I rake a hand through my hair. An all-expenses-paid weekend in the Hamptons sounds like a blast—it's my growing crush on the guy I'm supposed to be fake-dating that I'm afraid will blow up in a different way. Theo's not the only one in this room I can't trust.

I hold up the Revolc Foundation envelope. "I do this, and we're even?"

Theo grins. "I can put it in writing, if you want."

Chapter 6

The takeout's closed on Mondays, so Aunt Jade and I are in the kitchen for our first mooncake-making session. I haven't heard back from the contest organizer about whether I've been chosen as a contestant, but both of us are excited about getting a head start.

"Some people assume snow-skin mooncakes are easier to make than baked ones since they go into the freezer instead of the oven, so you don't have to worry about burning them," Aunt Jade says. "But as you can tell from its name, getting the snowy texture is the trickiest part. We'll work on the mooncake skin today."

In front of us is a large bowl of cooked glutinous rice flour—the main ingredient in the mooncake skin, made by steaming a mixture of raw glutinous rice flour and plain rice flour at high heat. Unlike other types of flour, the texture is rough and sandy, not smooth or fine.

"Once you add water, the concoction becomes sticky, like mochi dough," Aunt Jade tells me. "You can't use anything else, or the whole mooncake will fall apart." She points at a bowl of dried blue petals. "These flowers are from the butterfly pea plant.

Your grandma had one in her backyard, but I got these flowers from the Indian specialty store around the corner. They're used in a lot of South and Southeast Asian dishes."

Aunt Jade adds hot water to the bowl of petals. While waiting for them to steep, we put on gloves and mix the flour with sugar, wheat flour, shortening, and water. Aunt Jade keeps an eye on the consistency, adding water from a jug in small increments as we knead the soft, messy clumps.

There's something else I need to talk to Aunt Jade about. I've been putting it off, but I can't delay the inevitable any longer.

"So, uh . . . Theo invited me to his family's party in the Hamptons this weekend." I don't mention that it's a wedding and I'm pretending to be his boyfriend to return the favor we owe him. "Can I go? We'd leave Friday afternoon, and I'd be back on Sunday."

Aunt Jade sets down the jug. "I was wondering when you were going to talk about him."

Her meaningful tone puts me on alert. "What do you mean?"

She grins. "Oh, drop the act, young man. I know about your little plan with Theo."

My heart skips a beat. How did she figure it out? "I can explain. This isn't what—"

"Theo called the takeout earlier," Aunt Jade cuts in. "He introduced himself—"

Oh God. Did he tell her about the fake-dating?

"—and wanted to make sure we received the check from his family's foundation! He said applying for the grant was your idea, and all he did was help with the paperwork!" She throws her arms around me in a tight hug. "Oh, sweetie, why didn't you say anything?"

50

Good thing she can't see me miming a goldfish over her shoulder. "Um . . . I wanted it to be a surprise?"

"And you didn't want to take the credit." She pulls back, beaming. "This grant comes at the perfect time. And yes, you can go with Theo this weekend. School just started, but we shouldn't turn down the invitation after his family's nonprofit helped us out." Aunt Jade nudges me. "Meg thinks he's really into you."

"She has an overactive imagination."

"Well, Theo was a real gentleman on the phone," Aunt Jade says. "He seems like a great catch. Feel free to tell your nosy aunt to mind her own business . . . but what's holding you back?"

I shrug. "He lives in a huge mansion and drives a Ferrari. I ride a bike with a squeaky front wheel. Our worlds are as far apart as the sun and the moon."

"They align every now and then," Aunt Jade points out. "Eclipses are pretty memorable."

But they're over before you know it, I don't say.

We add the butterfly pea tea to the dough, kneading until the lump becomes pale blue. When Aunt Jade's satisfied with the texture, she divides the dough into smaller lumps, which we then roll into flattened discs of around three inches in diameter.

"The filling today will be red bean paste," she says. "I have some left over from last night's crispy pancake. We'll make the lotus seed paste the next time, okay?"

We scoop some red bean paste onto the center of the circle of dough and press the edges together so they completely wrap the filling.

"The skin is pretty sticky, and we don't want the mooncake to get stuck in the mold." She dusts the inside of a wooden mold with flour. "Shake off the flour before putting the dough ball

51

inside. Push down firmly, but not too hard. If it doesn't fit, re-shape and try again."

She inverts the mold, taps it against the surface of the work-table, and lifts it away to reveal a small blue mooncake embossed with floral patterns. My mooncakes emerge from the mold oddly shaped, but at least they look like mooncakes.

I bite into one. The taste seems fine to me, but Aunt Jade frowns. "The skin is too uneven. The texture should be smoother. I haven't made mooncakes in a while, so I'm a little rusty. But don't worry. We'll get everything right before the contest."

Aside from the contest, I've been racking my brain for other ways to generate publicity for the takeout. Aunt Jade's always experimenting with different recipes, and every now and then she'll add new dishes and phase others out. Churning out the same food over and over isn't why she became a chef, and she prides herself on the variety of dishes she can cook.

"Why don't we launch a special Mid-Autumn Festival menu for the takeout during the eighth lunar month?" I ask. "We could come up with a slightly different version of our popular dishes using Mid-Autumn foods like osmanthus, duck, pumpkin, pomelo, crab. . . ."

Aunt Jade's face lights up. "Brilliant idea, Dylan! We could have egg fried rice with duck meat. And chopped pumpkin could go well with the chye tow kuay?"

"Crab meat would be perfect with the fried Hokkien prawn mee," I add.

" 'Top Singapore Hawker Center Favorites, Mid-Autumn Edition.' " Aunt Jade mimes a headline for the menu. "What do you think?"

The phrase is a little long and could be catchier. I'm not

even sure most New Yorkers will know what a hawker center is. They're a unique Singaporean thing: open-air complexes in the heart of public housing estates with as many as a hundred food stalls selling all kinds of cheap local food. Each stall is tiny, so every vendor specializes in one or two dishes. People buy food from different stalls and eat at communal tables. Everyone enjoys the variety, and vendors get to keep costs low.

"How about Fry Me to the Moon?" I suggest. "Most people know Mid-Autumn's around the corner, so they'll make the connection. Megan can design a special menu to put outside our shop and post on social media."

"I love that! We can launch the promo next week, after your trip out of town with Theo." Aunt Jade winks. "You deserve to have a little fun."

Chapter 7

After the last bell, as I step out of school, my phone rings.

I answer the call. "Theo?"

"Hey, Dylan," he says. "We have an appointment with my tailor this afternoon."

I blink. "Sorry, we? What for?"

"The wedding's black tie. You'll need to get measured for a custom suit."

I have a black jacket, but I don't think it even has a label. Aunt Jade got it for me to wear to Mom's funeral, so I definitely don't want to put it on again.

I pinch the space between my brows. "In your world, you probably don't wear a tailored tux more than once—but in mine, I just rent one. This whole thing is supposed to be part of me returning your favor, remember? I don't want to owe you more stuff."

"If the rules were up to me, you wouldn't need a suit for the wedding," Theo replies. "You could show up in that cute otter T-shirt you're wearing."

My head snaps down to the goofy-looking otter on my T-shirt, which says I'M NOT LIKE THE OTTERS. I spin around, searching the crowd of students on the sidewalk. A few of them are pointing across the street—

Theo's leaning against his Ferrari, his phone held to his ear. He's in a long-sleeve white shirt with its collar upturned and a couple more buttons undone than what's probably allowed at his prep school.

A flurry swirls through my chest and pools in my stomach. I'm acutely aware of my schoolmates' stares as I dart across the street toward him.

Theo gives me a lopsided grin. "Come on. Hop in."

He hits a button on his key fob. The folding metal roof retracts, revealing a pair of plush red leather seats. Some kids whistle. Megan would say this'll give my reputation a boost, but my cheeks still burn. I don't belong in a car like this.

I concentrate on not looking as if this is the first time I'm getting into a vehicle worth half a million dollars. The seat is slung way lower than I expect, and I have to stretch out my legs to get comfortable. I fasten the seat belt and test it to make sure it's secure like I do whenever I'm regretting whatever terrifying roller coaster Megan talked me into trying.

Theo floors the gas pedal. We shoot down Third Avenue like a rocket being launched. The grind of asphalt feels five inches beneath my ass—and probably is. I grip the edges of my seat.

Theo glances at me. "You all right?"

The wind slaps my face and whooshes past my ears. "Yeah. Just getting used to my intestines wrapping around my spine."

Theo chuckles as we speed toward the Battery Tunnel.

Truth is, I'm not excited about getting fitted for an outrageously expensive suit. I buy my clothes from bargain bins and thrift stores. My family washes our own laundry, and when we bring clothes to the dry cleaners, we go to the ones in Chinatown that charge the same price for any garment. This visit to Theo's tailor is another reminder of how different we are.

We park in front of a nondescript shop on Madison Avenue with full-length panels so darkly tinted I can't see inside. They evidently don't need glass windows to attract customers, and the STRICTLY BY APPOINTMENT ONLY sign confirms that.

As we approach, a young lady in a black-and-white striped pantsuit opens the door for us. "Good afternoon, Mr. Somers. Please come in. Mr. Kashimura will be with you shortly."

"Thank you, Sue," Theo replies. "Mr. Somers is my dad—please just call me Theo."

Inside, a wooden worktable is covered with books of fabric swatches. Bolts of cloth and completed suits hang from paneled walls. A pair of vintage armchairs stand next to a glass display case, its shelves filled with cuff links, tie clips, and neckties. None have price tags.

Sue sets two porcelain cups of matcha tea in front of us. Before I can take a sip, a man in his sixties with gray hair and a measuring tape looped around his neck appears from a staircase at the back of the shop.

"Ah, Theodore! Wonderful to see you again." He shakes our hands warmly. "It has been . . . what's the phrase you young people like to use? A hot minute?"

Theo laughs. "Did you pick that up from your granddaughter, Mr. Kashimura?"

Mr. Kashimura's eyes crinkle. "Yes. My Mika just started seventh grade." His gaze slides toward me. "You said on the phone you need two suits, one for yourself and the other for your friend?"

"This is Dylan," Theo tells him. "We need the suits for this weekend. Sorry for the short notice. Do you think you can swing it?"

"Can I *swing* it?" Mr. Kashimura arches a brow. "A suit is more than a few pieces of cut fabric stitched together. Every garment is a work of art. Like any masterpiece, it takes time. I wish you wouldn't wait until the last minute for something this important."

I'm pretty sure Theo has a custom suit that his relatives have never seen him in—so my lack of sartorial options is probably the reason we're on this emergency trip to Mr. Kashimura's.

Theo grins. "Everyone knows rushed work from you is better than a six-week job anywhere else."

Mr. Kashimura looks at me with mirth. "Ah, your friend has a silver tongue. He can talk his way out of anything."

Something about his words prick at me, but I can't put my finger on what.

"I'm telling the truth," Theo says. "And I insist you add a rush fee to the bill."

Mr. Kashimura chuckles. "I wouldn't dare. When I came to New York and set up this shop twenty years ago, your father was one of my first customers. He took a chance on me—and I've tailored every suit of his, and yours, ever since. How is he, by the way?"

"He's great." Theo's answer is glib. "He received many compliments on the suit you made for his wedding."

"Ah, good to hear!" Mr. Kashimura takes the tape from around his neck. "Shall we get to the measurements?"

Theo nods. "Dylan, you're up."

Sue puts a wooden footstool in the middle of the room. I step onto it, feeling ridiculous in my scuffed sneakers and faded jeans.

"Do you know your inseam, young man?" Mr. Kashimura asks.

"Uh, a medium? I think?"

Mr. Kashimura exchanges an amused glance with Theo, who saunters over.

"I think charcoal gray will look fantastic on him," Theo says. "Let's go with soft shoulders, peaked lapels, and a slight nip to the waist."

I have no idea what any of that means. Mr. Kashimura takes my measurements and writes them down in a notepad. He and Theo talk about the details of the suit, and at one point, Theo runs a hand down my left thigh as they debate the pros and cons of a slim cut or a taper.

His touch sends a tingle through me that's . . . unambiguous. Worst time ever to have such a reaction.

"Let's go with a flat front," Theo says.

If Theo doesn't pull his hand away, the front of these pants is going to be anything but flat.

Thankfully, Mr. Kashimura gestures for me to step off the footstool. "Does the young gentleman have a matching pair of dress shoes?"

"Great catch," Theo replies. "Give him the works: leather shoes, dress shirt, belt, and tie."

Sue brings out a device to measure my foot size while Mr. Kashimura double-checks Theo's measurements and tells him to collect the suits on Friday before going out of town.

As we leave the tailor and walk to the car, Theo holds out his key fob to me. "Want to jump into the driver's seat for a change?"

I stare at the Ferrari badge on the key fob. "I don't think that's a great idea."

"Don't worry, you'll get the hang of it. Just go easy on the throttle—it's pretty sensitive and shifts into high gear quickly." He winks. "Nothing quite like your first time."

The double meaning in everything he said might've been a turn-on if I wasn't so embarrassed about the other thing. "I, uh, I don't have a driver's license."

"Oh." Theo takes this in stride. "You and half of New York City."

We drive back to Brooklyn, and Theo stops in front of the takeout.

"It's a two-hour drive to the Hamptons if we don't get stuck in traffic," he says. "I'll pick you up here on Friday at four o'clock?"

"Sure." I reach for the door handle. "I'll pack the night before so I can leave once I'm home from school."

"Don't forget to bring your trunks," he adds. "If this hot weather keeps up, we can go for a swim."

Suddenly, I'm praying for sweltering heat this weekend. "Sounds good."

• • •

On Thursday night, while I'm sitting on my bed with a chemistry textbook and a highlighter, my phone dings with an email from Mr. Wu, organizer of the mooncake contest.

Dear Dylan Tang,

Great news! Out of dozens of applicants, you and your sous-chef, Jade Wong, have been selected for the Mid-Autumn Festival mooncake-making contest at celebrity

chef Lawrence Lim's culinary studio. We especially want
to feature contestants who are actively involved in the local
foodie scene, and your work experience at Wok Warriors—

Megan barges into my room without knocking.

I look up. "Guess what? I got selected for the mooncake contest!"

"Awesome!" She grabs my phone and reads the email. "Lawrence Lim is that hottie on *Off the Eaten Path,* right? Too old for me, but since Mom's going to be your sous-chef . . . wouldn't it be wild if they fell in love during the contest, like a rom-com? Not to mention it would totally help Wok Warriors. We'd have a line stretching around the block!" She jumps onto the foot of my bed. "Speaking of romance, have you packed for your date weekend with Theo?"

"No. And it's not a date—"

"Yeah, yeah. Because showing up at school and whisking you off in his Ferrari sounds really platonic." She rolls her eyes. "You have no idea how lucky you are. I'll be seventeen in a few months, but Mom refuses to let me sleep over at Hannah's because her two older brothers live at home. Can you believe that? And yet she's cool with you spending a weekend in the Hamptons with a guy you have the hots for, and there's probably—big surprise—only one bed for both of you to share?"

I didn't even think of that. Hmm. "Maybe it's because I'm unlikely to get pregnant?"

"That's such a gross double standard." Megan sits pretzel-style and tilts her head. "So this party's the first time you'll be meeting Theo's family, right? Have you figured out how to sweep them off

60

their feet with your adorable middle-class charm, like Rachel did in *Crazy Rich Asians*?"

I snort. "They left a dead fish on her bed with blood and guts everywhere. And all her boyfriend could say was 'Is that all that happened?' Talk about gaslighting."

"Theo got ALLERGIC-TO-DUMBASSES to back off, didn't he? I bet he'll smite anyone who dares to make a snarky comment about you. Listen, when you get there, I want all the details. And lots of photos."

"I'm sure I can send a few nice sunrise shots."

"Very funny. I'm serious. You'd better let me live vicariously through you." She pulls a stern face. "And if any of Theo's relatives give you a hard time, you let me know."

I raise a brow, amused. "And you'll . . . do what, exactly?"

"I'll think of something. Pretty sure Chung has some triad connections back in Hong Kong." Megan gets up. "Got to run. I have to log into the booking website and camp there before everyone else makes the stupid thing crash."

Megan has been talking nonstop about the Blackpink concert since they announced their U.S. tour.

"Tickets going on sale tonight?" I ask.

"Yeah. If I can't get them directly, I won't be able to afford them on the black market."

"The black market?" I quip. "Should you try the pink market next?"

"Dork." She heads out the door.

I close my textbook and go to my closet. Maybe the reason I've been putting off packing for the trip is because nearly everything I own isn't good enough. The suit's settled, but what about the rest of my clothes? None of them have a flashy brand logo. The nicest pants I own are my Levi's jeans and Uniqlo chinos.

I put the only oxford shirt I have and a few polo shirts into my backpack. I hate wearing shirts in hot weather, but feeling out of place because I'm underdressed at some fancy resort will be a lot more uncomfortable than a sticky collar.

Something else has been bugging me. When I asked Theo why he isn't bringing Adrian as his plus-one, he said Adrian already had plans. He didn't try to pretend I was his first choice. Theo claims nothing's going on between them any longer—but Adrian has his own ringtone, and Theo has no problem being half naked around him. Even his relatives have seen them making out under the mistletoe. When I show up with Theo, they're going to compare me to Adrian—no prizes for guessing who's a better fit in their rich, fancy world.

Aunt Jade asked if there's anything holding me back from falling for Theo. His smile can light up my entire day, but that's the thing—it seems as easy for him as flipping a switch.

Your friend has a silver tongue. He can talk his way out of anything.

I'm not sure why Mr. Kashimura's words made me uncomfortable, but my uneasiness has only deepened. Because when Theo flips off the switch, I'll have to face the truth—my growing feelings for him might be the only thing between us that isn't fake.

Chapter 8

"**D**ylan!" Aunt Jade calls from downstairs. "Theo's here!"

I'm in front of my dresser mirror, trying to style my hair, which is too long and has lost its shape. I should've gone to the hair salon this week, but I didn't have time.

"Coming!" I grab my backpack, barrel down the stairs—and stop in my tracks.

Theo is in the middle of our shop. He's wearing khakis and a white Lacoste button-down shirt with the alligator icon on the left side of his chest. His sleeves are rolled back, and his aviator sunglasses rest on top of his head. He's so handsome that my brain cells fall out of formation for a whole moment.

"You're here," I say dumbly.

Tim laughs. "My mom literally just said that."

I try not to look like a goldfish out of water that's just been put back into its tank. "I thought she meant he was waiting outside. In his car."

"I wanted to come in and say hello to your aunt," Theo says. "This is the first time I'm meeting her in person."

"Like I said, the perfect gentleman," Aunt Jade says. She beams at my polo shirt and chinos ensemble. "You look so handsome!"

I turn red. Theo is standing *right there*.

Megan cuts in. "It's the Hamptons, Mom, not Coney Island."

Aunt Jade snaps her fingers. "Did you bring sunscreen?"

"Yeah, I did." I give her a one-armed hug. "See you on Sunday."

She pecks me on the cheek. "Have a great time, boys!"

"Send pictures!" Megan calls as Theo and I head outside.

Theo opens the trunk, which is hidden behind the folded roof. Inside are a bunch of garment bags, shoeboxes, and a large carry-on. Just for a weekend. I can't imagine what he brings on a two-week trip. I dump my backpack next to the carry-on and get into the car. Aunt Jade, Megan, and Tim are still waving at us through the window.

Theo chuckles. "Your aunt and cousins look like they're sending you off to college."

"You didn't have to park and come in just to say hi," I tell him.

"Bernard says it's rude to pick someone up without stopping for a minute to greet their folks." Theo pauses. "Should I have brought your aunt a gift as well? Is that a thing?"

"No, definitely not," I assure him. "Chinese culture has a bunch of gifting taboos, so it's better to show up empty-handed than with a wrong gift. A British minister once made a huge blunder by giving the mayor of Taipei a pocket watch."

"Is that supposed to be a bad omen?"

I nod. "The Mandarin phrase for giving a clock or a watch—sòng zhōng—sounds the same as attending a funeral, which implies you're waiting for the other person to die. Probably not the message the minister wanted to send."

Theo laughs. "Yikes. Anything else I should know?"

"Hmm. Aunt Jade says fruit baskets are safe as long as there aren't any pears in them—'sharing a pear' in Mandarin has the same pronunciation as 'parting ways.' And never give anything in multiples of four, because 'four' and 'death' sound similar."

"I think I'll stick to gifting a bottle of wine." Theo starts the engine. "That should be a safe bet, right?"

"Yeah. You'll score top points if you bring my aunt Moscato. She'd love that."

I lean against the leather headrest as we join the busy street ahead. Heads still swivel toward us everywhere we go, but I'm getting used to the speed, the rush, the power of the machine we're riding in. This isn't me—I'm usually rushing to catch the R train—but then again, I'm not supposed to be me this weekend. I'm supposed to be the kind of guy Theo Somers would bring to meet his family.

"How do you want me to act in front of your relatives?" I ask, since the pretend-dating handbook wasn't on my senior year reading list.

Theo shrugs. "We'll behave like a couple when they're around. When we're alone, we can be ourselves. Anytime you're not sure what to do, just follow my lead."

Not exactly helpful, since "being ourselves" isn't something we've gotten around to defining. Now that I'm his fake boyfriend, it's going to be even harder to make out . . . uh, figure out.

"Relax," Theo says, as if sensing what's going through my mind. "It's the Hamptons. You might actually have a little fun."

"What about your dad? How's he going to react?"

Theo shakes his head. "He won't be there. He's out of town on business, as usual."

Apart from getting me a tailored suit, Theo doesn't appear too concerned what kind of impression I'll make on his relatives. I try to stop worrying. Not like I'll see them again after this weekend.

When we're out of Brooklyn and cruising east on the Long Island Expressway, Theo turns on the music. It's hard to talk with the top down and the wind whipping our faces, anyway. His playlist has a good mix of artists, like Taylor Swift, Sam Smith, Cardi B, Olivia Rodrigo, and BTS. Megan would definitely approve.

When a Two Steps from Hell track comes up, I can't help raising a brow. "Seriously?"

"You don't like epic instrumental? Their music's on a bunch of film soundtracks."

"I love them. Just that most people blast Two Steps from Hell to imagine their old Honda's a Ferrari."

Theo grins and cranks up the volume.

The last time I was in the Hamptons was three summers ago. Mom wanted to go on a short trip before I started high school, and we bundled into a rental with Clover and came here for a few days. We stayed in a pet-friendly B&B in East Hampton within walking distance to Main Street and the beach. The owner, Barbara, was one of Mom's former coworkers, and she gave us a discount. We were fostering Clover at the time, and she was still skittish and restless. But being at the beach . . . something changed. She blossomed into a different dog. Mom and I beamed at each other as Clover ran around in circles on the soft, white sand. That was the moment we knew we wanted to be her forever family.

Theo drives past Main Street and continues north. Barbara told us the road leads to the northernmost tip of the bay, where a cluster of private bungalows and luxury homes have their own private beach.

Theo gestures as we pass a signpost marked THE SPRINGS. "What do you think of Jackson Pollock?"

I've heard the name before, but I'm not sure who that is.

"Pollock lived in the Springs," Theo says, sounding enthused. "Abstract expressionism began in New York, and he was one of the pioneer artists. His studio used to be an old storage shed for fishing equipment, and his home's now a museum. Want to check it out while we're here?"

"Yeah, sure." I have no clue what abstract expressionism is. I'm the weird in-between, someone who's not interested in either the arts or sports. I don't know which play picked up the most Tony Awards this year, and I have no idea which team has the most Super Bowl appearances. But I can tell you the breed or breed mix of almost any dog, or how fresh an egg is just by holding it in my palm.

We pull up at the main gate of a sprawling villa. Theo shows his invitation, and he's greeted and waved through. Guesthouses are spread across the compound, and the main building's a three-story country manor with a pitched roof and mosaic stonework on the walls. It's as pompous and lavish as Theo's mansion, which is probably why he doesn't bat an eye.

Theo stops in the sheltered driveway in front of the foyer. A porter helps with our bags. Theo hands his key fob to a young valet with a tip. I stand there, unsure of what to do. I'm not used to having people wait on me.

A shrill exclamation rings out. "Theo?"

A blond woman in stiletto heels is walking briskly toward us. She looks elegant in a wrap dress with frilly sleeves, and her pearl earrings must've been wrested from a pair of Godzilla-sized oysters. The only thing that doesn't match the rest of her appearance is the furrow between her flawless brows. Maybe my polo shirt and chinos aren't good enough for her?

"What are you doing here?" she demands. I realize she's glowering at Theo, not me.

"Hello, Aunt Lucia." Theo gives her a blithe smile. "It would be incredibly rude of me to miss Nora's big day."

Lucia crosses her arms. "I'm sorry to disappoint you, but the villa's fully booked. We didn't provide for unexpected guests."

Wait, what?

Theo holds up the invitation, unfazed. "So, I wasn't supposed to get one of these?"

Lucia stares at the card. Shock turns into annoyance.

"I suppose this is Terri's idea of a practical joke," she snaps.

Oh, shit—Theo wasn't even *invited*?

"Speaking of Terri, she just turned twenty-one last month, didn't she?" Theo has a glint in his eye. "I'm not old enough to drink, but for everyone else's sake, I hope the wedding won't be dry because of her."

Lucia's jaw clenches. She doesn't look in my direction even once. I thought she was offended by my clothes—but I'm invisible to her. Like a ghost.

"Theo?" comes another woman's voice. "I can't believe it! Is that you?"

Great. I brace myself for another onslaught of hostile relatives as two women around Aunt Jade's age—one Black and the other white—hurry toward us. They're dressed in matching pantsuits.

"So wonderful to see you, Theo!" The women take turns hugging him. "It's been too long! When was the last time? Two years ago?"

The white woman turns to me, her smile as bright as her curly red hair. "And who's this handsome young man?"

"Aunt Catherine, Aunt Malia, this is Dylan." Theo takes my hand, and I almost jump out of my skin. "My boyfriend."

"Oh! Delighted to meet you, Dylan." If Catherine notices that I look as if I've been zapped by a defibrillator, she doesn't show it.

Malia's braids are tied down with a silk patterned headscarf. "Did you know Theo was the ring bearer at our wedding when he was four?"

"No, I didn't." Another one of *many* details Theo conveniently failed to mention. "I can't wait for him to fill me in."

"I'm so glad you invited him," Catherine tells Lucia, squeezing her hand. "Whatever's going on between you and Malcolm shouldn't have anything to do with his son."

Lucia's expression looks like it's been blasted with liquid nitrogen.

Theo chuckles dryly. "To be honest, Aunt Catherine, I'm not officially on the guest list. But I've really missed everyone, and I wanted to congratulate Nora and Angelo in person. Unfortunately, Aunt Lucia just told us there aren't any spare rooms."

"That's too bad!" Catherine exclaims, while Malia looks crestfallen. "There isn't one extra room in this whole place? Why don't you guys bunk in with us?"

"Oh, no, we couldn't possibly," Theo says. "I owe Aunt Lucia an apology for crashing the wedding. It must be stressful to have unexpected guests popping up. Dylan and I will get a hotel in town—"

"Theo, you're just like your father, never letting me finish what I'm trying to say," Lucia cuts in, putting her hands on her hips. "There are no more rooms with pool views, but we can certainly have one of the other rooms prepared for you and your guest." She lets out a perfectly executed laugh. "How preposterous to suggest I'd make my own nephew get a hotel in town! I'm sure Nora will be touched that you made all this effort to give us a . . . surprise."

"Excellent!" Catherine says. "Now, if that's settled, we're headed to the bar. It's been a long drive from Boston, and there was an awful pileup on the I-95—"

"Like I said, we should've taken the Cross Sound Ferry," Malia interjects.

"After we were stuck for two hours on that half-sinking ferry between Montego Bay and Ocho Rios, I prefer transport that doesn't involve possibly being overwhelmed by ocean." Catherine turns to Theo. "Word of advice, kiddo. When in doubt, listen to your partner. If their plan doesn't work out, at least you won't get an *I told you so.*"

Malia gives her a playful jab, and both women laugh as they head off, arm in arm.

As soon as they're out of sight, Lucia's effusive demeanor slides. Giving us a room is clearly the last thing she wants to do. She signals to the concierge, who's waiting with a clipboard.

"The staff will bring you to your room." Her tone is like yogurt that's gone bad. "Feel free to use the private beach."

Theo gives her a broad smile. "So great seeing you again, Aunt Lucia." He doesn't let go of my hand. "I'm looking forward to catching up with everyone else."

Well, I'm not—especially after finding out the bride and groom didn't even invite us. From Lucia's face, that's probably the only thing she and I can agree on.

Chapter 9

Each guesthouse in the villa is divided into individual suites. The concierge opens the door to ours and gives us our key-cards.

I step inside the suite, which has an open layout. The four-poster bed is so big that if we sleep on opposite sides, it'll be as if we're in separate beds. There's a huge plasma TV on the wall, as well as a walk-in closet, a velvet chaise lounge, and a full-length mirror framed in rose gold. The Jacuzzi is out on the balcony—but that's not what catches my attention.

In the middle of the room is a rain shower. With clear glass panels on all sides. They aren't even frosted.

My stomach drops. Sharing a large bed is one thing—Megan will love this—but I wasn't expecting to watch Theo shower. The thrill is promptly drowned out by the sinking realization that *I'll* have to shower in front of *him*.

I push the thought aside. I'll deal with it later.

As Theo tips the concierge and shuts the door, I turn to him. "Want to fill me in on what's going on? Maybe starting with the part where you aren't actually supposed to be here? Did you fake the invitation too?"

"No, the invitation's real—my aunt Lucia just didn't know I got one." Theo sounds wry. "I might've forgotten to mention that she and my dad are locking horns in a billion-dollar lawsuit right now. The *Economist* ran a feature a couple of weeks ago with all the gory details. That's why my dad and I aren't on the guest list."

"So you decided to crash the wedding to get back at your aunt?"

"My aunt's not the target. My dad is."

I blink. "Your dad? But you said he won't be at this wedding."

"And he forbade me from attending any family gatherings after most of them took my aunt's side. When he finds out I showed up, he's going to lose his shit."

Alarm bells should've gone off when Theo said this was a family wedding. *Crazy Rich Asians* made one thing clear: rich people can be . . . crazy. Mom used to say that if you don't want to be fed to the sharks, don't wade into the water. But it's too late now.

I pin him with a glare. "I agreed to be your fake date, Theo, not an accomplice to some diabolical plan to spoil your cousin's big day!"

Theo shakes his head. "I'm crashing the wedding to piss off my dad, but I have no intention of ruining Nora's celebration."

"Most kids piss off their parents by breaking curfew, wrecking their cars, skipping school. Stuff like that." My scoff comes out a pitch higher than intended. "They don't show up at a big, splashy family wedding they aren't invited to."

Theo shrugs. "I've never had a curfew. I like my car, and I love getting a 4.0 GPA." A shadow crosses his face. "Doing stupid things and jeopardizing your future only works if your parent actually cares about you."

Unlike sliding down the banister, staying away from the relatives—especially Lucia—is the one rule Theo's dad still cares about. And Theo's determined to break it in the most spectacular way possible. Would he have done this if his mom were still around?

"What about your cousin Terri?" I ask. "You were pretty snarky to her mom about her drinking problem. Is she next on the list of people you're trying to piss off?"

Theo's expression darkens. "If you must know, she got wasted at a sorority party at Columbia last year and crashed her Benz. Her blood alcohol level was twice the limit. She could've killed someone."

Theo's mom died in a car crash. It wasn't a drunk driver, but what happened with his cousin must've hit too close to home. I let this argument go, but something else occurs to me.

"If you weren't invited, you wouldn't have needed a plus-one." I narrow my eyes. "Why drag me along as your date? Will your dad be even more furious because you brought some middle-class guy who works at his aunt's takeout and delivers food by bike? Is that why you asked me instead of Adrian?"

Theo's brow furrows. "Of course not—"

"Theodore Oliver Somers!" comes an impatient female voice from outside, followed by loud knocking. "I know you're in there! You've got some major explaining to do!"

I tense as Theo opens the door. A young woman in a swishy floral dress stands there, her strawberry-blond hair done up in a messy but stylish bun. Her frown and crossed arms remind me of Lucia.

"You show up with your new boyfriend, and I have to find out from my mom?" She stalks in and pokes Theo's shoulder.

Her manicured fingers are decorated with 3D butterfly art. "Why didn't you tell me?"

"I wanted it to be a surprise, chipmunk," Theo replies. "Dylan, this is my cousin Terri."

"Hi, Dylan!" Terri brightens and gives me a hug. "Theo has told me absolutely *nothing* about you—which means you must be special, since he always keeps his secrets closest to his heart."

Theo groans. "Terri, stop. I'm getting a toothache."

Terri cackles. "Mom was absolutely *livid* that I invited you. She yelled at me for trying to upstage my own sister's wedding. Seriously, though, I'm so glad you came! Being a lowly pawn pushed around the board in service of the queen is exhausting."

"Really? Nora doesn't strike me as the bridezilla type," Theo says.

"I'm talking about Mom. Nora's close to the end of her rope too. A few nights ago, I caught her making yogurt at three in the morning when I went to the kitchen to stress-bake cupcakes. I swear, if I survive this wedding and find someone I want to do this whole marriage thing with, I'm eloping."

Theo looks concerned. "You sure you're all right?"

"Of course. Why wouldn't I be?" Terri shrugs. "Okay, I'll be stuck at the rehearsal dinner tonight, which could take forever since Mom will probably go through the schedule at least twenty times. Our photographer, Georgina Kim—she's the Annie Leibovitz of Korean celebrity weddings—wants a head start on the wedding party shots after brunch tomorrow. Family photos are after the ceremony—you're not on the list, obviously, but you should show up anyway."

Theo chuckles. "Your mom will never forgive me if I'm immortalized in the album."

Terri checks the time. "Damn, I've got to go. Nora won't start the rehearsal dinner without me. Beverly, our resident gossip queen, will probably spread a rumor that I was busy making out with a cute waiter or something." She looks at me. "The three of us *have* to find some time to hang out this weekend. I want to hear all about how you stole my favorite cousin's heart."

"Go easy on him," Theo says mildly. "I don't want you scaring him off."

"Nah, pretty sure any guy who can handle you can handle himself." Terri glances at the rose petals scattered on the bedsheets. "Speaking of handling . . . Nora has the honeymoon suite, but it seems like you guys got the sexy-time room. Condoms are in the dresser drawer, by the way."

My face burns. Theo sounds amused. "That's a very thoughtful wedding favor."

Terri winks. "We want to make sure our guests have a wonderful stay."

After she leaves, I turn to Theo. "She's the cousin you were bad-mouthing earlier?"

Theo nods. "But I wasn't throwing shade at her drinking problem. That jab was meant for her mom. If Aunt Lucia hadn't been so obsessed with making her daughters seem perfect instead of letting them be messy and real, Terri might not have ended up the way she did. Good thing the prosecutor agreed to drop charges if she went to rehab. Otherwise that DUI would be on her record for the rest of her life."

"Terri thinks we're actually a couple too? She doesn't know we're fake-dating?"

"I'll tell her after the weekend. She's got enough going on for now." Theo has the grace to look contrite. "Listen, I'm sorry I wasn't up-front about crashing the wedding. I have a thick skin, obviously, but I should've thought about how awkward you might feel. If you really don't want to be here, I can drive you home."

"But we just arrived." I tilt my head. "What's everyone going to say if they find out your boyfriend walked out on you before the wedding?"

Theo's expression is self-deprecating. "Guess I'll have to pick up a cute bartender in East Hampton on my way back and pay him to show up tomorrow."

"Good to know I'm fully replaceable."

"If you want the truth . . ." Theo reaches for my hand, pulling me closer. "I'd much rather be with you."

I suck in a sharp breath. Smart move. First, disable my executive function by frying my brain with his touch. Then add a little flattery to sweeten the deal. I'm still annoyed he didn't say we'd be gate-crashers. Terri invited him, but technically, she doesn't have the authority to do so, and she didn't give anyone a heads-up. But I can't leave him in the lurch, not after he gave our takeout the lifeline we needed. I owe him this favor. The circumstances don't matter, right?

I pull my hand away. "Fine. I agreed to be your fake date. I'm going to keep my end of the bargain." I pause. "How did your dad and aunt wind up fighting in court? Have they always been rivals?"

Theo shakes his head. "Growing up, he and my aunt Lucia were the closest among the four siblings. They're a year apart, like you and Megan. They got on so well that my grandfather gave them joint control of his biggest company before he died. But my aunt was more interested in the socialite life than running a business, and my dad resented having to pick up the slack. A couple of years ago, she discovered he'd been channeling his ideas and siphoning the company's talent into a new venture of his own."

"I guess that didn't go down too well."

"They had a huge falling out, and she sued him for compensation." Theo sounds grim. "But she wasn't after his money. She was hurt and angry that he went behind her back. The whole family knows the most important thing to my dad is his reputation. The lawsuit was the biggest slap in the face she could give him."

Now Theo's doing the same thing by showing up at this wedding. Question is: What did his dad do to make Theo hurt and angry enough to get back at him this way?

Theo grabs a jacket. "Come on, dinner's on me. Promise I won't say anything if you flirt with the waiter."

No one we've met so far, not even Terri, has asked about my family. They all seem to assume I'm also from a wealthy background . . . because who else would Theo Somers date? From his track record, nothing less than a spoiled snob like Adrian.

"Terri won't be the only one who's curious about how we met," I tell him. "I'm not ashamed my family runs a takeout, but are you sure you want yours knowing? Especially since we don't have any Michelin stars?"

"You're my fake date, but I never expected you to come with a fake identity," Theo replies. "I don't think it'll hold up, anyway."

I cross my arms. "What's that supposed to mean?"

"You looked at me like you thought Jackson Pollock was a kind of Atlantic fish."

Oh, oops. "Yeah, well, art history isn't offered at my school."

"Which is why you should be yourself. Don't worry about my relatives. My dad's the black sheep, and I'm unfortunately his biological lamb, but they won't give you a hard time."

"How can you be sure?"

He flashes an infuriating grin. "Because I won't let them."

Chapter 10

Theo and I drive out to East Hampton for dinner. Main Street is rowdy with tourists, and the queues outside the clubs have started to form.

"What do you have in mind?" Theo asks.

"I'm fine with anything." My family rarely goes out to eat—there are always lots of leftovers—and when we do, Megan chooses Japanese nearly every time. "You decide."

I expect him to head for one of the fancy, upscale restaurants, but we pass those and he picks a burger bar instead. The atmosphere is chill and laid back, and we sit at a table in the alfresco dining area. I choose the grilled lemon pepper chicken with salad and crinkle-cut fries. Theo decides to get a black Angus beef burger with applewood bacon on a brioche bun.

His order reminds me that Clover always gets a special bacon treat on Fridays. Not sure if dogs have a concept of calendar days, but I don't want her to think I forgot about her.

When Theo goes to order, I send Megan a text: *Help me give Clover a bacon treat?*

I glance at Theo to make sure he's at the counter before I

start Googling his last name. Something I should've done *before* I agreed to come to the Hamptons as his fake date.

Google reveals that Malcolm H. Somers is the CEO of Somers Technology, a Fortune 500 semiconductor company that counts Intel and Qualcomm as its top rivals. His second marriage to Natalie Cruz—heiress to one of Silicon Valley's top ten tech companies—made national news last summer, along with their twenty-million-dollar mansion on Long Island designed by Moshe Safdie. Recent news is dominated by the ongoing lawsuit with his sister, socialite Lucia Leyland-Somers, with headlines such as *The Somers Standoff* and *Framing Britney Spears—Family Feuds of the Corporate World*.

"Pro tip: narrow the search by adding my name," comes Theo's voice over my shoulder. "Or you'll get a ton of boring stuff about my dad instead."

I quickly put down my phone. "I wasn't Googling you."

"You sure?" Theo's hip brushes my shoulder as he sets the order number sign on the table. "You might find a really unflattering photo of me from the third grade buried in the search results."

Instead of sitting across from me, he takes the chair next to mine. My proximity sensor goes off. "What are you doing?"

"I thought we'd try some method acting while waiting for our meal to arrive." Theo gazes at me like I'm the only person here. "Good practice for tomorrow."

He doesn't know it, but "fake-dating" actually means something different for me—stop trying to pretend I *don't* have a huge crush on Theo and start behaving like I *do*. Which is a lot harder than it should be.

Theo leans in. His lips brush my earlobe, turning my stomach into a ball of nerves. "Listen, if you can't act as if you're attracted to me, then can you at least not look like I'm holding a knife to your thigh under the table?"

I gulp. "Sorry. I suck at this—"

"Theo? Is that you?"

Theo pulls back as a skinny white man comes up to our table. He's sporting the kind of facial hair that only looks good if you're Michael Fassbender. Next to him, an Indian woman is carrying a baby and clutching her Hermès handbag in a way that shows off the brand logo. Their other four kids run circles around them.

"Hello, Uncle Herbert, Aunt Jacintha." Theo stands and shakes their hands instead of giving them a hug, the way he did with Catherine and Malia.

"We've been following reports about the lawsuit," Herbert says. "Catherine and I were hoping your dad and Lucia would settle the matter out of court before the wedding. That obviously didn't happen, but I'm glad you were still invited."

I resist the urge to roll my eyes. Theo gives the baby a serene smile. "She's adorable. What's her name?"

"Asha," says Jacintha. "It means 'hope' in Hindi. Do you want to hold her?"

Theo's expression is hilarious as she thrusts the infant into his arms. I've never seen him so uncomfortable. You'd have thought she passed him a bomb. Asha fidgets and starts to cry. Theo hurriedly hands her back to her mother.

I stifle a grin. Apparently, he's only great with kids over ten who can play the violin.

"Have you seen Terri?" Herbert asks. "I heard she's in the wedding party. How's she doing?"

"She's fine," Theo replies. "She stopped by our room on her way to the rehearsal dinner to meet Dylan, my date."

"Ah, your date!" Herbert looks as if he just noticed my existence. "Are you from Theo's school?"

I glance at Theo.

"No, we met when I went to his aunt's takeout," Theo says. "Their soup dumplings are the best. You should check them out if you're in Sunset Park. The shop's called Wok Warriors."

Herbert nods. "A number of my hedge fund clients are from China as well."

"My family's from Singapore," I say. "It's six hours from Beijing by plane."

"Oh, Singapore!" Herbert snaps his fingers. "I can never tell the difference. You're all Chinese, though, right? I love your food, but Jacintha's really into clean eating, and the amount of MSG you guys put into your cooking . . ."

My jaw tightens. Before I can think of a response, Theo speaks up.

"Actually, Uncle Herbert, MSG is a naturally occurring amino acid in tomatoes and cheese, which is extracted and fermented in a way similar to yogurt and wine," he says. "I know you love a glass of cabernet sauvignon—so the myth that MSG in Chinese food is bad for health isn't just untrue but actually xenophobic."

Herbert blinks. Jacintha nudges him.

"Yes, of course." Herbert looks at me with a chuckle. "No offense, son."

Not his son, but whatever. Their actual kids have escalated to shrieking and chasing one another, nearly running into a server balancing several plates of burgers.

"Stop that!" Jacintha chides. "All right, kids, we're leaving!"

With a baby to carry, she and Herbert don't have enough hands to grab hold of all their children.

"See you boys at the ceremony!" Herbert calls out as they drag their brood away.

The server arrives with our food. He gives us an unfriendly glance as he rearranges the chairs the kids pushed around. I can't blame him. I hate when people let their kids wreak havoc in public. Once, some kids ran around the takeout and knocked over an antique vase Aunt Jade brought from Hong Kong, and their parents didn't even apologize.

Theo exhales. "Sorry. My uncle can be clueless about how offensive his words are."

"How did you know all that stuff about MSG?" I ask. "Do you take AP chem or something?"

"Nah, I'm terrible at science. I read Eddie Huang's memoir, *Fresh Off the Boat,* for an extra-credit assignment in AP lit. Then I watched one of his interviews, and he brought up a few fascinating misconceptions about MSG."

"Eddie Huang and Lawrence Lim are good friends," I tell him. "They're always making guest appearances on each other's shows."

Theo has a twinkle in his eye. "Does this earn me some culinary cred?"

"Sure does." I snag a shoestring fry from his plate—I like my crinkle-cut fries better but sharing food with him just feels good. "Are you taking any other AP classes?"

"U.S. history, psychology, music theory, and art history."

"Pre-law?"

He nods. "Not that I have much of a choice. My dad made that a requirement if I want to use my college trust fund."

Another rule. I can't help thinking of the impeccably pruned, stunted bonsai at Theo's mansion. Seems his dad expects him to fit the Somers family mold in the same way.

"But I'll let you in on a secret," Theo adds. "Once my senior year of tuition is fully paid, I'll switch to a double major in art and music instead."

"What do you plan to do with that degree? Teach? Work in a museum?"

Theo shrugs. "I'm not sure yet. I just don't want to be stuck in some corporate job where I have to spend all day in a suit. What about you?"

"I'm taking AP biology, chem, physics, and calculus," I reply. "I wasn't planning on calculus, but the guidance counselor said the pre-vet tracks at most colleges require that. I'm hoping to land a scholarship to NYU."

"Why vet school?"

"Oh . . . my mom was a vet. She worked in a clinic in Greenwood Heights." I have fond memories of volunteering there during the holidays. "I thought rescuing animals and taking care of them would be a great way to follow in her footsteps."

"Like Clover?" Theo asks. "Did you adopt her from your mom's clinic?"

"Yeah." I'm surprised but touched that he remembered. "Her former owner kept her leashed all day with not enough food and water, and my mom was one of the volunteers who rescued her. When we fostered her, she was always crying or growling or ripping something to shreds. Once, she hurt herself hiding behind the TV console. My mom tried to bandage her paw, and Clover bit her. But my mom didn't get mad. She just took the first aid kit and bandaged her own hand. Clover was watching. Later, when my mom tried to bandage her paw again, Clover let her."

"Sounds like Clover realized you guys wanted her to be part of your family."

"For sure. When my mom was recovering from chemo, Clover wouldn't leave her side." I force down the emotions threatening to spill over. "After she was gone, Clover needed a while to understand that my mom didn't abandon her. She was just . . . not coming back."

"Clover's lucky to have you," Theo says. "I think you'd make a terrific vet."

"That's the thing." I hesitate. "Mom always knew she wanted to be a vet, and Aunt Jade was sure she would go to culinary school. At first, I taught myself to cook recipes from YouTube whenever my mom had to work late at the clinic and I didn't want to waste money ordering in. Then I learned to cook her favorite food so she could relax on weekends. After I moved in with my aunt and cousins, I've been spending even more time in the kitchen, learning to cook the dishes my mom ate and loved when she was growing up in Singapore. . . ."

"And you're wondering if being a chef might be your true calling?" Theo asks.

I chew on my lip. "I love taking care of animals, like my mom did. But at the same time, I want to help Aunt Jade fulfill her dream of running her own restaurant someday. The Culinary Institute of America has a campus in Hyde Park. Anthony Bourdain was one of their alumni."

I haven't told anyone this, not even my family. Not sure why this idea came out in front of Theo—but somehow, it doesn't feel weird at all.

Theo tilts his head. "So you're seriously thinking of going to culinary school?"

"Yes? Maybe? I don't know. It's a tough choice. And I'll need to drop physics for statistics."

"You know what will help you make up your mind?" Theo's expression turns playful. "A sign from the universe."

I stifle a snort. "That sounds really scientific."

"Hey, I'm not the guy who's figuring out whether to drop physics." Theo snaps his fingers. "How about this: if you get picked for that mooncake contest at Lawrence Lim's studio, you're meant to be a chef."

I break into a grin. "You're not going to believe this, but they emailed me last night. I got in!"

"What?" Theo laughs. "There you go. The universe has spoken. You're destined for great culinary things."

I ponder for a moment. "I don't know . . . maybe the sign should be something more challenging?"

Theo raises a brow. "You mean like winning the contest and getting your aunt's takeout featured on the show?"

I feel a little sheepish. "Yeah, I know, that's—"

"Perfect," Theo says. "That'll be your sign."

I blink. Is Theo secretly trying to nudge me toward picking vet school, or does he genuinely believe I have a shot at the prize? Or am I just overthinking a throwaway comment that he'll probably forget about in a couple of minutes?

We head back to the villa after dinner. When we enter the room, the sight of the rain shower sends another jolt through me. At some point this weekend, each of us will have to take off our clothes and step inside—and the glass leaves nothing to the imagination.

Delaying the inevitable sounds like a good plan for now.

Theo jumps onto one side of the bed and scrolls through his phone. I go to unpack my stuff, but when I open my backpack, I stop in horror.

All my nice shirts are gone. In their place are a bunch of my favorite T-shirts. I frantically dig deeper. My Levi's jeans are still there, but all my shirts have vanished except a light blue polo.

No way. This can't be happening.

I pull out a crumpled T-shirt with a bulldog in professor glasses holding a bone and the line I FOUND THIS HUMERUS emblazoned on the chest. A piece of notepaper slips out and falls to the floor.

BE YOURSELF!!! The words in gold ink are scrawled in Megan's handwriting. HE LIKES U FOR WHO U ARE—

"Everything all right?" Theo asks from the bed.

My head snaps up. I crumple the note. "Uh, yeah. Everything's fine."

"You sure? You look like you found a dead lizard inside your backpack."

I stuff Megan's note into the front zipper pocket. I'm going to kill her when I get back. "I have a feeling I didn't pack something important."

"I get that every time I go on a trip," Theo says. "Don't worry. If you need anything, we'll drive into town and pick up whatever you're missing."

I'm pretty sure there isn't a factory outlet in the Hamptons. I should own up and tell him what Megan did. She pranked him, too, so he'll believe it. Probably laugh it off. But I don't want him thinking this wouldn't have happened if he'd brought Adrian instead.

Theo stands and starts unbuttoning his shirt.

My heart collides with my rib cage. "What are you doing?"

He stops. "I was going to jump into the shower. Or do you want to go first?"

"No!" I burst out. He looks startled. Oh God. This is embarrassing. "I mean, you go ahead. I'll, uh, head to the villa reception desk and get another . . . pillow."

Theo points at the wardrobe. "There should be an extra two on the top shelf."

"Um, I need more, like, five." Theo arches a brow, and I hastily add, "I have this super weird idiosyncrasy. . . . On the first night I'm sleeping in an unfamiliar place, I have to be surrounded by a lot of pillows."

I can imagine Megan cracking up if she heard this. Nice job, Dylan. You can't even come up with a story that *doesn't* make you seem like a complete nutcase.

Theo shrugs off his shirt. "We can call room service and they'll bring more pillows."

I'm seeing him shirtless for the second time—and I don't have the excuse of a wrong order to gracefully exit the scene with.

"Nah, I need to stretch my legs after the long drive," I babble, snatching one of the keycards on the dresser. "I'll be right back."

Before Theo can protest, I flee the room.

Chapter 11

The villa's footpaths are well lit at night, and there's a faint tinge of wood smoke in the air. I take the long way to the reception desk to get the pillows I don't need. Maybe I should use them to build a rampart in the middle of the huge bed we have to share. I don't want to roll over and accidentally cuddle Theo while I'm asleep or something.

As I pass the patio, voices drift from the heated pool. I duck behind a tall hedge and peer around. A bunch of twentysome-things in bikinis and swim trunks are in the pool, sipping from champagne glasses.

"Pass the bottle," says a brunette with a big hibiscus in her hair.

One of the guys—he's cute in a Harry Styles kind of way—refills her glass. "Hey, Amber, did you see Terri taking off right after the rehearsal? She looked like she was crying."

"Whatever." Amber sounds bored. "She and her little drinking problem seriously screwed with the vibes of our bachelorette. Right, Beverly?"

"Oh, total buzzkill," replies a blonde with electric-blue

highlights. "Instead of a boozy weekend on Amber's dad's yacht, we had a spa retreat in the middle of the woods. I mean, we did yoga by the lake, and a hot French chef cooked our meals—but my grandma got more alcohol at communion than we did the whole weekend."

A lanky Asian guy with chest and shoulder tattoos laughs. "Lucky for us, Angelo's family knows how to throw a stag party. They own a distillery in the Valle de Guadalupe, and we had the place to ourselves. Free flow of tequila, bourbon, and whiskey . . . I got so plastered I don't even remember how much I lost at poker."

Amber flicks water at him. "Humblebrag."

I back away and slip off.

Is this what rich kids do? Brag and talk shit about people behind their backs? Is this what Theo's like with his prep school friends? If I have to act shallow and superficial to pretend I belong in this world, then I don't want to fit in. I'd rather go back to being invisible.

The villa suddenly feels stifling, and when I pass the gate leading to the beach, I wave my keycard and go through. The briny scent of the ocean wafts on the breeze as I walk across the sand. Good thing it's late and no one else is around.

Unlike the soft, velvety beaches along Main Street, the shore out here at the head of the bay is rougher, grittier. The moon is nowhere to be seen, which means we're at the end of the Hungry Ghost Month. No Chinese couple would ever have their wedding in the seventh month. It's bad luck.

Up ahead, an unlit wooden pier stretches about fifty yards from the beach into the ocean. Probably for fishing, since the platform is too high above the water for boats to dock. There are no railings between the posts, so people can sit with their legs dangling over the edge.

At the far end of the pier is a silhouette of a young woman. I'm not alone after all. Any other time, I'd just keep going—but something's off about the way she's leaning against one of the posts. When I get closer, I realize who she is.

"Terri?"

She turns, startled. Blunt recognition dawns.

"Oh. It's you." She's wearing the same dress as earlier, but her hair's a mess and she has a liquor bottle in her hand. It's too dark to tell what's inside. "What's your name again?"

"Uh, Dylan." I hesitate. "Are you all right?"

"Why won't everyone just *stop* asking me that?" Terri's voice is slurred, and she waves the bottle in my face. "Why *wouldn't* I be all right? We're here for a wedding! I mean, it's not every day I get to watch my big sister walk down the aisle with my ex, right?"

Whoa. Definitely didn't see that coming. After what Theo told me about the DUI, I understand why he seemed concerned earlier.

"Watching the man you loved riding off into the sunset with someone you also love . . . isn't something they prepare you for in rehab." Terri lets out a shaky, hollow laugh. "I didn't want to be in the wedding party, and Nora was cool, but Mom was like, 'Absolutely not! What will the relatives say?' That's all she worries about. Maybe she wouldn't have cared that I crashed my car if the *New York Post* hadn't found out. Theo told you, didn't he? Not like anything can stay a secret in this family."

It feels intrusive to know something so painfully personal about someone I just met. But there's no point denying anything. I let my silence be my answer.

"After the crash, Angelo broke up with me." Terri rubs an eye, smearing mascara over the tear tracks on her cheek. "He said I was lucky I didn't kill anyone. Next time I saw him after I got out of rehab, he was dropping Nora off at home after their first date. Awkward."

Damn. Poor Terri. She was with Angelo first, and now she has to watch him marry her sister. Being the scandal of the wedding must be particularly rough. The gossip, the glances . . . from the wedding party's conversation in the pool, they probably didn't even try to be subtle in her presence. The rehearsal dinner must've been the breaking point.

"Listen, it's getting pretty cold." I need to get her off this pier before she does something reckless. "Why don't we head inside and look for Theo?"

"Nah, don't need a lecture from my younger cousin about this." She takes another swig from the bottle. "What are you doing out here by yourself, anyway? You guys have a fight or something? He can be a pain in the ass sometimes, but"—she pokes me in the chest—"he's got a good heart, you know?"

She sways a little. I reach out to steady her, but she pushes me away and stumbles alarmingly close to the edge—

I start forward. "Terri, watch out!"

Her eyes go wide as she steps back and finds only air. She flails—before I can catch her, she teeters and falls over. Her scream cuts off in a splash below.

"Terri!" I rush over. She's bobbing in the water beneath the pier. I jump in.

The ocean isn't very cold, but plunging in is still a shock to the system. Kicking without anything under your feet is a lot scarier when you're not in the deep end of a pool. I push my wet bangs away from my face. It's dark everywhere, and Terri's nowhere to be found.

Something else makes my chest constrict with dread.

Sharks roam the waters off Long Island in late summer. The last time I was here with Mom, the beaches were closed to swimming after a great white was spotted offshore. And most of them hunt at night.

When I envisioned getting fed to the sharks in the Hamptons, I didn't imagine the situation would end up being literal.

I dive underwater, but I can't see anything. I flounder, my hands sweeping in wild circles until I brush against what feels like a human arm. I sure as hell hope it's Terri's.

I break the surface, spluttering. Terri's motionless in my arms. Her eyes are closed, and I can't tell if she's breathing. I keep her head raised so she won't inhale a lungful of water. My heart beats as if it's trying to send out a distress call in Morse code. I shout for help, but all I can hear is the thunderous crash of waves around us. The shore seems impossibly far—the longer we're in the water, the harder fighting the current will be.

I take a deep breath, kick as hard as I can, and swim toward the shore. Suddenly, something tugs at my feet, trying to yank me down. I panic, kicking frantically. But my legs are tiring out, and Terri feels heavier with each passing moment—

A pair of arms reach around my torso, pulling me against a solid form. Theo's face is a dark blur inches from mine. "Dylan?"

I lift my head, gulping for air. I can't even gasp his name. Terri's weight lightens in my arms. Together, we haul her toward the shore and onto the beach.

Theo leans over her, alternating between rescue breathing and CPR. My elbows and knees sink into the wet sand, and my breath comes in harsh stabs. People run toward us from the villa, their flashlights strobing the night.

"Someone call nine-one-one!"

"Is anyone here a doctor?"

Terri's not moving. Fear rips like a hook through my chest.

"Is that her?" comes a woman's hysterical voice. "Terri!"

Lucia rushes forward, still in her wrap dress and heels. She trips and falls onto the sand not far from us, crawling to Terri's side.

"Oh God, no!" she wails. "My baby—"

Terri's body jerks. Lucia screams. A guttural noise emerges from Terri's mouth, and Theo quickly rolls her onto her side as she vomits water. A burly guard pushes through and lifts Terri like a rag doll, carrying her back to the villa. Lucia and the others hurry after him.

Theo doesn't follow. Someone gives him a towel, which he wraps around me instead of himself.

"Dylan? You okay?" He runs his hands over my arms and back, as if searching for unseen injuries. "Are you hurt?"

My teeth are chattering. "Will she be all right?"

"I think so. She's breathing again." Theo pushes my wet bangs away from my forehead. I've never seen him so pale. "Damn, you're freezing. Let's get you back inside."

The air feels like water in my lungs. I'm not sure if my knees can hold my weight. Theo's arm tightens around my shoulders as he leads me back to the villa.

When we reach our suite, he goes to the shower and turns on the faucet, testing the temperature like Mom used to do when I was a kid.

"Careful, the water's a little hot," he says.

94

I mechanically peel off my soaked clothes. I just pulled someone who wasn't breathing out of the ocean. Being naked in front of Theo Somers won't be the most dangerous thing I've done tonight.

I step into the shower and stand under the spray, letting the warm rivulets stream down my body. My muscles are twitching, sending tiny aftershocks through me. The shower is getting too hot, but I can't stop shivering.

Theo left a fresh towel for me on the shower handle. I quickly dry myself and put on a clean sweater along with sweatpants. Theo has changed into dry clothes, and his damp hair is sticking up in spikes. There's a knock at the door, and he goes to answer it.

My chest is still wound tight. Each breath takes more effort than when I was battling the ocean. My fingers hum with a weird tingling sensation, like pins and needles.

Theo shuts the door. His arms are full of four large, fluffy pillows.

"I got these from room service. I figured you didn't get a chance to request them yourself," he says. "There are another two in the wardrobe, and you can have one of mine. Are nine pillows enough?"

A surge of emotion rises in my chest. I can't believe he remembered that stupid little lie.

He dumps the pillows on the bed and comes toward me with an oversized plaid button-up shirt.

"Here, put this on. It'll keep you warm." I glimpse the Burberry label before he maneuvers my arms through the long sleeves and does up a few buttons in front. "I'll go check to see if they have news about Terri. Be right back, okay?"

I nod numbly. Terri could have died tonight. *I* could've died.

Thank God we're both alive—but I'm exhausted, boneless. I just want to hide underneath the covers until this wedding's over.

After Theo leaves, I climb into the huge bed and bury my face in one of the pillows. He thought I needed them—as ridiculous as it sounded—and he got them for me. He wanted me to feel safe. His shirt around my body is warm, like he's holding me in a hug. With each breath my panic recedes, a tide drawing away from the shore.

I curl up, shut my eyes, and hope I don't dream of drowning.

Chapter 12

When I wake up, I'm engulfed in a sea of pillows. Sunlight streams through glass and hits me in my eye, making everything overly bright. I'm not sure where I am.

On the nightstand is a gigantic basket bursting with colorful daisies. A note card reads:

THANK YOU, DYLAN!

Memories from last night rush back: Terri. The pier. The ocean. The cold.

I'm still wearing Theo's Burberry shirt. The clean, musky scent of the soft flannel reminds me of him. His side of the bed is creased, which means he was sleeping beside me at some point during the night.

I extricate myself from the pillows and reach for my phone. Good thing I didn't take it with me when I headed out last night, or it'd be at the bottom of the ocean.

There's a bunch of messages from Megan with photos of different dog treats: *Which is bacon? This one? Or this one? Never mind.*

I gave her all 3. She likes me more than you now. Two texts are from Aunt Jade: *Having fun? Good night!* and *Morning, everything ok?*

I don't know how to tell her that Theo's cousin nearly drowned last night. Or that we *both* could've been fish food. I don't want her to worry. I text back: *Sorry for the late reply. Having a great time. Love you!*

My head snaps up as the bathroom door opens. Theo steps out.

"Hey. You're awake." He's dressed in dark blue pants and a shirt with narrow gray and white stripes. He comes over and sits on my side of the bed. "How are you? Feeling better?"

"I'm fine. How's Terri? Is she all right?"

"Yeah. She stayed overnight at the hospital just to be sure. Her father's driving her back to the villa now." He gestures at the basket of flowers. "Nora sent this."

I look at him. "Now I understand why Terri invited you without telling her family."

Theo nods. "I wanted to give her moral support and divert some attention. Pissing off my dad is the cherry on top."

I can't imagine growing up in this glossy world where money can buy anything and appearances mean everything. Lucia put Terri through the ordeal of being in the wedding party when she clearly wasn't coping well with the whole situation—all for what? So the relatives wouldn't talk? From the way Herbert asked Theo about Terri, they're talking all the same. Still, Lucia's distress when she rushed up to her daughter's unmoving body on the beach was terrifyingly real.

"Sure you're okay?" Theo touches my forehead and neck. Suddenly I'm unbearably warm. "Your aunt will kill me if she finds out what happened last night."

I shake my head. "Don't worry. I didn't say anything to her. And I don't intend to."

Theo gets to his feet. "Well, if you're feeling up to it, we're in time for brunch."

I glance at the clock on the nightstand—quarter to eleven. My stomach growls on cue. "Yeah, I'm starving."

As I'm brushing my teeth, I realize I have no proper brunch clothes. Given what Theo's wearing, even the single polo shirt that survived Megan's carnage is too casual for the dress code. I'm pretty much doomed for the rest of the weekend. Maybe I can tell Theo I have a headache and ask him to bring back a few bread rolls or something.

When I walk out of the bathroom, Theo has put on a navy blazer, which he leaves unbuttoned. He looks smoking hot, but I'm too stressed to enjoy the view.

"Listen, I'm really sorry to break this to you now, but I have nothing to wear to brunch," I blurt out. "I swear, I packed the nicest shirts I own, but Megan's idea of a hilarious prank was to replace them with . . . these."

I cringe as I show him the T-shirt with the bulldog in professor glasses holding a humerus bone. Theo takes out a white T-shirt with a dozen scowling rabbits and the line EVERY BUNNY WAS KUNG FU FIGHTING.

"I think this one's my favorite," he says.

"I'm not joking. Your aunt Lucia is going to freak out if I show up in any of these." I take the Kung Fu Bunnies T-shirt from him and stuff it into my backpack. "Can you lend me one of your spare shirts? You've packed a dozen extras of everything in that huge carry-on, right?"

Theo points at my black Levi's. "Put those on. I'll find something to match them with."

I change into the jeans and follow him into the walk-in closet. I look around. "Where are our suits?"

"They got a little creased in the garment bags, so I asked the staff to have them pressed and sent back before the ceremony." Theo waves at two blazers on the rack, one tan and the other gray. "I always bring at least one extra blazer and a pair of loafers. A server might spill a drink on your sleeve, or you might step on some doggy poo on the lawn. True story."

To my surprise, Theo gives me a white crew neck T-shirt.

"A collared shirt isn't the only way to pull off a semi-formal look," he says. "A turtleneck is great in winter, but in hotter weather, you can wear a blazer over a plain T-shirt. Try it on."

"You're as good in the closet as I am in the kitchen," I joke, hoping Theo won't notice how self-conscious I'm feeling as I take off my sweater. I realize, too late, how my words came out and turn red. "I didn't mean you're in the closet! I'm not, either. What I was trying to say . . . You know what? I'm just going to shut up now."

Theo chuckles. "I get it. We're two guys standing in a wardrobe. It's cool."

Although I don't have time to hit the gym, hauling around fifty-pound bags of rice and gallons of cooking oil is pretty good weight training, so I'm not lanky or anything. But being shirtless in front of Theo sends an anxious tingle up my spine. I duck my head and quickly pull on the T-shirt. The cotton blend is soft and luxurious. The Tom Ford label probably has a lot to do with that.

Theo takes the tan blazer off its hanger. "In any wardrobe

emergency, you can't go wrong with neutrals, clean lines, and layering."

I stand in front of the full-length mirror while Theo helps me put on the blazer, which complements my denim jeans perfectly.

"The trick is to mix and match in a way that *doesn't* seem as if the pieces were put together at the last minute." Theo meets my eyes in the mirror. "We want them to look like they were made for each other."

His enigmatic tone makes me wonder if he's talking about more than just clothes.

"Thanks," I tell him. "You really saved the day."

Theo shakes his head. "No, Dylan, you did. I didn't get a chance to thank you last night. For saving Terri. What you did was . . . really dangerous but incredibly brave."

"I didn't know if I could save her. But I had to try."

"You didn't just save her, you saved the whole wedding," he replies. "If not for you, what should be the happiest day of Nora's life would've ended up being the worst."

I don't say that Terri was drinking when I found her. The hospital would've run blood tests and disclosed her alcohol level to her parents—but no one else has the right to know unless Terri decides to tell them herself.

"How did you know I was out there?" I ask.

"You hadn't come back by the time I got out of the shower, so I went looking for you," Theo says. "A member of the staff saw you heading out to the beach. When I was close to the pier, I heard someone shouting over the waves. I thought I imagined your voice at first."

Terri might not have survived if Theo hadn't helped me drag

her to shore. And he was the one who resuscitated her. I didn't expect a rich kid who never had to lift a finger for anything to know CPR.

Theo's just half a shoe size bigger than me, and his pair of dark tan loafers complete my outfit. I face the mirror again. I should feel like an imposter, dressed up in Theo's T-shirt and blazer and trying to squeeze myself into his world—but for the first time, I don't.

Theo moves closer, adjusting the lapels of the blazer and dusting invisible specks off my shoulders. As I stare at our reflections, I find myself daring to hope that maybe all this glitz and glamor isn't who he really is. That his world is closer to mine than I expected—and like his Burberry shirt, it's somewhere I can fit in.

Chapter 13

As soon as Theo and I step into the dining hall, a woman in her mid-twenties wearing an elegant white toga dress hurries toward us. I guess who she is before Theo can introduce us.

"Thank you for saving Terri!" Nora's voice cracks as she grasps my hand in hers. She has a simple French manicure, in contrast with Terri's elaborate 3D butterfly nail art. "I can't tell you how grateful we are. If you hadn't been there . . ."

Her composure crumbles, tears spilling onto her cheeks. She has the same blue eyes as Terri, the same strawberry-blond hair—one glance and anyone can tell she and Terri are sisters.

Apparently, the guy in a suit who comes over and puts a comforting arm around her thought the same thing. So, this is Angelo—the groom and the ex.

"We're so thankful you were there to save Terri." Angelo formally holds out his hand as if he's going to award me a medal. "You have our deepest gratitude."

I shake his hand stiffly. I don't know the whole story, and he wasn't the one who pushed Terri off the pier or put the alcohol bottle in her hand—but he *had* to marry the one person in the world who shares her DNA?

"Honey, stop crying or you'll ruin your makeup!" comes a shrill voice.

Instead of a bikini, Amber's now in a wine-red cocktail dress with a plunging neckline.

She sees me and lets out a shriek. "You're the guy who rescued Terri! Derek, right?"

I speak up. "My name is Dylan."

"You must be the guardian angel of this wedding!" Amber gushes. "We all LOVE Terri like she's our own sister. We felt SO terrible that we didn't notice she wasn't around. . . ."

From the conversation I overheard last night, I highly doubt that. I give her an unsmiling stare. Too bad it's lost on her as the other bridesmaids appear and usher Nora off to fix her makeup.

Theo must've noticed my surly manner toward Amber. But he doesn't get the chance to ask, because the next thing we know, we're mobbed by his relatives. They're surprised he's here, and they want to know who I am and what happened with Terri.

Theo introduces me and gamely fields the barrage of questions.

"We decided to come to the wedding at the last minute, but Aunt Lucia was gracious enough to accommodate us." "Exactly—whatever's going on in court, Nora's still my cousin, right?" "Oh, Dylan and I met at his aunt's takeout in Sunset Park." "Yes, we were very lucky that he was on the beach last night." "You know what? The details aren't important—what matters is Terri's fine."

I plaster a smile on my face. I'm like a puppy someone brought to their friend's birthday party that everyone wants to pet. The names and faces soon become a blur.

Theo seems to sense I'm overwhelmed.

"We'd love to chat more, but we're starving, and those bagels over there aren't going to eat themselves," he tells his relatives. "Let's catch up later, maybe during cocktail hour?"

As Theo steers me away from the throng, I look at him. "Smooth. Thanks."

He doesn't let go of my hand. "I promised I wouldn't let anyone give you a hard time."

Catherine and Malia wave at us from their table. I noticed they were watching us although they didn't join the crowd. Theo and I check out the buffet spread, and Malia comes over to us.

"Too bad you boys can't try the mimosas, but check out these yogurt parfaits in martini glasses—they're nonalcoholic," she says. "The yogurt's made with milk from happy, free-grazing cows that spend their free time doing Pilates or something."

The bagel bar has over a dozen flavors, and the bread counter is stocked with different kinds of jams and marmalades. There are also apple turnovers, vanilla twists, and ultra-flaky butter croissants.

Malia points at a basket of square puff pastries. "Angelo's grandma grew up in Cuba, and she used to make these pastelitos for him when he was a kid. They're filled with guava and cream cheese."

I wait for Theo and Malia to help themselves to the food, in case it's bad etiquette to take more than a few pieces at a time. But they both stack their plates, so I do the same.

"Come join us!" Malia says. "Our table's laid out for four."

Theo glances at me to ask if I'm okay to sit with them. I nod. They seem chill. Turns out, Malia is a poli-sci lecturer at Harvard, and she and Catherine met at one of her public lectures.

"When she stepped off the podium, I introduced myself and said, 'I'd love to take you to dinner,'" Catherine says.

Malia cuts in. "And I was like, 'Hang on, you're Catherine Somers? If you think a six-figure donation to our faculty means I'll agree to go out with you, think again.'"

Theo mimes a stab to the heart. "So how did you win her over?"

"I quoted her paper on Supreme Court confirmation hearings," Catherine replies. "Told her not just what I agreed with, but what I didn't. We got there in time for our reservation at a cozy, family-owned Moroccan restaurant."

"She did her research on me and found out I spent a sabbatical year in Marrakesh," Malia says. "I still thought she was a smartass, but I couldn't pass up a spicy seafood bastilla with crispy warqa pastry. I felt like I was back in the Jemaa el-Fna Square again."

I haven't traveled outside the States except to visit my grandparents in Singapore. We'd always have a layover in Hong Kong on the way. Aunt Jade would take us for the best dim sum (Megan's favorite Chinese food), and we would stuff our faces with egg tarts (Tim loves them) and pineapple buns (I couldn't get enough).

"How about you two?" Catherine asks. "How did you guys meet?"

"The first time I walked into his aunt's takeout, Dylan was making xiao long bao," Theo replies. "He steamed them and told me how they get the soup inside the dumplings. Of course, they were delicious, but the best part was knowing he made them by hand."

Malia beams. "Aww. That's got to be the most adorable meet-cute ever."

I don't know about "most adorable," but this story is a thousand times better than *I defended him against Adrian, aka ALLERGIC-TO-DUMBASSES, over spring onions.*

"Clearly the universal love language is food," Catherine adds.

Theo and I are supposed to act as if we can't take our eyes off each other, but I drop my gaze. I feel like the guava and cream cheese pastelito on my plate, with its sweet, mushy filling oozing through the diagonal cuts on top. The last thing I want is for him to suspect this is more than pretend for me.

After brunch, we say goodbye to Catherine and Malia, who're headed to the beach. The weather's perfect, and most of the guests are working on their tans, playing volleyball on the sand, or taking a dip in the water.

"Did you know Chinese people stay away from lakes and oceans during the Hungry Ghost Month?" I tell Theo before pulling a wry face. "Sorry—my family and I are total nerds about the origins of our culture's myths and beliefs."

"Are you kidding? I love learning all these details," Theo says. My heart swells. "Why do Chinese people avoid water?"

"They think drowned spirits might cast a spell and draw you in. Once you're close enough, they'll pull you into the depths to take their place." Last night, when an unseen force yanked at my ankle in the ocean, I almost believed it. "But there's a logical explanation. Hot weather increases the chances of getting leg cramps. You know how crippling those can be."

"So you're saying those drowned spirits are actually . . . muscle cramps?"

I laugh. "Scientifically, yeah."

"To be safe, though, let's not jump into the water anytime soon." Theo checks his watch. "We have a couple of hours before we need to get ready for the ceremony. Anything you want to do? Fair warning—if you say, 'you decide,' we'll end up going to the Jackson Pollock museum in the Springs. So choose carefully."

"Why don't we head into town and check out the Saturday farmers market?" I suggest. "They're open until three. I went with my mom the last time, and there was a stall selling handmade mooncake molds."

He grins. "Sounds like a plan. Let's go."

Chapter 14

The farmers market in East Hampton is in full swing when we arrive. A couple of large tents are set up near the beach, and stalls are selling everything from kombucha to kimchi. There are more vendors of color than the last time I was here with Mom, which is good to see in a vacation spot that's mostly white. It's lunchtime, and the stalls with hot meals and freshly baked pastries have the longest lines.

The sun is high in the cloudless sky, and we leave our blazers in the car. Theo doesn't attempt to hold my hand. Right. We only need to act like we're a couple when his relatives are around. I can't help wishing one of them would pop up.

We explore the market, sometimes going our own ways to check out different stalls. One sells organic soap in the shape of rainbow kueh—colorful, bite-sized desserts popular in Southeast Asia. Aunt Jade will love them. I buy shea butter and mango lip balm for Megan and a small succulent in a hand-painted ceramic pot for Tim. Clover gets gourmet dog biscuits. She'll love the BBQ chicken and cheddar cheese flavors.

"So what's special about these mooncake molds you want to check out?" Theo asks.

"The last time my mom and I were here, an elderly woman called Auntie Chan was selling handmade wooden molds with Chinese characters engraved on them," I reply. "I'm hoping to find her again. Buying a couple of new molds might bring good luck for the contest."

We spend some time searching before finding Auntie Chan's stall tucked in an inconspicuous corner of the market. With short, curly hair and a round, kindly face, she reminds me of my Por Por.

"Hi, Auntie Chan," I greet her. "You probably don't remember, but my mom bought agar-agar molds from you three years ago. I'm back to buy mooncake molds for a Mid-Autumn contest."

"Ah, yes, I remember you and your mom! She spoke to me in Cantonese." Auntie Chan gestures at the wooden molds on display. Some are square, others round. Each is engraved with a Chinese character surrounded by petal designs. "I'm afraid 'zhōng' and 'qiū' have sold out."

"Zhōng means 'middle,' and qiū means 'autumn,' " I explain to Theo. "Together, they form the word zhōng qiū—'Mid-Autumn.' "

"Let me see what else I have." Auntie Chan pulls a box from under the table and takes out two square molds with 團圓.

"What do they mean?" Theo asks. "Sorry, I can't read Chinese."

"Tuán yuán means 'reunion,' " Auntie Chan replies. "I used the traditional Chinese characters for this pair. The additional strokes make them more . . . classic? Graceful? I don't know how to describe it in English. I didn't put them out for sale because I didn't want someone to buy one and not the other. They must go together."

"I'll take both," I say immediately. "I love how they come as a pair." Another round-shaped mold inside the box catches my eye. "What about this one?"

"Ah, niàn." Auntie Chan hands me the mold. "You don't find this character on mooncakes often, but no celebration about family is complete without remembrance."

My throat constricts as I stare at the character 念. *Remembrance.*

I never performed any Hungry Ghost Month rituals for Mom—not just because she didn't believe in them, but because I don't believe she's only close to us for a month in every year. And I want to remember her, not by leaving food on an altar, but by making a mooncake she would've loved.

Theo speaks. "It's beautiful."

I choke up. This time, the swell of emotion is different— almost like I've carved out a piece of my grief and shaped it into something else. "It's perfect."

I pay for the three molds, and Auntie Chan returns more change than she should. I try to give it back, but she pats my arm. "You're a good boy. I'm sure you'll make lovely mooncakes."

"Do you have any tips?" I ask.

She leans forward conspiratorially. "Here's a secret I don't share with just anyone. When you're making the mooncake dough, don't use room-temperature water." Her eyes twinkle. "Ice-cold water will make the mooncake skin extra smooth and velvety."

"Thanks." I beam at her. "I can't wait to try that out."

As Theo and I walk away from Auntie Chan's stall, my phone beeps with a quick-fire barrage of messages from Megan.

You replied to my mom's texts but not mine
R U IGNORING ME??

Got a death wish or something?

Ok where are the pics??? She adds a string of kissy and heart emojis.

Theo falls into step beside me, and I quickly pocket my phone before he sees Megan's messages and incriminating emojis.

We stop at a stall selling homegrown strawberries. The vendor has a mini fondue set up, and I buy two sticks and twirl them until all the strawberries are coated with a thick layer of chocolate. I give one of the sticks to Theo, and we stand facing the sea, nibbling on strawberries and getting melted chocolate all over our mouths. This has been the most normal time we've had since we got here.

Theo speaks. "Those mooncake molds you got to remember your mom are incredibly special. They'll bring good luck for sure."

"I hope so." The five grand from Theo buys us some time, but we need more to keep the business afloat. I overheard my aunt talking to the bank about getting a temporary loan. "I really want to get us on *Off the Eaten Path*. You've seen the queues at the restaurants after they're featured on the show. I know this might sound crazy, but imagine this." I mime a headline: "*On the top ten list of New York City's best Chinese takeouts, hailing from Sunset Park, Brooklyn . . . Wok Warriors!*"

"Doesn't sound crazy at all," Theo replies. "Hey, maybe I can help you and your aunt make mooncakes for the contest? Wait, scratch that—the rules say you can only have one assistant, right?"

"Yeah. But you're welcome to come over and watch," I say shyly. "I bet your mom would've been happy to know you're learning more about her culture."

He smiles. "I think she would've loved that too."

Mom used to say there's good in the worst of things, and bad in the best of them. Theo and I come from completely different social and economic backgrounds—but whenever we talk about our moms, we understand each other in a way no one else in our lives can.

I point at a spot on his cheek. "You've got some chocolate on your face."

He brushes the spot with his fingers, smearing it more. "Is it gone?"

"Nope, still there." I reach out and swipe my thumb over the smudge. Theo's gaze holds mine, and a squiggly feeling goes through me—I step back, letting my hand drop. "Got it. All good now."

"Thanks." The wind grazes the top of Theo's hair, and I get a flash of how it might feel to run my fingers through it. I quickly push the thought aside.

We leave the farmers market and head back to the villa to get ready for the ceremony, which starts at five. When we step into the room, Theo waves at the shower.

"You can jump in first," he says casually.

Last night, I was too dazed to be self-conscious. This time, I'm not. I try to act nonchalant as I undress, but my chest is a cage of butterflies. Stripping down in front of other guys before hitting the showers after PE has never bothered me—but getting naked in front of Theo makes me keenly aware of every part of my body.

I dart into the shower and turn on the faucet. At least the droplets streaking the glass give some illusion of privacy. Theo moves around the suite, checking his phone, going in and out of the walk-in closet . . . all the while not looking in my direction. Not once.

A sharp twinge goes through me, but I ignore it. He's just being polite.

I didn't notice the bath gels when I showered last night. They're luxuriously lathery and smell of tangerine and mandarin oranges. Too bad I can't enjoy them since I'm determined to get my shower over with as soon as possible.

I step out and wrap a towel around my waist. "Um, shower's all yours."

"Cool." Theo takes off his shirt and unzips his pants. I can't grab a keycard and escape like I did last night—I avert my eyes, mumble something about getting dressed, and find safety in the closet. I end up mismatching the buttons on my shirt twice before I get them right.

Twenty minutes later, I'm standing in the middle of the room, still fiddling with my shirt cuffs. Theo's already got his bow tie on—he looks like he just walked off the set of a Ralph Lauren photo shoot.

"Need any help?" he asks.

"Uh, I'm not sure if your tailor made a mistake . . . but my cuffs have two buttonholes and no buttons."

Theo chuckles. "French cuffs don't have buttons. They're supposed to be worn with cuff links. Here, I brought you a pair."

He takes a pair of square cuff links from the safe. They're made of brushed platinum with parallel black stripes. I extend my wrists, and Theo slides each one through the buttonholes, fastening the tiny metal bar with a deft twist.

He picks up a strip of burgundy silk. "Should I help you, or do you want to tie this yourself?"

I stifle a grin. "Depends on whether you want it to look more like a shoelace or a bow tie."

Theo flips up my collar and loops the strip of silk around my neck, tugging on both sides to pull me closer. I have to dig in my heels to stop myself from lurching forward and colliding with his lips. Theo takes his time, teasing the bow into perfection, apparently oblivious that I might pass out any moment from forgetting to inhale.

Theo raises his gaze, appraising my unruly hair.

"Sorry," I say. "I should've gotten a haircut."

Theo's mouth twitches. "Then let's make you look like you didn't on purpose."

He goes to the dresser, giving me a chance to catch my breath. But no breathing technique's going to work with Theo Somers in such close proximity.

He comes back, rubbing some styling wax between his hands. I try to be still as he runs his fingers through my hair, but his touch turns my nerves into live wires. Instead of brushing my too-long bangs back, he makes a side part and combs them into obedience until they're neatly swept to one side, held in place by just enough product.

"There." Theo steps back, satisfied. "Watch out, some guests might mistake you for a K-pop star."

My cheeks color. We stand side by side in front of the mirror and put on our jackets. My burgundy bow tie contrasts with the gray of my suit, while Theo's bow tie and suit are in matching shades of dark green. He's wearing knot-shaped gold cuff links. Next to him, I'm like a kid playing dress-up.

Theo winks at our reflections. "Let's go crash a wedding."

Chapter 15

The celebrity photographer, Georgina Kim, is taking pictures of the couple and the wedding party in the villa's landscaped gardens. Palm trees sway in the wind and rustic wooden barrels teem with tropical blooms. Angelo's in a black tux, and Nora looks gorgeous in her wedding gown, which has a deep V-neck top, lace sleeves, and intricate embroidery along the lower half of the skirt. Her gown doesn't have one of those long trains—I've always thought it's weird to have someone scrambling behind the bride, trying to make sure the train doesn't bunch up.

Terri stands between Beverly and Amber. She's wearing the same Tiffany-blue dress as the other bridesmaids, but unlike them, she doesn't pose with her head tilted to catch her best angle. She doesn't need to. With her hair and makeup done, no one would guess she spent last night in the hospital after being pulled out of the ocean unconscious.

Terri catches my eye and mouths, "Thank you."

I smile and nod.

Lucia's hovering around the patio, micromanaging one of Georgina's frazzled assistant photographers, who's snapping pictures of the ceremony venue before guests are seated. An elegant white gazebo at the front is surrounded by concentric circles of white chairs. The aisle is lined on both sides with champagne and pink roses. Fancy lettering on a wooden sign reads: LOVE IS SWEET; PLEASE CHOOSE ANY SEAT.

As more guests arrive, the wedding party stops posing for pictures to get ready for the ceremony. A lady in a pantsuit—probably the wedding planner—says something to the couple. Nora's face instantly falls. Lucia hurries over, and they huddle close, wearing grave expressions.

I nudge Theo. "Seems like there's a problem."

"Let's find out," he says.

Terri's the only one who notices us walking in their direction. She breaks away from the rest and comes over.

"Something wrong?" Theo asks.

"Nora's favorite violinist, who's supposed to play a solo as she walks down the aisle, just passed out in the villa bathroom and hit her head pretty hard," Terri replies. "She's conscious now, but they still called an ambulance. Obviously, she can't play for the ceremony, which is starting in exactly ten minutes."

"Can someone from the wedding band cover for her?" Theo suggests. "They should be here to set up for the reception by now, right?"

"Nora loves this particular Vivaldi concerto, and we aren't sure if the band violinist knows how to play it," Terri says. "The planner's gone to check. Mom's freaking out that starting the ceremony late will mess up the timing. Nora's close to tears. You should've seen her face when Amber asked if we could find the concerto on Spotify."

Theo tilts his head. "Vivaldi's 'Winter' Largo?"

Terri blinks. "How'd you guess?"

Theo sidesteps her and walks toward Nora and Angelo. Terri and I exchange puzzled glances and follow. When Angelo sees Theo, he tries to put on a nonchalant face. Nora's still distraught, and Lucia narrows her eyes, as if she thinks Theo's coming to gloat.

"I can do it," Theo tells Nora. *The Four Seasons* is my favorite Vivaldi composition. I can play the 'Winter' Largo by heart."

Nora looks stunned. Even Angelo's speechless. But no one can match the utter disbelief on Lucia's face.

"I'll borrow a violin from the band," Theo continues. "Can someone run and get it for me? I'll need a few minutes to tune the strings."

Everyone springs into action. The Harry Styles look-alike sprints off. Angelo and his best man hurry to the front with the officiant. Lucia and the bridesmaids usher Nora to wherever they're supposed to wait for the procession to begin. Terri stays with us until Harry Styles returns, winded, a violin case in both hands.

Theo takes out the violin and rests it under his chin, his brow pinching in concentration as he turns the pegs forward and backward by the smallest of fractions. "All right, I'm ready."

As Theo heads to the gazebo and Terri rushes off to join the bridesmaids, Catherine appears and catches my arm. "Dylan! Come sit with us!"

She leads me to the third row, where Malia, Herbert, and Jacintha are seated. Their kids are nowhere to be seen, so the villa must've arranged for childcare.

"What's Theo doing up there?" Malia asks. "Is he going to play for the ceremony?"

"It was a last-minute thing." I sit next to Catherine, leaving an empty chair by the aisle for Theo. "The violinist had an accident, and Theo volunteered to take over."

Herbert is surprised. "Lucia's okay with that?"

"That boy sure has a way of making his presence known," Catherine says. "I can just imagine Malcolm's face when he finds out."

On each chair is a kraft paper envelope with the words PLEASE HAVE A SEED! Inside is a packet of seeds. According to the printed card, they're from locally sourced plants native to Long Island. Mine is prairie rose.

"This must be Nora's idea," Catherine tells me. "She's big on nature and sustainability."

Yeah, Lucia doesn't strike me as the environmentally friendly kind. Or the type to like kitschy slogans.

The officiant announces the ceremony is about to begin. Everyone settles down as the groomsmen file in from the right and stand next to Angelo. Theo's waiting on the other side of the gazebo. The officiant signals him to start.

Theo brings the violin to his chin and draws the bow across the strings. Rich, resonant notes lilt and fill the air—one moment strong and sharp, the next soft and smooth. Some in the crowd have their phones out, recording his performance. Theo's face is an image of perfect focus, which sends a prickle up my neck. He has the same intent, inspired expression he had earlier when he stroked his fingers through my hair to wax it into shape.

Beverly's the first bridesmaid to make an entrance with Harry Styles. Terri comes next with the Asian dude. When Terri steps aside at the end of the aisle, she doesn't see Angelo's gaze following her. It's a blink-and-you'll-miss-it glance, but I catch it.

Amber, the maid of honor, comes last, smiling at the guests like this is her own wedding.

We rise when Nora appears, flanked by both parents. As Nora walks down the aisle, Malia nudges Catherine. "Told you, it's Oscar de la Renta."

When the music ends, Nora's father puts her hand in Angelo's. Theo lowers the violin, and Nora gives him a grateful nod.

As the officiant starts speaking, Theo exits from the side of the gazebo and disappears. A few minutes later, he slips into the chair next to mine so abruptly that I don't get a chance to take the envelope of seeds before he sits on it.

Catherine reaches across me and squeezes his arm. Herbert gives him a thumbs-up.

Theo grins at me. "What'd I miss?"

I shrug. "Not much. Some guy played the violin as the bride walked down the aisle."

"Was he cute?" Theo's expression turns impish. "Is he your type?"

I stifle a smile. "You have a packet of seeds under your ass, by the way."

"Oh." Theo extracts the envelope and peers inside. "I got beach plum. What did you get?"

An elderly woman from Angelo's side of the family shushes us. Theo looks apologetic, but when she faces front, he leans in.

"You didn't answer my question," he whispers in my ear.

"I got prairie rose."

"Not that question." His lips brush the edge of my earlobe. "The other one."

My heartbeat quickens. I bite the inside of my cheek and keep my gaze fixed ahead. Out of the corner of my eye, Theo smirks as he sits back in his seat.

When Angelo slides a ring onto Nora's finger, Terri briefly glances away. But when the officiant says, "I now pronounce you husband and wife," she's clapping along with everyone else as the newly married couple kiss, and her smile feels real, like she's truly happy to be here.

At the end of the ceremony, Nora comes straight over to us, beaming.

"Oh my God, Theo, the way you played the 'Winter' Largo . . ." She presses a hand to her heart. "I've never heard anything so beautiful. How did you know it's my favorite?"

"You played it on the piano a few times at family gatherings," Theo replies.

"You actually remembered!" She embraces him, teary-eyed. A flurry of camera flashes go off around us. "Thank you. I had my favorite violinist at my ceremony after all."

Theo smiles. "That's the least I could do after crashing your wedding."

Nora's expression turns somber. "I feel really bad that I didn't invite you. I wanted to, but my mom refused. And I just let her have her way." She looks at Terri, who's chatting with Catherine and Malia. "I should've stood up to her about a lot of things."

Angelo thanks Theo before he and Nora are ushered off by the photographer's assistants. In the meantime, the villa staff have transformed the patio from a ceremony venue into a cocktail space. Waiters make their rounds with glasses of wine and platters of hors d'oeuvres. I snag a fig with bacon and chile as Theo and I head over to the bar by the poolside. We each get a glass of nonalcoholic passionfruit sangria flavored with slices of orange, kiwi, and starfruit.

Terri's head appears between us.

"Why are you two over here?" she demands. "Everyone's waiting!"

She grabs our arms and pilots us away from the cocktail area to the gardens, where family photos are in progress. Theo's relatives are already in formation around Nora and Angelo.

"Terri, wait," Theo protests, backing away. "I don't think I should—"

"Stop." Lucia's sharp tone makes us skid to a halt. "Where do you think you're going?"

Chapter 16

I didn't notice what Lucia was wearing when she walked Nora down the aisle, since we were all focused on the bride. Lucia appears ethereal in her sequined golden gown with long bell sleeves—but her glare is enough to send anyone crashing back to earth.

"These family photos are meant to be lifelong memories of Nora's special day." Lucia glowers at Theo. "How thoughtless of you."

He looks sheepish. "Sorry, Aunt Lucia, I wasn't planning to—"

"How thoughtless of you to make everyone wait for you to show up," Lucia cuts in. "Go over there and stand next to your aunt Catherine. Quickly, now."

Theo can't hide his surprise. Terri grabs his wrist and drags him toward the group.

"Dylan, you too!" Nora calls out.

It's my turn to be stunned. She can't be serious. They don't know I'm Theo's fake date—which makes joining in feel more wrong. I catch Theo's eye, hoping he'll tell them to go ahead without me.

Instead, Theo beckons me over. "Come on, Dylan!"

Lucia gives me an exasperated stare. "I hate to be rude, young man, but please get over there and stand next to Theo right now. We're running dreadfully late."

Lucia hurries to her place as I make my way to Theo. He pulls me closer, linking our arms. Before I can make sure my suit looks okay, the camera shutter goes off a few times—and I'm officially part of the poshest wedding I was never actually invited to.

When we head back to the cocktail area, the rest of the wedding party, who had their pictures taken before the ceremony, are talking loudly and laughing near the bar. Amber is swirling a glass of red wine. As I walk past, her head swivels toward me.

"Oh my God!" Amber grabs my wrist. "Theo got these cuff links for you?"

"Uh, yeah." Her nails hurt—I try to pull my hand away, but she refuses to let go.

"These are from Cartier's latest collection! I wanted to buy them for my fiancé, but they sold out on the first day." She looks at Theo. "How did you manage to get them?"

Theo extricates my wrist from Amber's grip. "My butler has excellent connections. He can get almost anything done."

Amber pouts. "I was SO disappointed. I mean, they were only ten grand—no wonder they got snapped up so fast!"

She flutters off. I turn to Theo with wide eyes. He looks shifty. I take him by the elbow and steer him to a spot away from the others.

"These are Cartier cuff links?" I hiss. "Have you lost your mind? What if they fell off?"

"Relax, I made sure I put them on securely—"

"I'm here at this wedding because of the five grand you helped me with. And you thought it was a good idea to put cuff links on me that cost *ten thousand dollars*?"

"Dylan, I'm sorry." Theo sounds chastised. "You're right. I should've told you. I didn't mean to make you uncomfortable—"

"Let's go back to the room and put them in the safe." Two tiny pieces of metal worth five figures should be behind a combination lock, not dangling from my shirt cuffs, where they could fall off at any moment. "Right now."

Some guests steal glances at us. I take a breath and soften my expression so it doesn't seem like we're fighting.

"I have an idea." Theo steps closer, resting his hand on my hip. "People might notice us leaving abruptly, so why don't we pretend we're sneaking back to our room to make out? When you show up at the reception without the cuff links, they'll assume you forgot to put them on after we messed around."

Considering I was mad at him two seconds ago, this shouldn't sound as hot as it does.

We leave the poolside and return to our room without running into anyone along the way. Theo shuts the door, and I hold out my wrists for him to remove the cuff links.

"I'm sorry I didn't tell you they're Cartier." He looks rueful. "I didn't want you thinking I was using you to impress my relatives. I definitely wasn't trying to make you someone you're not."

"I'm not used to wearing stuff that costs more money than my family's ever had at one time." I gesture at my suit. "I know this is the dress code, but slapping on a pair of designer cuff links won't make me feel any less out of place."

"I know. I'm really sorry." He puts the cuff links back into the safe.

Now that we're by ourselves, away from nosy stares, I feel

bad about being snippy a few minutes ago. I can't blame him. This luxury is all he's ever known. Everything in his life costs way more than it should.

A glint of mischief in Theo's eye makes me pause. "What?"

"If we want them to think we slipped back to our room to make out, we should look like we're trying to hide something." He tilts his head. "Any ideas?"

My mouth goes dry. I can't believe he just turned this into a risqué Choose Your Own Adventure.

"Okay, I'll go first." Theo leans in. "We started making out as soon as we got in the door, so the first thing to go was our jackets. . . ." He runs his palms over my lapels, crinkling them before smoothing them down. "They have a few creases we can't get rid of. Your turn."

Even through two layers of insulation, I'm sure he can sense my heartbeat going crazy. I reach between us, touching his bow tie and throwing off the symmetry by a fraction.

"You didn't have time to tie it as perfectly as you did before," I whisper.

"Brilliant. And I ran my hands through your hair, messing it up. . . ." Theo's voice is low and teasing as he grazes his fingers over my once neatly styled hair. "You tried to fix it after we finished, but it wasn't the same."

A heady buzz rushes through me, like I'm at the top of a roller coaster, waiting for the drop—but instead of shutting my eyes, I want to keep them open all the way. Our faces are so close I can see the curl of Theo's lashes, and if we both move forward at the same time, our lips will meet—

A keycard beeps. The door opens, and the housekeeping lady comes in. She sees us and gasps.

126

"I'm so sorry, sirs!" She sounds flustered. "I thought everyone was at the wedding, and the Do Not Disturb sign wasn't on the door—"

"Don't worry, your timing is perfect." Theo smoothly steps back. He walks toward her with a charming smile, takes out his wallet, and puts a hundred in her hand. "My date reminded me we forgot to leave a tip, and we came back to do that."

As we head to the door, the housekeeping lady glances at the ten pillows on the bed. My face burns. She probably thinks we used them for something kinky last night.

When we're outside, Theo's gaze rakes up and down my body. "They'll totally believe we were all over each other."

Trust Theo to make *not* making out the biggest turn-on ever. He looks unfazed, as always—but the faint flush of color on his cheeks is something he can't hide.

I stifle a grin. *I* made Theo Somers blush. I'm taking the wins where I can get them.

Chapter 17

By the time we get back, cocktail hour's almost over and most guests have made their way into the main manor for the reception. As we walk to the ballroom, the photo booth attendant waves us over.

"Instead of a guestbook, the couple would like some fun photos of their guests," she says. "Grab a prop or two and come on in!"

Theo takes a top hat and hands me a sign with the words I DO. We climb inside the old-school photo booth. He puts an arm around my shoulders, though we don't need to huddle close to fit in the frame. I'm too self-conscious to make funny poses, so I grin widely and hold up the sign as the flash goes off.

When we step out, the attendant gives us each a photo. "You both look great!"

I've got a goofy smile in the picture, while Theo manages to look blasé even with the ridiculous top hat. I zoom in on my missing cuff links, the wrinkles on my lapels, the barely perceptible tilt of Theo's bow tie that probably no one else will notice.

Theo nudges my shoulder. "Hey, we now have our first picture together."

I can't suppress a smile. "It's a good one."

Everything about the wedding has been a perfect illusion of grandeur and glamour, and the ballroom's no exception. The banquet tables are arranged in long rows perpendicular to the bridal table so everyone can see the couple. Next to the bridal table is the wedding cake, a formidable tower of confectionery with seven tiers of white icing piped with gold frosting and silver swirls. The wedding band's set up near the dance floor, and a female singer is crooning a jazzy tune I don't recognize.

We take our seats, which are marked by place cards. Catherine and Malia sit across from us. On each place mat is a large porcelain plate with a gold rim, four forks, three knives, and two spoons. Aunt Jade would have a fit if we used this much silverware for one meal. Since we weren't officially on the guest list and thus were never offered a choice for tonight's meal, a waiter discreetly asks what we want for our main course: meat, fish, or vegan. I feel a little weird, since I'm usually on the receiving end of orders Tim sends through the serving window.

I choose the oven-baked sea bass fillet and parmesan polenta with roasted Mediterranean vegetables. Theo picks the seared wagyu filet mignon with shallot and red wine sauce. Wagyu stir-fry with scallion and ginger is one of Aunt Jade's specialties, but at two hundred dollars a pound, she only cooks that dish during our reunion dinner. In China, large families would reunite once a year when siblings living and working in different provinces returned to their hometown to celebrate the Lunar New Year. To Chinese people, dinner on New Year's Eve is the most important meal families can have together—and we've never missed a single one.

The host announces that the wedding party is ready for their grand entrance. The band bursts into a spirited instrumental rendition of "Viva La Vida" as Lucia and her husband come in first, followed by Angelo's parents. Terri smiles at us as she walks past.

"And now," the host says, "please welcome Angelo and Nora, the new Mr. and Mrs. Sanchez!"

Everyone stands, clapping and cheering. Angelo's in a white tux with black lapels, and Nora looks radiant in her strapless white evening gown with bold black embroidery along the hem.

"Vera Wang," Catherine and Malia say in unison.

After the couple's first dance, waiters stream in with the appetizers, and the band plays an upbeat theme song I immediately recognize. I nudge Theo. "Hey, that's from—"

"*How to Train Your Dragon.*" He grins at my surprise. "What, you think I only know Vivaldi and Mozart?"

I'm in love.

A waiter puts a freshly made gourmet salad in front of me. I want to show Megan, but no one at our table is taking photos. I surreptitiously watch which fork Theo picks up and do the same. The butter knife with the blunt end and the dessert fork and spoon are obvious enough, but the other forks and knives seem pretty much the same. The salad is crunchy and tangy-sweet, with baby greens, endives, toasted pistachios, and citrus vinaigrette.

As we eat, servers come around with flutes of champagne. Theo and I get nonalcoholic sparkling cider. At the bridal table, Terri's the only one who opts for it too. Good thing they're feeding us while the wedding party gives their toasts, because all the speeches sound the same after a while. When Terri stands, though, a hush falls over the ballroom and the incessant clinking of silverware fades. Everyone must know she's the younger sister of the bride and used to date the groom. A mix of pity and intrigue crosses a few faces.

"When I was a kid, I told Mom no one dared to bully my best friend because she had a big brother." Terri's voice is clear, but there's something fragile about it, like thin glass. "My sister was a boring bookworm who never wanted to go outside and play. It wasn't fair. Why didn't I have a big brother instead?"

At any other wedding, this would've elicited a couple of chuckles, but everyone is silent. Angelo drops his gaze. Nora seems unsure how to react. Lucia fixes Terri with a stare that might've turned a lesser person to stone. Catherine and Malia exchange glances. I'm not sure which knife on my place mat is for cutting the tension.

"Mom took my hands and told me that although my sister might not be a lot of fun, there's something about her I should know," Terri continues. "I was six weeks premature, and the day I was born, my parents had planned to take Nora to Disneyland. She was four, and she was so excited. When Mom brought her to the neonatal unit, she asked if Nora was mad the trip got canceled because of the baby. But Nora told her, 'I'm not mad. She's my sister. I love her. I would give her my whole world.'"

Terri looks at Nora.

"Now it's my turn to say it back." Terri's smile shines more brightly through a sheen of tears. "I love you, sis. I would give you my whole world."

And she did. From the way Nora sobs into her palm and Angelo averts his gaze as he hands her a bunch of tissues, they both know it too. Lucia's eyes are glassy with emotion.

Everyone claps hesitantly and takes a bigger gulp of champagne.

The servers bring our main courses, and I watch which silverware Theo picks up for his filet mignon. I follow suit.

"Wrong ones," Theo mutters out of the corner of his mouth.

I stop. "But that's what you took."

"You ordered the fish. Since it's a fillet, you should use the fish fork with the dinner knife. My knife's for steak. The waiter must've forgotten to take yours away."

I quickly make the switch, hoping no one noticed.

Theo nods. "All good."

My sea bass is baked to perfection, falling into firm yet tender flakes when I cut into it. During the Lunar New Year, we always eat steamed whole sea bass seasoned with ginger, spring onions, light soy sauce, and sesame oil. The word for *fish* in both Mandarin and Cantonese—yú—sounds like "abundance." Eating a fish cooked with its head and tail is a popular tradition to herald a new year that will be auspicious from beginning to end.

"Hey, Dylan, check this out." Malia shows me a picture on her phone. "Good thing we posted our wedding pics on Facebook, or I wouldn't have been able to find this."

Theo's about three or four years old in the photo. He's dressed in a suit with a turquoise bow tie, and he's holding a small pillow with two rings secured with ribbon ties.

"Aunt Malia," Theo mock-groans.

"First time this boy rocked a tux, even with a clip-on tie." Catherine laughs. "Isn't he the cutest thing you've ever seen?"

I smile. "Yeah, he is."

Malia pats my hand, looking pointedly at where my cuff links should be. "Your boyfriend's come a long way from the innocent little kid in that photo."

Heat rises to my cheeks.

Catherine leans forward. "I'm going to be the insufferable aunt who puts you on the spot. Tell me—what do you like about my darling nephew?"

"If he breaks up with me after this weekend, I'm blaming you and Aunt Malia," Theo says, although there's no rancor in his tone.

Catherine's question catches me off guard. I've barely gotten the hang of acting as if we're a couple—admitting out loud what I like about Theo is legit more terrifying than jumping off that pier last night.

I take the plunge anyway. "There's a Chinese saying my aunt loves: yǒu yuán qiān lǐ lái xiāng huì."

"What does it mean?" Catherine asks.

" 'We have the destiny to meet across a thousand miles.' " I don't dare to look at Theo. "That's kind of how I felt when we met. The way our paths crossed was so out of the blue that I couldn't help but think something in the universe must've aligned."

I'm almost always in the kitchen with Aunt Jade instead of on a bike delivering orders. Except on the night I first saw Theo.

Malia's eyes light up. "I love that! When you guys get married someday, you must tell this story."

"If you don't, I'll be the crazy aunt who jumps up and makes a toast when she's not on the list of speeches," Catherine adds.

"Please don't jump, you might pull something," Theo jokes.

Catherine reaches across the table, and Theo dodges her smack aimed for his arm. Other guests turn at the commotion.

Malia grins at them. "There was a big mosquito on him."

Theo's shoulder bumps into mine—and under the table, his hand lands on my leg. I suck in a sharp breath. Even through a layer of fabric, his touch radiates heat . . . and something else. Before I can react, Theo lifts his palm away and shifts back into his seat, chuckling. Catherine glowers at him, although she's smiling.

After the parent dances and cake-cutting, the band kicks off a mix of classic and newer hit songs to get older and younger guests on their feet. Catherine and Malia head to the dance floor, where Amber is turning up the heat level a little too much with her fiancé.

Theo and I check out the affogato station. A barista puts two small scoops of vanilla ice cream into a parfait glass, pours an espresso shot over it, and adds shaved dark chocolate and chopped hazelnuts on top.

"Mmm, ice cream and coffee." Theo admires the marbling of the dark espresso and ice cream in the glass. "Whoever thought of this was a genius."

"I downed a ton of those at weddings when I was a teen," comes a young woman's voice behind us.

We turn around. It's Beverly, the resident gossip queen.

She waggles her brows. "So what's it like being the most popular couple at this wedding?"

Theo doesn't miss a beat. "I thought that title belonged to Nora and Angelo."

She laughs. "Oh, you know what I mean!" She steps toward Theo and lowers her voice conspiratorially. "I definitely didn't mean to eavesdrop or anything, but during cocktail hour, I overheard your date saying he's only here because you gave him five grand? What's going on? Are you two just *pretending* to be a couple?"

My gaze darts toward Theo, but his expression gives nothing away. If it gets out that Theo paid someone to be his fake boyfriend . . . I don't want him to be embarrassed in front of everyone. The incriminating words came out of my big mouth, so I have to handle damage control.

"You heard right," I tell Beverly, keeping my tone cool. "I like paying for my own stuff, but Theo insisted we both get suits tailored by Mr. Kashimura." I put a hand on Theo's shoulder and purposefully slide my palm down his bicep. Not sure if it's my imagination, but Theo goes very still at my touch. "If not for the five grand my boyfriend dropped on me, I wouldn't be fancy enough for this party."

"Aww, baby," Theo plays along. "Did you think I wouldn't get you something for our first monthiversary?"

He leans in and nuzzles my neck, which renders me incapable of a response.

Beverly pouts, clearly hoping for something juicier. "So you two are really together?"

Theo takes my hand and feigns a shocked look. "Where're your Cartier cuff links?"

"Dammit. I must've left them behind when we went back to the room." I pretend to think hard. "I'm sure they're on the dresser. I took them off before we, uh, you know. . . ."

Theo smirks. "Oh, I definitely remember that part."

Beverly rolls her eyes. "I'm going to get a drink."

As she slinks off to the bar, I exhale in a rush. That was close. I triple-check that no one's within earshot. "Sorry. I almost blew our cover."

"Quick thinking back there," Theo replies. "I'm impressed."

"Glad you caught on. Bringing up the cuff links was a nice touch."

He grins. "We make a good team."

The opening chords of Ed Sheeran's "Perfect" start playing. Couples on the dance floor move closer, arms linked around their partner's neck or waist.

Theo holds out his hand. "Come on. I love this song."

A lump forms in my throat. It's *that* kind of song. "You want to dance? With me?"

"You're my date. I don't think I should be asking anyone else."

People are watching us. My pulse ratchets. "I've, uh, never slow-danced before."

"It's easy. Just shuffle your feet from side to side." He winks. "Follow my lead."

I lick my lips nervously as I take his hand. Theo doesn't need to do this for show—he's in the family photos, not to mention the footage of his violin solo at the ceremony. So why is he asking me to dance in front of everyone?

As we step onto the dance floor, a space promptly opens for us. Catherine and Malia give us an excited thumbs-up.

Theo faces me. I have no idea where my hands should go. He puts one palm on the middle of my back and the other on my arm, close to my shoulder. I mimic his actions. We're around the same height, but I still feel a little awkward. He pulls me closer, and the front of my suit brushes his.

As the chorus plays, I shut my eyes and let my other senses take over. The weight of his hands around me. The nudge of his chin resting on my shoulder. His breathing close to my ear, quiet and steady. As we move in a circle, I imagine we're two planets in the same orbit, his gravity the only thing holding me in place.

When the song ends, my eyes flutter open. Theo's face is inches from mine.

He leans in and kisses me.

My mind goes blank. I barely register the light touch of his lips. Then he pulls back, a half-smile curling the edges of his mouth. People around us are clapping and cheering. I'm rooted to the spot, a deer in the headlights.

Oh my God. Theo Somers just *kissed* me.

The host announces that cake will be served, and most of the guests go back to their seats. My mind is racing as we return to ours.

Malia grins. "Aww. You two are the cutest."

But what did it *mean*? Did he kiss me just to prove we're a couple, in case there are other skeptics like Beverly? Was it just another part of the charade?

There are two wedding cake flavors—I choose the vanilla with salted caramel, and Theo picks the chocolate ganache with peanut butter.

He cuts a piece and holds it out on his fork. "Here. Try mine."

Right. Couples usually share. I nearly forgot. Catherine and Malia also chose both flavors, and Catherine's cutting the cakes so they can have half each.

I eat the chocolate cake from Theo's fork and offer him a square of my vanilla one. He takes it with gusto, his tongue darting out and licking a dab of buttercream from his lip.

The reception ends with the send-off, and waiters bring out platters of gold bells with satin ribbons monogrammed *N&A*. We line the aisle and ring them, filling the air with a tinkling symphony as Nora and Angelo make their fairy-tale exit.

It's already eleven, and at least half the guests leave as well. Herbert and Jacintha wave good night as they hurry off to pick up their kids from childcare. At the bridal table, Lucia and her husband head off along with Angelo's parents.

The best man grabs the mic. "Ladies and gentlemen, the real party starts now!"

A Cardi B song blasts from the speakers, and Amber jumps onto the bridal table and starts dancing. The groomsmen pop bottles, spraying champagne onto the young ladies on the dance floor, who shriek. I feel bad for the cleanup crew.

"Hey." Theo grabs my hand. "Let's get out of here."

I'm surprised. "You don't want to stay?"

"To be honest, I'm not much of a party person."

I chuckle. "Funny how the only party you're not invited to is the one you have to crash in the most dramatic way possible."

Theo looks wry. "Seems like what I can't get is always what I really want."

As we leave, I can't help but wonder if he's still talking about party invitations.

Chapter 18

The night air is balmy, tinged with the scent of salt and rain. The sky is moonless, the stars blotted out by the heavy thunderheads on the horizon. A storm is coming.

As we hurry back to our guesthouse, Theo casts a sidelong look in my direction.

"Sorry for not giving you any heads-up about that kiss," he says. "It seemed like what a real couple might naturally do after a romantic slow dance. So I went for it."

"Uh, yeah. Sure." Just thinking about the brief brush of his lips against mine sends goose bumps up and down my arms again. "It felt totally natural to me too."

"Oh, good. I was worried it might have been awkward."

Nope, not awkward. Just shorted out a bunch of neural pathways in my brain, that's all. They'll regenerate.

Thunder rumbles as we step back into our room. Theo drops his suit jacket on the chaise, pulls the knot of his bow tie loose, and tosses the strip of silk onto the dresser. I reach for my own tie but pause. I don't want to pull on the wrong end and wind up with a dead knot.

"Glad that the wedding's almost over?" I ask.

"This might sound hard to believe, but I don't think anything could be worse than the last wedding I went to," Theo replies. "My dad's."

My ears prick up. I want to know what Theo's issue with his dad is. "What happened?"

"They had a private ceremony in Napa Valley. Bernard and I were the only ones from my dad's side." Theo rubs his neck, ruffling the hair at the back of his head. "When I went to the housewarming party at his new home on Long Island, guess how many pictures of me he had in the entire place? One. At the corner of the mantelpiece. From when I was five."

There's nothing I can say to soften that blow. "The family portrait in the hallway of your house is a beautiful picture of the three of you."

Theo shakes his head. "Not like the photos you have with your mom, aunt, and cousins on the wall of your takeout. That portrait's nothing more than a snapshot from the past. Even before my dad remarried, he was out of town on business nearly all the time. Bernard was the one cheering in the stands when I won my first junior tennis tournament." He lets out a mirthless sound. "It's like the day my mom died, I stopped mattering to him. Well, except when he expects me to shun my relatives and take his side in a public scandal."

Now I know why emptiness doesn't just fill Theo's mansion—it pervades it. He grew up within those walls, with every need taken care of, surrounded by everything one could want . . . except family. My dad's barely been in my life since he left for Shanghai, but the difference was, I still had Mom. She did everything she could to make sure I knew I was loved. Theo's dad should've done the same after Theo lost his mother.

Theo goes to the minibar and takes out two small bottles. "Want any? We've got red and white, vodka, and tequila."

"No, thanks." I tried some at a party once, but I got a headache. "Knock yourself out. As long as you don't accuse me of taking advantage of you."

Theo laughs. "Seeing how hard it's been to get you to take advantage of me so far, I don't think I have anything to worry about."

I'm confused for a second before I realize he's talking about the fake grant—the reason I'm at this wedding with him in the first place.

Theo twists open the bottle and tosses back the vodka without a gag or cough.

"So, what's a Chinese wedding like?" he asks. "I've never been to one."

"That depends on who you ask," I tell him. "In traditional families, the tea ceremony is even more important than the wedding reception. My mom told me that in ancient China, they believed the tea plant could only be grown from seed. That's why tea is supposed to represent lifelong love."

"Sounds romantic." Theo's eyes twinkle. "Like that saying you told my aunts earlier . . . the one about destiny. What is it again?"

He remembered. I feel a quiver of excitement. "Yǒu yuán qiān lǐ lái xiāng huì."

"Yǒu yuán qiān lǐ lái xiāng huì," Theo repeats. "Did I get that right?"

I chuckle at his accent. "Close enough."

Theo moves forward, bringing us closer than two people who aren't actually involved with each other should be. "Do you believe in destiny, Dylan?"

His eyes meet mine—there's something mercurial in them, something magnetic. Even though our lips locked on the dance floor, now the air between us feels even more charged, crackling with a different kind of anticipation.

I swallow hard. "I think if fate brings two people together, nothing can keep them apart."

Theo reaches for my bow tie, pulling it loose with a light tug. The perfect knot he tied for me unravels. I don't breathe as his fingers brush my skin, undoing the top button of my collar. The pressure around my neck loosens, but my throat tightens. It's as if the storm outside has electrified the invisible molecules in the air, forcing them to collide and creating an imbalance that's waiting to be discharged somehow.

What do you like about him? Catherine asked. And a reckless part of me wants to show Theo, right now, exactly what that is. To move forward until our lips touch again, to run my hands through his hair and kiss him senseless—

Theo steps back, and just like that, the moment vanishes.

He eyes the mountain of pillows on the bed. "You said you only need a lot of pillows on the *first* night sleeping at a new place, right?"

"Uh, yeah." My heartbeat is still reverberating in my ears.

"Cool. Let's get rid of some of these." He tosses aside half the pillows, picks up the TV remote, and jumps onto the middle of the huge bed. He flicks through the channels but stops when Lawrence Lim appears on *Off the Eaten Path*. "Hey, isn't he the guy who's sponsoring the mooncake contest?"

I nod. "This is a rerun of last week's episode."

"Good taste," Theo says approvingly. "He's hot. Another motivation to get on his show."

I laugh. "He's a little old for me. Megan thinks we should set him up with Aunt Jade."

"Is that so?" Theo fluffs the pillow behind him. "I happen to have a weak spot for cute chefs too."

My stomach does a somersault. Or more like a clumsy backflip.

Theo pats the spot next to him. "Come on, scoot closer. So that if Terri asks, you can confirm I'm an excellent cuddler."

I climb onto the bed. He puts an arm around my shoulders, pulling me against him, and I can't help leaning into his embrace.

As Lawrence introduces a hole-in-the-wall Indonesian eatery in Queens with the best nasi goreng he's ever had, I stretch out my leg, letting my foot brush against Theo's shin.

He doesn't move away, and neither do I.

Chapter 19

When I wake up in the morning, I'm alone in bed. Again. The sheets on Theo's side are rumpled, and on his pillow is a piece of paper with the villa's logo.

Morning, sleepyhead. Went for a run. Brunch at 11.

The curtains are parted, and sunlight floods the room. The sky is blue and cloudless. It's a beautiful day. Brand-new. No trace of last night's thunderstorm except for the dried water stains on the balcony glass.

A few minutes later, a keycard beeps outside. The door opens and Theo walks in, wearing a T-shirt and athletic shorts. He grins. "Hey. Sleep well?"

I run a hand through my hair, which probably looks like a bird's nest. "Yeah, thanks. You?"

"Pretty good," he says. "We're checking out before brunch, so we should probably start packing."

It's already ten. I head to the bathroom, and when I come out, Theo's in the shower. I avert my eyes—but the splashing sounds conjure an incredibly detailed image of Theo that makes me feel like I need a shower too. A cold one.

I pack the mooncake molds and the gifts for Aunt Jade and my cousins into my backpack. As I put my suit jacket into the garment bag, something in the inner pocket rustles stiffly.

I pull out the picture from the photo booth. Theo's arm is around my shoulders, and I've got a goofy smile as I hold up the I DO sign. That squiggly feeling returns to my chest . . . but now there's an emptiness too.

Last night, when Theo asked if I believed in destiny—it felt as if we were on the brink of something . . . inevitable. I still feel it, like a question left hanging between us. And I don't know if we'll get to find out the answer.

I slip the photo into the front zipper of my backpack.

We can dress down for brunch, since everyone will be traveling home after. I put on the light blue polo shirt that escaped Megan's scourge and match it with the Levi's I wore yesterday. Hopefully no one will notice.

Theo steps out of the shower, a towel around his waist.

"Hey, I thought you'd wear your 'Every Bunny Was Kung Fu Fighting' T-shirt." He winks. "Maybe next time."

As he goes to get dressed, I can't help but wonder if he means that. If there'll ever be a next time.

At the start, I wanted to get this weekend over with as quickly as possible. In a couple of hours, we'll be going home. Back to our different lives. Our different worlds. I help out at my aunt's small takeout, while Theo's dad owns a Fortune 500 company. His family is splashed all over the news, while I barely have time to read the papers because I'm too busy trying to juggle work and school.

We leave our bags in the luggage room and go to the dining

hall. The women are mostly in sundresses, and the men aren't wearing jackets or blazers. As Theo and I greet Nora and Angelo at the entrance, Terri appears. She's in a bohemian-style dress with flouncy sleeves and a ruffle skirt Megan would love.

"Where have you guys been?" Terri grabs our arms. "I've been looking all over for you! Come on, let's get something to eat. I'm beyond hungry."

Nora smiles fondly at her as we head in. Angelo seems relieved he doesn't have to make small talk.

Terri ushers us to the buffet. The breakfast favorites have a colorful theme: rainbow bagels, confetti pancakes with sprinkles and icing sugar, and multicolored waffles with fried chicken. There's a raw bar with oysters on the half shell. Terri makes a DIY acai smoothie with chia seeds, coconut flakes, and honey. A bunch of hungover guests are clustered around the coffee bar.

"Heard from your dad yet?" Terri asks Theo as she sits across from us.

"Nope. Maybe he'll send a cease-and-desist letter demanding I take out a full-page apology ad in the *New York Times*." Theo puts down his plate loaded with French toast and prosciutto pizza. How does he manage to keep his abs in such good shape? "I'm going to grab a mocktail. You two want anything?"

Terri glances at a handsome brown-skinned guy at the mocktail bar. She can't contain a grin. "Nope, I'm good."

Theo looks at me. "Dylan? Want to try Kissing on the Beach?"

I almost choke on my first bite of pancake.

Terri laughs. "Sex on the Beach . . . the nonalcoholic version."

Theo doesn't stifle his amusement.

"Uh, orange juice is fine, thanks," I manage hoarsely.

As Theo leaves, Terri's expression turns serious.

"Hey, Dylan, we haven't had a moment to talk, just the two of us," she says. "I can't remember anything after I fell off the pier . . . but thank you for what you did." She squeezes my hand, like Nora did yesterday. "You saved my life. And I'll never forget it."

"I'm just glad you're okay." I hope that drink was only because she was overwhelmed this weekend. "You were great at the wedding, by the way."

"After what happened, Nora and my mom told me I could step down from being a bridesmaid," Terri says. "I'd been trying to get out of it for so long."

"But you didn't quit the wedding party."

"Yeah. Not for my mom, or even for Nora . . . but for me. I needed to look Angelo in the eye and then step aside and let my sister marry him. And somehow find it in my heart to be happy for them." She shrugs. "Once I did, I felt liberated. Like I could finally move on."

"And did John Boyega at the mocktail bar help with that?" I tease.

Terri breaks into a wide smile. "Oh my God, he could totally pass for John's younger brother, right? His name's Lewis, and he's a college buddy of Angelo's. We got to talking at the after-party—turns out, he just started his master's in geology at Columbia last week!"

I glance at Lewis, who's talking to Theo at the bar. "Did you offer him a private campus tour?"

"It would be rude of me not to." Terri beams. "As luck would have it, the Psychology Library, where I spend *all* my time as a psych major, is in the same building as the Geosciences Library. Who knew rocks could be so sexy?"

I chuckle. When Angelo broke up with her after her DUI, he must've thought he was taking the safe path by distancing himself from her drinking problem—but he was also taking the easy way out. I hope she finds someone willing to weather the storms together.

Terri rests her elbows on the edge of the table.

"You know, I've never seen Theo as happy as he's been around you this weekend," she says. "It's been pretty lonely for him . . . not just after his dad moved out, but since he lost his mom. Seeing you guys now, having a great time together, is the best thing ever."

I remember the feeling I had when we bought mooncake molds at Auntie Chan's stall and ate strawberries covered in melted chocolate and watched *Off the Eaten Path* together. . . . I haven't enjoyed a weekend so much since before Mom died either. Theo's never met her—but spending time with him made me think of her without guilt or grief. Maybe that's what remembrance truly means.

Theo returns with his mocktail and my orange juice, bringing me back to the present.

"So, what'd I miss?" he asks.

Terri smirks. "I was just telling Dylan what a pain in the ass you can be."

"Pretty sure he already knows that." He leans toward Terri. "Your new friend at the mocktail bar was very interested to hear how you and I know each other. Couldn't hide his relief when he found out I'm your cousin."

Terri grins and raises her glass of sparkling water with a strawberry inside. "To moving on."

"To moving on," I repeat. We toast.

At the end of brunch, Catherine and Malia give Theo and me a farewell hug. When we say goodbye to Nora and Angelo, Lucia steps forward.

"The family's Christmas party will be at our place this year," she tells Theo. "Your father's still not welcome, but I'm giving you advance notice so you won't have any excuse not to attend." She looks at me. "Dylan, we'd love for you to be there as well."

I don't even know if I'll see Theo again after this weekend. But I smile and nod back. "Thanks. I'm looking forward to it."

Terri walks us to the foyer. A valet brings the Ferrari, and Theo palms him a generous tip.

Terri hugs me warmly. "I'm so glad Theo brought you to the wedding. And not just because you pulled me out of the ocean." She turns to Theo. "Thanks for saving the lecture for another time that isn't in front of your boyfriend."

Theo gives her a playful nudge. "No lecture. I'm proud of you, chipmunk."

"Ugh, you know I hate it when you call me that! I got my teeth fixed years ago." She laughs, then jumps into Theo's embrace when he holds out his arms.

I smile. I'm glad he has Terri, like I have Megan and Tim.

Theo and I get into the car, and Terri waves at me. "We'll be seeing each other soon!"

She shrinks and disappears in the rearview as we drive out of the villa.

On the road leading back to East Hampton, I look at Theo. "Let's visit that Jackson Pollock museum along the way."

Theo sounds surprised. "You sure? You might be bored."

"You went to the farmers market with me to get mooncake molds," I tell him. "We should do something you want before heading home."

He doesn't need more convincing. We stop at Jackson Pollock's home and check out the old shed that used to be his studio. Theo kneels to admire the floorboards, which are covered in splashes and streaks of paint.

"Can you imagine?" he says, touching them almost reverently. "We're standing in the same place Pollock did when he created his famous drip paintings."

"That's what they're called? Drip paintings?" I ask. "I figured abstract expressionists would've come up with a more sophisticated name."

He laughs. "Who says simplicity isn't sophisticated?"

We leave the shed and go inside the house, which has been converted into a study center and research library with two thousand volumes on modern American art. Theo wanders around, admiring Pollock's artwork and his jazz record collection. Art appreciation isn't my thing, but Theo appreciation certainly is.

By the time we leave the Hamptons, the afternoon sun is high in the sky. As we cruise along the Long Island Expressway, I steal a sidelong glance at Theo. "You should, you know."

"Should what?"

"Major in art and music. Not just in your final year or whatever, but from the start. When you played the violin during the ceremony . . . it didn't matter if there was one person or a hundred or a whole concert hall listening. You were amazing. Many people go through their entire lives never finding anything they love *and* are good at."

The edges of Theo's mouth curl. "In that case, you should pick culinary school. Don't get me wrong, I think you'd make a great vet, and I know we're still waiting on the universe . . . but I'm sure your mom would've wanted you to follow your heart, not just in her footsteps."

I chuckle. "Yeah, she knew how much I suck at physics."

"You can still volunteer at animal clinics and welfare groups in your free time," Theo adds. "Maybe organize an adoption drive on her birthday or something like that."

"That's a fantastic idea." Lightness buoys my heart, and the career I should choose is suddenly clear.

All too soon, we pull up in front of Wok Warriors. There's a lull in orders between three and five in the afternoon, and Megan's at the counter with her earbuds plugged in, probably watching a K-drama episode on her phone.

Theo gets my backpack from the trunk. "Sure I can't convince you to keep the suit? Maybe for the next wedding you get invited to?"

I shake my head. "In my world, teenagers don't wear tailored suits that cost more than their family makes in a month." Besides, I told Aunt Jade that Theo invited me to a party, not a wedding. Bringing the suit home will blow my cover.

"Oh, I almost forgot." Theo takes something out of his pocket. It's a leather bracelet with a tiny glass vial. "Got you this from the farmers market. I always thought rice writing started in China, but the vendor told me it came from Turkey."

He loops the bracelet around my wrist and secures the clasp. A single grain of white rice is suspended in colorless liquid inside the vial. The word written in black ink is so minuscule that I have to lift my hand to the sunlight to see it clearly. It's my name.

"The oil in the vial preserves the ink on the grain," Theo adds.

His eyes are inscrutable, as if he wants to say something . . . or he's waiting for me to. But my tongue seems stuck to the roof of my mouth.

"Thanks." I mask my nerves with a strained laugh. "I guess we're finally even, huh?"

Theo's expression is hard to read. "You don't owe me anything, Dylan. You never did."

I stand on the sidewalk as he gets back into his car. I never knew my heart could feel so full and hollow at the same time.

Eclipses don't last long—but I can't help wishing this one could go on for a little longer.

Chapter 20

The chime on the door dings as I walk into the shop. Megan takes out her earbuds and grins. "You're back! How was your romantic weekend with Theo?"

"It was okay."

"Just okay? You sure?" Megan waggles her brows. "You took *hours* to reply to my texts. You two must've been really busy."

"Dylan!" Aunt Jade steps out of the kitchen. "Did you have a good time? Where's Theo?"

"He dropped me off and left," I tell her.

Aunt Jade frowns. "He didn't walk you in?"

"No. Why would he? It's not like he's my boyfriend."

Aunt Jade and Megan exchange a knowing look. Megan takes a copy of the *New York Post* from under the counter. "Guess you guys were also too busy to read the papers."

Shocking Wedding Twist in Somers Family Feud is splashed in block white letters over a cover photo of Theo and Nora smiling and embracing. A smaller headline reads *Son Defies Father, Performs at Once-Estranged Cousin's Ceremony.*

Below that is a photo of Theo kissing me on the dance floor.

An electric jolt goes through me.

"Family party, huh?" Aunt Jade says.

I look at them guiltily. "I . . . didn't know how to tell you."

"Well, letting us find out in the news is one way of getting around that," Megan remarks. "Auntie Heng came in earlier—she was waving the paper and bursting with excitement about how you're famous now."

"I'm sorry I wasn't honest with you," I tell Aunt Jade. "I was worried if you knew, you wouldn't let me go, and I'd already given Theo my word—"

"Well, this is the first time you haven't been truthful with me," Aunt Jade replies. "Which means this boy must be something special."

"No," I immediately say. "We aren't together—"

"You sure?" Megan grabs the paper and flips to page two. "'Sources report that Theo was smitten with his boyfriend, Dylan, rumored to be from a working-class immigrant family. He was seen sporting cuff links from Cartier's limited-edition, sold-out collection. Theo was also heard crediting his beau for his presence at the wedding: "Dylan's my inspiration. I'm only here because he reminded me why I should show up for family—my real family."'"

I turn red. "It's a tabloid! They'll print anything to sell more copies. That's why they get sued all the time."

"Actually, E! Online picked up the story. CNBC too." Megan shows me her phone. "Damn, your first kiss is going viral! It's your first kiss, right?"

My face is still burning. "That wasn't real! Theo wanted to bring a fake boyfriend so his relatives wouldn't set him up with every wealthy young gay guy they know. Since he helped us with the grant . . . uh, I mean the grant paperwork, I agreed to go with him. Only to return the favor."

"What about this Somers family feud?" Aunt Jade asks. "Won't his dad hit the roof when he finds out Theo was at the wedding? Will you get dragged into their mess because you were his date?"

"Don't worry, I doubt Malcolm Somers cares who I am," I tell her. "He'll be pissed with Theo. Like I said, that kiss was just for show. There's nothing going on between Theo and me."

I must be pretty convincing because Megan shrugs and goes back to her K-drama. As Aunt Jade heads into the kitchen, I stare at the photo of Theo and me on the front page. Obviously not a Georgina Kim–level shot—one of the guests or waitstaff members must've taken pictures and sold them to the tabloid.

Did Theo really appear smitten with me? When did he tell his relatives that I'm his inspiration? Did he mean that?

My gaze drops to the bracelet around my wrist. I didn't expect him to get me a thoughtful souvenir. I didn't get him anything. Though that's not the only thing that took me by surprise. Last night, the expression in his eyes when he asked if I believed in destiny, the way he leaned in and pulled my bow tie loose . . . In that moment, the only thing I didn't know was who would kiss whom first.

A bittersweet feeling wells up inside my chest. I never imagined anything would come of pretending to be Theo's date. But we aren't in the Hamptons anymore.

We're finally home.

• • •

I'm upstairs on the living room couch, trying to study. Two days have passed, but I can't stop thinking about Theo. About our weekend in the Hamptons. How we slept in the same bed for two nights without touching . . . There's an ache somewhere deep in my chest, like I've pulled a muscle. The heart's a pretty major one, so I guess I have.

My phone dings with a message. I bolt upright . . . but it's not from Theo. I haven't heard from him since Sunday afternoon, after we got home. He said he had a busy week coming up with school and tennis. I texted him a couple of times, asking how he's been. But he hasn't replied.

Clover comes over and paws my leg.

"Remember Theo, the guy who came into the shop the other day?" I tell her. "You should've seen him in a suit. Woof."

Clover gives me a look, like I'm not using *woof* correctly. She barks at the bag of BBQ chicken and cheddar cheese biscuits from the farmers market, clearly more interested in a treat than my love life.

"Okay, let's try something." I take a biscuit in one hand. "Do I tell myself what happens in the Hamptons, stays in the Hamptons, and try to forget about him?" I hold a second biscuit in the other hand. "Or do I tell him the guy who played the violin is totally my type and hope he feels the same way?"

Clover moves forward and eats both treats.

I sigh. "Thanks a lot, buddy."

"Try structured questions. Like bark twice for yes, once for no." Megan appears at the top of the stairs, slipping through the safety gate that stops Clover from going down to the shop. "I've got to say, though, getting relationship advice from your pet is a sign you need a break. How about a delivery run? A bike ride might clear your head."

Aunt Jade hasn't asked me to help with deliveries since the incident with Adrian. We must be shorthanded. I close my textbook. Not like I'm getting any work done. "Where to?"

Megan holds out the order slip. "He specifically asked for you."

It's Theo's address. My heart leaps.

"Hurry up and put on a clean T-shirt." Megan yanks me to my feet. "Your hair's a mess, by the way. You're overdue for a haircut."

My hair's stubbornly sticking out, and the humidity is seriously messing with my bangs. I try to fix them with styling wax, but they end up weird and flat and still sticking out.

Tim waves from the counter as Megan and I step outside. Aunt Jade pokes her head through the serving window. "Ride carefully!"

Megan hands me my helmet. "Speaking of riding carefully, you have condoms, right?"

I eye her, askance. "Why would I need those for a delivery?"

"Pretty sure Theo's got more than takeout in mind." She grins. "You know, Netflix and chill. Or should that be IMAX and climax?"

"Meg!" I glance over my shoulder to see if Tim overheard. She cackles.

I strap on my helmet, climb onto my bike, and set off. The night air is cool and crisp against my face, and the half moon overhead is like a round snow-skin mooncake that's been cut in two. I feel as if someone just took the lid off a jar of butterflies inside my chest. Now we're not in the Hamptons, and everything's more . . . real.

I pedal faster than usual, and by the time I reach Theo's mansion, my T-shirt has damp circles on my back and under my arms. I take the food out of the warmer bag and ring the bell.

"Delivery for Theo," I say.

I'm buzzed in without question. The hike up the driveway to the mansion seems longer than the last time. Before I can knock, the front door swings open—

Adrian steps out.

My smile freezes.

"Hope you got the order right this time." Adrian's wearing cutoff shorts and a fancy plaid shirt that's unbuttoned down the front. He pauses, as if clocking my stunned expression. "Hang on—you were expecting Theo to answer the door, weren't you?"

I can't tear my eyes away from Theo's Burberry shirt. I try to swallow the hurt, the disbelief, but I can't.

Adrian lets out a scornful laugh. "Did you think he's your boyfriend because he kissed you? Hate to break it to you, but you're nothing but a charity case to him. Theo pities your family, that's all." He snatches the bag of food from me. "If there are spring onions in this again, you'll be getting a letter from my dad's firm."

He goes back inside without shutting the door. I'm still rooted to the spot.

Bernard appears. He shoots a disapproving stare in the direction Adrian went.

"I should've been the one to come to the door." He gives me a sympathetic smile that doesn't quite reach his eyes. "I'll tell Theo you said hello."

A knot tightens inside my chest. "Don't bother."

That shirt Theo put on me, which I slept in, which made me feel safe . . . seeing it wrapped around Adrian's body is a sucker punch to the gut, knocking all the wind out of me.

Somehow, my legs carry me to the end of the driveway and out the gate. My eyes sting and blur as I fumble with my bike lock. I only manage to open it on the third try. My head is spinning, and a sour taste rises in the back of my throat as the truth hits home.

There was never going to be a next time for us.

Chapter 21

Our airflow system breaks down again, and our landlord refuses to do anything because we're still behind on rent. Aunt Jade has to pay for repairs, and we close the takeout for an extra day to get the system fixed. After I help her clean up, we make the best of the free time by diving into our second mooncake-making session.

Aunt Jade admires the wooden molds I bought from Auntie Chan. "They're so meaningful." She points at the round-shaped mold with the character 念. "Especially this one."

A pang goes through me. After we bought the molds at the farmers market, Theo even said he wanted to help make the mooncakes. The seventh lunar month is over, but guys like him seem to be good at ghosting all year round.

"All right! Let's start on the lotus seed paste filling," Aunt Jade says. "I've got everything we need: alkaline water, sugar, groundnut oil, maltose, and of course, lotus seeds. Most shops sell the ones stripped of their coats, since removing them is a ton of work. But the seeds lose their flavor once they're exposed, so we want those that haven't been skinned."

Some shops in Chinatown sell the paste ready-made—but like our xiao long bao, Aunt Jade would never take that shortcut.

"The mooncake skin makes a first impression, but the filling is its heart," Aunt Jade adds. "Making the lotus seed paste from scratch gives you a chance to put your heart into it too."

I put my heart into making things happen with Theo, and look how that turned out. Worst part is, I can't even fully blame him. He was clear from the beginning that I was only his fake date. This was supposed to be strictly business with no strings—or feelings—attached. I was an idiot to think anything real could be built on a lie.

No one knows Adrian answered the door on that delivery. Not even Megan. When I got back, I just told her Theo had friends over. Which wasn't a lie. I went upstairs, took off the bracelet, and threw the thing to the bottom of my dresser drawer. I should've tossed it into the trash, but I couldn't bring myself to.

We boil the lotus seeds. Aunt Jade wasn't kidding about how much work goes into removing the coats. We also have to pluck out the tiny green shoot inside each seed. Leaving them in will make the paste bitter. When we're done, we boil the seeds again and blend them into a smooth puree. I jot down the right amount of sugar and groundnut oil to add. Aunt Jade watches as I stir-fry the puree with maltose until the mixture thickens into a paste in the wok.

"Keep stirring so the paste won't burn," Aunt Jade reminds me. "Take it out only when it becomes thick enough to be scraped away from the sides of the wok."

After I scoop out the paste, she pours some grayish white melon seed kernels into a pan and gives them a quick fry before adding them to the paste.

"Aren't these the melon seeds we eat during the Lunar New Year?" I ask.

"Yeah. They're supposed to bring good fortune, but their hulls are super tough. Your Gong Gong once tried to crack one open with his teeth and broke a molar. He definitely didn't feel lucky when he saw his dental bill." She holds up a packet of white powder. "Guess what? I figured out where we went wrong with the mooncake skin. I should've used wheat starch, not wheat flour. Pop quiz: What's the difference?"

I furrow my brows. "Wheat flour contains the starch as well as other parts of the wheat, including the gluten and protein. Wheat starch is pure starch and gluten-free."

"I've taught you well, young Padawan." Aunt Jade opens the packet. "Wheat starch is also a thickener, which gives the snow skin a translucent sheen. Dough made with starch is less elastic than dough made with flour. That's how we can get the soft, smooth texture we've been missing."

"The lady who sold me the wooden molds gave me another tip," I tell her. "Use ice-cold water instead of room-temperature water for the dough."

Aunt Jade considers this. "I don't remember your grandma mentioning that. But why don't we give it a try?"

I add the wheat starch and the rest of the ingredients to the cooked glutinous rice flour along with ice-cold water before kneading the mixture.

"Okay, that's enough." Aunt Jade pokes the dough to test its consistency. "Too much kneading will squeeze out the moisture. We want the dough to be smooth and bouncy. Make sure you roll it evenly. When we were kids, your Por Por used to grumble that your mom's mooncake skin was wafer thin and mine was as thick as a cookie."

We wrap the dough around our homemade lotus seed paste and put the dough balls into the molds. When we're done, I bite into one of the mooncakes. The homemade filling is smooth, almost like ice cream, and the snow skin is softer and more velvety than our first attempt.

Aunt Jade looks pleased. "The paste is fragrant, and that tip was great: the ice-cold water gives the skin a perfect texture. Nice work. We'll tackle the white chocolate truffle core next time, okay? I have to grab a few things at the store before I get our dinner going."

"I'll pick them up for you," I volunteer.

The air is cooler but still humid, turning my hair into a shapeless mop. Instead of going straight to the store, I take a detour to the hair salon. I'm sick of bangs. When I brush them aside, I remember how Theo ran his fingers through them—and it's like an invisible hand has reached into my chest and squeezed the air out of my lungs.

"Same style, just shorter?" the hairstylist asks.

I need a complete refresh. "Chop off the bangs. I want them gone."

A part of me hoped Theo would try to explain why Adrian was there. But it's been two days and I haven't heard a word from him. Fake charity, fake dating . . . as much as I hate to admit it, Adrian was right. Theo just wanted to help the takeout. That was all.

I walk out of the hair salon in a crew cut with tapered sides. By the time I get back to the takeout, Aunt Jade's cooking our dinner and I can hear Megan in the kitchen as well. The aroma of

Hainanese pork chops sizzling in the wok drifts through the serving window. My stomach lets out a growl. It's my favorite dish—slices of pork loin coated in cream cracker crumbs, deep fried, and topped with a thick gravy of ketchup sautéed with onions, green peas, and tomatoes.

I bring the bags of groceries I bought to the storeroom. As I head back to the front of the shop, the chime on the door dings.

"Sorry," I automatically say, "but we're closed—"

I break off.

Standing in the doorway—dressed in jeans and a gray shirt, with a bottle of wine in hand—is Theo.

Chapter 22

My chest constricts. It's a replay of the morning he first walked into our shop—except that time, he hadn't smashed my heart into bits yet.

"Hey, Dylan." Theo flashes a hesitant smile. "You got a new haircut."

I stare at him. "What are you—"

Megan must've overheard us, because she bursts out of the kitchen.

She sees me and lets out a shriek. "Oh my God, Dyl— What did you do to your hair? I told you to get a trim, not chop it all off! Ugh! It's your head. Do whatever you want." She beams at Theo and calls out over her shoulder, "Mom, Theo's here! And he brought you wine!"

WTF is flashing inside my head in neon letters.

"Theo!" Aunt Jade appears, wiping her palms on her apron. Theo holds out the bottle with both hands. "Wow, how did you guess Moscato's my favorite? Did Dylan tell you?"

"Yeah, he mentioned it," Theo says. He remembered that too? "Bernard had a bottle handy in our wine cellar."

"Theo called after you went to the store, so I invited him over for dinner," Aunt Jade tells me. "When I asked if he had any special requests, he said, 'whatever dish is Dylan's favorite.'"

"Stop, that's so sweet," Megan chimes in.

Aunt Jade passes me the bottle of wine. "Why don't you bring Theo upstairs? And put this in a bucket of ice, please. After going through our books with the accountant this morning, I sure could use a glass. Dinner will be ready in ten."

Megan winks as she follows Aunt Jade back into the kitchen. I shoot her the death glare reserved for traitors.

When they're out of earshot, I spin around to face Theo.

"You've got some nerve, showing up like this." I keep my voice low and hard. "What's the matter, Adrian's busy tonight?"

Theo's brow furrows. "I was worried about you. I wanted to know if you're okay."

A flush of heat curls up my neck. He came by to make sure I'm not a total wreck after running into Adrian at his place? As if I need his pity on top of his charity?

"I'm fine," I snap. "Since you have your answer, the door's that way. I'll tell my aunt you had to run off—"

"Theo, you're here!" Tim appears at the foot of the stairs with his violin. "Meg said you were coming over for dinner."

"Hey, Tim. I brought you this." Theo takes out a small eraser-shaped object from his pocket. "This is the brand of rosin I told you about. Works like a charm."

"Thanks!" Tim sounds excited. "I'm practicing Mozart's Contredanse Number One for my violin exam. Want to hear me play? You can tell me if I get any notes wrong."

"Sure." Theo gives me a measured glance. "That is, if Dylan doesn't mind."

Tim looks at me eagerly. Dammit. There goes any chance of getting rid of Theo.

"Yeah, go on," I say through gritted teeth.

Tim's face lights up. "Awesome. Let's go to the living room."

As Theo climbs the stairs with Tim, I make my way to the deep freezer around back and scoop ice cubes into a bucket. I fantasize about dumping them on Theo's head instead of sticking the bottle of wine inside.

When I go upstairs, Clover's hanging around the safety gate. She's usually cagey whenever we have people over, but she seems chill around Theo, who's showing Tim how to use that rosin thing on his violin.

"Make sure you get some onto the last inch, where the string goes into the peg," Theo says. "Don't put too much."

"Coming through!" Aunt Jade appears at the top of the steps with a large tray full of dishes. "Tim, have you set the table?"

I hold the gate open for her as Tim scrambles to set the table for five. We only have two wooden stools on each side of the dinner table, so Tim adds a fifth. Aunt Jade catches my eye and points at the seat next to Theo, but I sit diagonally opposite, the farthest I can get from him. Megan sits beside me, Tim takes the extra seat, and Aunt Jade ends up next to Theo.

"I added an extra dish of honey sesame chicken in case you don't fancy the pork," Aunt Jade tells Theo, putting the biggest, juiciest piece of pork chop in front of him. There's white rice, potato wedges, and broccoli sautéed with olive oil and garlic on the side. "My dad—Dylan's grandpa—used to sell pork at the wet market, so I know which cuts are the best."

Clover trots over to Theo and playfully tugs at the cuff of his jeans. Theo reaches down to pet her head. "I think she wants some of this delicious food."

Not only does Clover not bite his hand off, but she actually wags her tail.

"Clover, stop that," I say, annoyed.

I carry her to the other end of the living room. She barks in protest but stops when I give her an extra bunch of those gourmet biscuits she loves. When I look over my shoulder, Theo has opened the bottle of wine and is pouring Aunt Jade a glass. Megan's laughing at whatever he just said, and Tim's gazing at him like he's the big brother he never had.

Seems like Clover isn't the only member of my family I need to drag away from Theo. Only problem is, it won't be as easy as offering them some treats.

When I return to the table, I can feel Theo's eyes on me. I concentrate on murderously dissecting the pork chop on my plate. It's perfectly browned, and the gravy is fragrant and tangy—but my appetite is nonexistent with Theo sitting there. I don't want him hanging out with my family. I want to get this meal over with and get him out of here as soon as possible.

"So, the scalpers did it again," Megan says. "Snapped up all the tickets for the Blackpink concert. I waited forever for them to go on sale—but our internet connection sucks, as usual, and I got booted out. Amy managed to grab four tickets and promised to sell me one. But guess what happened today?"

"The organizer oversold tickets and canceled them?" Theo says. "Happened to me once."

"No." Megan's expression becomes stormy. "Another girl offered Amy an extra hundred, and she sold her my ticket. And you know what Amy told me? 'Sorry, Meg, nothing personal.' Like, what? In first grade, when a boy stepped on her sandwich, did I hoard my food and say 'nothing personal'?"

"You've got to be careful, Meg." I pin Theo with a cold glare. "Some people can't be trusted."

Discomfort crosses Theo's face.

When we finish our meal, Aunt Jade goes to the fridge.

"We have mooncakes for dessert!" she announces, putting them in the middle of the table with a flourish. "Dylan made them."

My heart sinks.

Tim pipes up. "Did you know a baked mooncake has as many calories as a double cheeseburger *and* a hot fudge sundae?"

"No one likes a party pooper, Tim." Megan grins at Theo. "You must try one of Dylan's mooncakes. You'll love them to the moon and back."

I kick her under the table, but she dodges with her taekwondo-trained reflexes and I make contact with Theo's ankle instead. He raises a brow. I quickly avert my eyes.

Aunt Jade gives each of us a fork. Theo reaches for the mooncake with the character 念.

Instinctively, I push it away with my fork. "Not this one. Take one of the others."

Megan and Aunt Jade look at me quizzically. I chose that mold especially for Mom. After everything Theo has done, I can't stomach the thought of him eating a mooncake with *remembrance* imprinted on top. As far as he's concerned, I just want to forget.

Tim turns to Theo. "Mooncakes always remind me of Chang'e. Do you know the story?"

"I've only heard bits and pieces," Theo says. "Something about an archer and the moon goddess?"

Megan groans. "Theo, don't encourage him."

Tim perks up, ignoring his sister. "Okay, here's how it goes. A long time ago, there were ten suns in the sky. People, plants, animals, everything was dying from the heat. An archer named Hou Yi used his bow and arrows to shoot down nine of the ten suns. As a reward for saving the world, the gods gave him an elixir that would make him immortal—"

"Chinese emperors were totally obsessed with that stuff," Megan interjects. "Some died trying to drink a bad batch that turned out to be mercury."

"Meg, stop butting in with your stupid trivia. I'm telling the story here." Tim shoots her a withering look. "So, where was I? Hou Yi got the potion—"

"You said it was an elixir," Megan cuts in.

"Elixir, potion, whatever. Isn't it the same thing?"

"Yeah, but a good storyteller shouldn't use different words. You'll confuse your audience."

"Well, you're not being a good audience if you keep jumping in and interrupting the storyteller," Tim counters.

"Why don't we just call it forever juice?" Theo suggests.

Aunt Jade chuckles. I stare at my fork and debate whether stabbing Theo or myself will make this nightmare end sooner.

"Hou Yi didn't want to drink the forever juice and become immortal," Tim continues. "He wanted to stay on earth with his wife, Chang'e. But one day, when Hou Yi wasn't home, one of his students tried to steal the forever juice. The only way Chang'e could stop him was to drink it herself. Instead of floating to the heavens, she flew to the moon . . . the closest she could be to her husband on earth."

Aunt Jade's eyes glint with mirth. "The roundness of the full moon represents reunion—not just among family, but also between lovers. Chinese dynasties had strict curfews, and women weren't allowed out at night except on special occasions. Young ladies would dress up and go out to meet young men. They would eat mooncakes and fall in love. That's why Mid-Autumn is sometimes also known as the Chinese Valentine's Day."

"Are you going to the festival this year?" Tim asks Theo. "You could come with us!"

"Nah, you should go with Adrian." I fix him with a hard stare. "You two can hold hands and walk under the full moon. It'll be really romantic."

Tim seems confused. Aunt Jade and Megan exchange "oh shit" glances.

Theo's mouth pinches. "I told you, Adrian and I are just friends—"

"Drop the act, all right?" I burst out. "He came to the door wearing *your* shirt when I showed up on that delivery *you* asked me to make!"

My voice echoes in the abrupt silence. Clover comes over, her big ears perked. I bite down hard on my lip. I didn't mean to explode in front of everyone, but I couldn't stop myself.

"You know what?" Aunt Jade forces a light tone. "I should deep clean the stove. And unclog the sink and scrub the floor." She gives my cousins a meaningful look. "All these dishes won't wash themselves. . . ."

"We'll help," Megan and Tim say in unison.

The three of them jump up, grab as many plates as they can carry, and disappear downstairs, leaving us alone.

Chapter 23

The plate of mooncakes between us remains untouched. Clover watches Theo closely, her hackles raised.

Theo stares at me, baffled. "Dylan, what's going on with you? What delivery? And what does any of this have to do with Adrian?"

"I still have the receipt from Tuesday night. With your address." I utter a short, acerbic sound. "I know we were just pretending, Theo, so you don't need to act like you care about my feelings while rubbing it in my face—"

"I have no idea what you're— Hang on, did you say Tuesday night?" Theo's brow furrows. "I wasn't even home. I was at a tennis boot camp with my teammates until midnight . . . but Adrian did text to say he was coming over to use my pool because the one at his condo was being cleaned."

I'm incredulous. "So you're saying Adrian went to your place when you weren't around and ordered takeout pretending to be you? That's the story you're going with?"

Frustration flashes in Theo's eyes. "I don't know what else I can say to convince you I didn't make that order. When you ghosted me after we got back, I wasn't sure what to think—"

"*I* ghosted you? Pretty sure it was the other way around."

"See for yourself." Theo pushes his phone across the table. "That's why I called the takeout today. I was worried something might've happened to you."

I reluctantly glance at his screen. There are over a dozen texts I never received.

"I never got any of these." I show him the unanswered messages I sent him on my phone. "You never replied to any of my texts, either."

Theo pulls up my contact details. "This is your number, right?"

"No, it isn't." I frown. "Wait—are you saying someone changed my number in your phone?" I tap on Theo's number in my contacts—but his phone doesn't ring, and the call on my side goes straight to voice mail.

Realization dawns on Theo's face. He swipes to his blocked contacts. "Is your number in here?"

It is. Everything makes sense now—we couldn't reach each other because my real number was blocked in Theo's phone and replaced with a fake one. His texts to me were sent to that number instead, and my calls to him never went through.

"Seems Adrian got into your phone again," I tell him. "This time, he did more than change your ringtone."

Theo's expression turns grim. "We need to have a talk with him."

I shake my head. "I'm not getting dragged into this. Why would he go through all this trouble if there isn't anything going on between you two?"

"Dylan, I swear, Adrian and I aren't seeing each other." Theo reaches across the table and puts his hand on mine. Clover lets out a warning growl. "Yeah, we have history. I never tried to hide that from you. But it's all in the past. And I sure as hell am *not* hooking up with him now. You have to believe me."

I rub a palm over my forehead. It feels weird that my bangs are gone. But for the first time in days, the hurt coiled inside my chest unspools. I still don't have a label on what Theo and I are to each other—just friends, or something more—but I like him enough to want to give us a chance to find out.

Theo's watching my reaction. Our eyes meet. "Okay."

Clover barks. She can sense the tension has broken. She trots to me, wagging her tail.

I ruffle the top of her head. "Good girl."

When we go downstairs, Aunt Jade, Megan, and Tim look at us anxiously through the serving window.

"We're going to sort some things out," I tell them, grabbing my jacket. "Don't wait up for me. I've got my keys."

We get into Theo's car and drive to Adrian's condo on 74th Street. I never thought I'd be back at the place we first met.

When we enter the lobby, the doorman nods at Theo. "Good evening, Mr. Somers." His gaze lingers on me. I doubt he recognizes that I'm the delivery guy from a couple of weeks ago.

"He's with me," Theo replies.

"Certainly. I'll let Mr. Rogers know you're on your way up."

"Please do," Theo says.

We breeze past the front desk to the elevators. Seems like Theo's on the approved visitors list. He must come over often. Does he spend the night? I push the thought aside as the elevator doors open on the top floor.

Adrian leans in the doorway, wearing a crisp Balenciaga T-shirt and ripped jeans. "Hey, dude, why didn't you text me that you're—"

He breaks off when he sees me. His mutinous expression says it all: busted.

Theo stalks toward him and holds up his phone. "If you don't give me a really good explanation for this crap you pulled, I'm going to block you from my life like you tried to block Dylan."

"All right, you got me. But I only did it for your own good." Adrian slants a disdainful look in my direction. "Seriously, Theo, you could have any boy you want—and you fall for the food delivery guy?"

"Insult Dylan one more time and I'll kick your ass." Theo's tone is deadly. "And when your mom asks me why, I'll tell her exactly what you did. Want to bet whose side she'll take?"

"Chill, leave my mom out of this, okay?" Adrian glowers at Theo. "In case you think I'm trying to steal you from Takeout Boy because I'm jealous, don't. We've known each other forever. We agreed our friendship is worth more than screwing around."

Theo shoves him on the shoulder. "Then why the hell are you trying to get between us?"

A warm prickle goes up the back of my neck. Us?

"I'm not, dumbass." Adrian lifts his gaze to the ceiling. "Shit, this is so messed up. I never should've agreed to help."

"Help?" Theo's eyes narrow. "What are you talking about?"

Adrian takes out his own phone and shows Theo a string of digits on the screen. "This is the number you thought was Dylan's. When you called, has anyone ever picked up?"

"No. You'd know since you're the one who swapped out our numbers. If you're planning to be a lawyer like your dad, you should read up on the Fifth Amendment, because you just incriminated yourself."

"You wanted a really good explanation, didn't you?" Adrian taps the call button and puts his phone on speaker. "Wait for it."

Ringing fills the silence before the call's picked up.

"What is it, Adrian?" comes a familiar male voice with a clipped British accent. "You're not supposed to call this number unless it's an emergency."

I stare at Theo, unable to hide my shock. Blood drains from Theo's face.

"I did everything you asked," Adrian replies, sounding bored. "He still figured it out."

Hardness coalesces in Theo's eyes as he takes the phone from Adrian.

"Hey, Bernard," he says. "I'm pretty sure this qualifies as an emergency."

Chapter 24

For only the second time, I'm setting foot inside Theo's mansion. There's a glass display case in the entranceway I didn't notice the last time. All the trophies and plaques inside are engraved with the same name: MALCOLM H. SOMERS.

Bernard is waiting for us. He spares me a glance before turning to Theo, looking resigned. "If you have words for me, I'd prefer if we spoke in private."

"No," Theo says flatly. "You gave up that right when you dragged Dylan into this. Sticking a knife in my back is one thing, Bernard, but you crossed a line when you got him involved. Did you ever think about how he might get hurt?"

"Did you?" Bernard's tone is calm. "I warned you not to spit in your father's face by attending the wedding. You refused to listen. You could've gone on your own—but you had to bring Dylan into this fray."

"So you tried to cause a rift between us by luring Dylan over and making sure Adrian answered the door wearing my shirt?" Theo's eyes darken. "I thought Adrian changed Dylan's number in my phone and blocked him—but that was you, wasn't it?"

Theo should really stop giving his passcode to so many people.

Bernard grimaces. "Publicly showing support for your aunt won't influence the court case, but as far as your father's concerned, what you did is the worst kind of betrayal. And thanks to your newsworthy quote about how Dylan inspired you to 'show up for your real family,' now your father suspects *Dylan* convinced you to go to the wedding so he could get his fifteen minutes of fame."

I'm aghast. "That's absolutely—"

"Correct," Theo says matter-of-factly. "Dylan gave me the idea of crashing the wedding."

My head snaps toward him. "What?"

"You had no idea, of course," Theo tells me. "But when I walked into your shop that morning and saw all your photos on the wall, I couldn't help but think of how my dad only had one picture of me in his new place. How he barely mentions a word about me in media interviews. I decided to remind him that the son he seems to have forgotten can make a headline or two of his own."

"Your father also knows about the five thousand dollars you gave to Dylan's aunt's business." Bernard's expression is troubled. "Malcolm has had his share of clout chasers trying to get close to him for his family's wealth and influence. And the court battle with your aunt is proof of how your father can be . . . ruthless when provoked. I was worried what extreme measures he might resort to, so I quickly stepped in and promised I'd take care of the matter."

Fallout from the wedding was inevitable—that was Theo's goal, after all. But I never thought I'd get caught in the middle. Turns out, Bernard was trying to defuse the situation—and of course, Adrian agreed to help because he thinks I'm not good enough for his BFF.

Theo's tone softens perceptibly. "Going behind my back and trying to get Dylan to hate me is a pretty screwed-up way of showing you're on my side, Bernard."

"I regret that." Bernard exhales heavily. "But this is a lot more complicated than having a broken stained-glass window replaced after I told you not to play with a tennis ball in the house."

"Then let's make my dad think his plan worked." Theo has a gleam in his eye. "Tell him Dylan and I had a big fight over Adrian and broke up. I could make a huge scene, maybe smash a few of his golf trophies. Dylan could, I don't know, set the bonsai on fire."

Bernard rolls his eyes but seems less tense. "The plants are innocent, Theo. Let's leave them out of this."

"So we're supposed to be fake . . . hating now?" I ask.

Theo grins. "Something like that. But we'll still find a way to hang out without my dad knowing."

"But he still thinks I'm the bad guy," I point out. "I'd rather not go around with a target painted on my back."

"Let me worry about that." Theo squeezes my hand. "It's getting pretty late, so Bernard will drive you home, okay? I don't want your aunt to be stressed. We'll figure something out. I'm not going to let my dad win."

The corners of Bernard's mouth twitch. "You are so much more like your father than you realize."

I step outside with Bernard and go to his Audi. Nice wheels. Maybe I should become a butler instead of a chef.

When we pull up in front of the takeout, Bernard puts the car into park.

"I owe you an apology, young man," he tells me. "My first priority is always to protect Theo, but I shouldn't have used Adrian to push you away. That was terribly deceitful. I hope you can find it in your heart to forgive me."

"I know you care about Theo, maybe like he's your own son," I reply. "But I care about him too. My whole family adores him . . . even my dog, and she doesn't trust most people. Seems like Mr. Somers is the only one who can't see what an amazing guy his son is. And I'm not going to let him get between us."

Bernard's expression turns contemplative. "Did Theo tell you how his mother died?"

"He said another driver blacked out and hit her car."

"The accident happened on her way to pick Theo up from kindergarten. Malcolm rushed to the hospital and forgot about him." Bernard sighs. "By the time the school contacted him, poor little Theo had been waiting for hours. Not knowing why his mother never came to pick him up. Not knowing why he was the only kid left behind."

Bernard doesn't say it, but we both know that feeling probably never left Theo. When you lose someone you love, you'll always remember, with unwanted clarity, exactly where you were and what you were doing when you got the news. When the hospital called about Mom, I was wearing my NO DRAMA, LLAMA T-shirt. I never wore it again.

When Theo lost his mom, he must've been so scared, so confused, so . . . abandoned. Maybe he still blames himself since she got into the accident on her way to pick him up.

I face Bernard. "Theo's dad trusts you. If you don't mind me asking, how do you two know each other?"

"When Malcolm was ten, Malcolm Senior moved the whole

family to London for a few years," Bernard replies. "My father was their butler, and we lived in a cottage on the estate. After Theo's mother died, Malcolm asked me to join the household and care for Theo full-time. He offered double my salary as an hotelier . . . but that's not why I said yes." Bernard pauses. "Theo's grandfather sponsored my university education. My family would never have been able to afford the fees."

"So you repaid his kindness by taking care of his grandson?" The bond between Theo and Bernard makes even more sense now.

Bernard nods. "Over the past twelve years, I've watched Theo grow up, and you're right: I don't have kids, but I love him like he's my own." A crease forms on his forehead. "I also admit, I had my doubts at first about your motives for getting close to Theo."

"And now?" I ask. "Why are you helping us get around his dad?"

"There's not much I can give a boy who has nearly everything. If something, or someone, can make him happy . . . I'll do my best to let him have that." Bernard holds my gaze. "As long as the other person has the right motives."

I open the car door. "Is this the part where you solemnly swear to hunt me down and kick my ass if I hurt Theo?"

Bernard unexpectedly chuckles. "I'm beginning to see why he likes you so much."

Chapter 25

Megan bites into her toast. "I can't believe we get to say the butler did it."

"I can't believe the nerve of that man." Aunt Jade frowns. "Trying to drive a wedge between you and Theo? He should be ashamed of himself."

I crack my soft-boiled eggs into a bowl. "Theo lost his mom, and now he's at war with his dad. He doesn't have many people left who care about him, and I don't want him to lose another. What Bernard did was awful, but I'm willing to let it go."

"Well, you have people who care about you too," Aunt Jade replies. "If I ever see that glorified babysitter, I'm going to give him a piece of my mind."

Megan takes the carton of milk and looks at me. "You should've seen your face at dinner. You looked as if you wanted to eat Theo. And not with a spoon—more like tearing him right off the bone."

"Sorry I blew up. I was too embarrassed to tell you guys what happened on that delivery."

"Nah, we figured something was off when you got back," Megan says.

"Even Clover knew," Tim adds. "She started bringing her spiky ball to me instead."

Aunt Jade stirs her mug of coffee. "We thought you boys had a fight and needed time to cool off. That's why I invited Theo over when he called the shop. I was hoping you two would patch things up." Her brow creases. "Do you think Theo's father might try something more drastic if he finds out you're still spending time together?"

"We pretended we had a big fight," I tell them. "But Theo will find a way for us to hang out."

"Well, I'm glad you guys made up," Tim says. "If you hadn't, Megan was going to make us wear T-shirts with 'Team Theo' across the front until you came around."

I laugh. "Can I get one too?"

Back in my room, I open the dresser drawer where I threw Theo's bracelet after I got back from that delivery. I hold the tiny glass vial to the fluorescent light. Sand drifts around the grain of rice with my name.

Theo and I didn't get the chance to talk about *us* last night. But for now, the mix of excitement and hopefulness is enough.

I loop the bracelet around my wrist and fasten the clasp, putting it back where it belongs.

• • •

On Saturday night, the first day of fall, I have a date . . . with a wok full of fried noodles.

Fried Hokkien prawn mee with pomelo is one of the signature dishes featured on Fry Me to the Moon, our special Mid-Autumn Festival menu. None of us has mastered the art of tossing egg fried rice without a single grain falling outside the wok, but I've learned to cook this dish on my own. Auntie Heng, one of our regulars, ordered two large boxes.

Stir-fry thick yellow wheat noodles and vermicelli with bean sprouts, prawns, eggs, squid, slices of pork belly, and crispy pork cubes—not the healthiest choice, and some people ask us not to add the cubes in, but seriously, they make such a difference in the taste of the dish. Then let the ingredients braise in prawn stock for a couple of minutes with a lid over the wok, allowing flavor to seep into the noodles.

We usually serve the dish with calamansi, a lemon-lime type of fruit, but this time, I sprinkle peeled pomelo for a crunchy Mid-Autumn twist. Pomelo is also citrusy, with a unique sweet-bitter tang like grapefruit. The last step? Serve with a scoop of sambal chili paste.

Aunt Jade has gone to the storeroom to get more satay for the grill, and as I'm opening the bottle of sambal chili paste, Megan's voice rings out through the serving window.

"DYLAN!" she yells. "GET OUT HERE NOW!"

Oh no. The last time she yelled my name this way was when one of my colored socks accidentally got rolled into the wash with the whites. Before that, it was the time I didn't have a pen and I used her eyebrow pencil to scribble down our new Wi-Fi password.

I come out of the kitchen in trepidation. Aunt Jade is in the corridor with a packet of frozen satay, her eyebrows raised. Megan is at the counter, smirking.

Theo is standing in the middle of our shop. He's drop-dead gorgeous in a dark suit and necktie. When he sees me, he breaks into a smile that almost makes me lose my grip on the bottle of chili paste I'm holding.

"Hey, Dylan," he says. "I'm here to take you to the ball."

"The ball?"

"A charity benefit at the Met," he adds. "Uncle Herbert and Aunt Jacintha had to bail because one of their kids ate a crayon and ended up in the ER. Aunt Catherine called and asked, 'What are you and Dylan doing tonight?' So I figured, why not?"

I glance down at myself. I have a couple of prawn shells and legs stuck to the front of my apron. "You mean right now?"

"Mmm-hmm. The event starts in an hour. I brought your suit with one of my button-downs and a different tie."

I'm still confused. "What happened to fake-hating?"

"That was the plan, but . . . the more I thought things through, the more this cloak-and-dagger situation didn't sit right with me. I asked your aunt and cousins for their opinions, and they agreed we shouldn't sneak around. We've got nothing to hide." Theo gives me a rakish grin. "Plus, I really missed you."

"Aww, stop it." Megan grabs the garment bag from Theo. "I'll take that. You wait here while I deal with"—she gestures at me from head to toe—"*this.*"

Tim snickers. Aunt Jade takes the chili bottle as Megan ushers me upstairs.

I jump into the shower and scrub myself with the leftover body wash I swiped from the Hamptons before we left. (I'm the kind of guy who cuts a flattened tube of toothpaste in half to get the last bit out.) I hurry to my room with a towel around my waist, smelling of mandarin oranges. The garment bag Theo brought is draped across my bed.

Megan, who's been waiting outside my room like a prison guard, barges in the second I zip up my pants. She accosts me with a hairdryer. "If Taylor Swift's there, you'd better get me her autograph."

I squirm as a blast of scalding air hits me in the face. "If Taylor's there, I think she'd want to enjoy the evening instead of being bugged by some random—"

"Don't get all bougie on me, Dyl." Megan brandishes the hairbrush. "You're not in a position to negotiate. I have an eyelash curler, and I'm not afraid to use it."

My hair is much easier to style since I cut my bangs short. Megan's next weapon is a makeup brush—I try to fend her off, but she gets a few swipes of tinted powder on my nose.

"You clean up real nice," she says, satisfied.

I put on the suit jacket, and we go back downstairs. Aunt Jade has packed the wok of fried Hokkien mee for Auntie Heng, who's chattering admiringly with Theo.

"Hello, Auntie Heng," I greet her. "I deshelled the prawns the way you like them."

"Dylan!" she exclaims. "I almost didn't recognize you—you're so handsome!"

"He is," Theo agrees. My cheeks flush.

Megan gives him the charcoal tie and pinstripe handkerchief. "I'll let you put the finishing touches on him. Don't want his pocket square looking like an origami crane."

Theo steps closer, looping the long strip of silk around my neck. It's like getting dressed for the ceremony in the Hamptons all over again—but this time, we're in my world, not his. Theo's eyes don't leave mine as he ties the knot, adjusts the dimple, and tucks the folded handkerchief into my pocket.

He takes out a pair of cuff links—different from the Cartier

186

ones, but I know better than to ask what brand they are. As he secures them onto my cuffs, just thinking about what happened the last time he took them off makes me hot around the collar.

"Go on, you two!" Megan says. "As delicious as our honey sesame chicken is, you don't want the greasy smell to stick to your suits."

We step outside, and Aunt Jade snaps pictures with her phone like we're on our way to prom. Theo opens the passenger door for me with a grin—and as we drive off, I can't help beaming like the half moon over our heads.

Chapter 26

I've been to the Met—but when I get out of the car on Fifth Avenue, I've clearly never *really* been to the Met. Not like this.

A valet whisks Theo's car away. Photographers circling the venue turn their lenses toward us as we climb the iconic steps. Theo takes my hand, and I almost jump. We haven't held hands in public since we got back from the Hamptons. After everything we've been through, his palm in mine feels fresh, exciting, like the first time all over again.

"Bernard bought an annual membership, and children under twelve can enter for free." The wonder in Theo's eyes reminds me of how enthralled he was at the Pollock studio. "We used to visit on Sunday afternoons and eat ice cream cones on the steps after. I loved the Musical Instruments galleries on the second floor."

I recall a random fact from a museum tour in my freshman year. "They have the world's oldest piano on display, right?"

Theo nods. "A Cristofori. Did you know most of the antique instruments in the Met are still in playable condition? I would absolutely kill to play one of their Stradivarius violins."

Catherine and Malia are hurrying toward us. Catherine's in a sleek ivory pantsuit, while Malia wears a yellow sequined gown that complements her brown skin.

We exchange hugs before Catherine pulls Theo aside and speaks in his ear.

Malia grins at me. "I love your new haircut!"

As Catherine and Malia go to greet other guests, Theo nudges me. "Before we go inside, there's something you should know."

"Don't lick the ice sculptures?" I joke.

"My dad's here too."

"Your— Wait, *what?*" I spin around like a trapped animal. How fast can the valet bring Theo's car? Or maybe we should run across the street and jump onto the first bus that arrives. "Pretending to date in front of your family at the wedding was enough to make your dad lose his shit. How do you think he'll react if we show up together in front of him?"

"Just hear me out for a sec." Theo holds up a hand. "My dad thinks you're this barnacle, which is totally untrue, but that's because he doesn't *know* you—"

"I'd like to keep it that way."

"I told your family that I don't want us to hide, and I mean that." Theo sounds earnest, but I'm too stressed out to ask what exactly *us* means to him. "This is the perfect chance to prove to my dad that he's wrong about you. That you're not hanging out with me for some ulterior motive."

There's no point running. The paparazzi already snapped us arriving. We'd just seem like we're jiàn bu dé rén, as Mom used to say—too ashamed to face anyone.

I brace myself. "Fine. But if he sees me and picks up a steak knife, I'm out of here."

Theo grins. "Don't worry. I know exactly where the Arms and Armor gallery is."

We walk into the Great Hall. The high domed ceilings are cavernous, with orbs of night visible through the circular skylights. The pillars are lit with electric-blue floodlights, illuminating about twenty tables in the center space, covered in white cloths and set with silverware and plates. The VIP tables at the front are decked in pale gold cloths—and one of the guests is strikingly familiar.

Malcolm Somers looks like he just stepped out of his portrait in his mansion. His dark blond hair has receded but still seems as if it was parted with a razor. He holds himself with a detached air that, uncannily, reminds me of Theo. His blue eyes are lasers, pinning us from across the room.

Theo halts. Catherine and Malia exchange glances. I don't know how to react.

"My dad's at the VIP table," Theo mutters out of the corner of his mouth. "Ours will be in the middle. Hope you don't mind."

Which table his dad will be seated at isn't the problem. I'd rather not be in the same building. Preferably not within the same borough.

"Come on." Theo doesn't let go of my hand. "Let's do this."

Malcolm raises his chin as we walk toward him. A sudden hush falls across the hall. Dozens of eyes are fixed on us. Tendrils of discomfort creep up the back of my neck.

"Hello, Dad," Theo says.

Malcolm's mouth twitches. "You should've told me you were coming, Theodore. Natalie's feeling under the weather, so there's a spare VIP seat for family."

Theo stiffens. Not sure if it's because of the use of his full name, the mention of his stepmom, or his dad's coldly pleasant tone as he said the word *family*.

"Thanks, but we've got seats for two." Theo pulls me closer to his side. Maybe it's the matching serious expressions on their faces, but there's definitely a resemblance between father and son. From the portrait, I think Theo has his mom's smile. Then again, I've never seen Malcolm's. "I came over to introduce Dylan. He was with me at the wedding last weekend."

Malcolm cuts a glance in my direction. I'm suddenly filled with the dread of a bug under a ray of sunlight passing through a magnifying glass.

"I've been wondering when I might meet the boy who has my son wrapped around his finger." Malcolm's tone is placid. "I see Mr. Kashimura's suit fits well."

"Dylan looks great, but guess what? He refused to keep the suit." Theo levels a gaze at his dad. "If you're worried about his intentions, you can relax. He's not that kind of person."

A few camera flashes go off at the corners of my vision before the photographers around us swivel toward the entrance. Lucia and her husband have just entered the Great Hall.

"Ah, your favorite aunt has arrived," Malcolm says dryly. "She must be eager to greet you. Don't keep her waiting."

Theo glares at him before we walk away.

"Theo! Dylan!" Lucia comes toward us in a perfectly choreographed strut. A cynical journalist might describe her as a preening peacock, but I have to admit, she has a certain elegance that reminds me of a swan. As she air-kisses our cheeks, more flashes go off. "Wonderful to see you two again so soon!"

A reporter comes forward. "Mrs. Leyland-Somers, congratulations on your daughter's wedding last weekend." She turns to

Theo. "Mr. Somers, what made you decide to attend your cousin's wedding despite the ongoing lawsuit between your aunt and your father?"

My hand slides out of Theo's as Lucia thrusts him into the spotlight.

"Theo and his cousins have been thick as thieves since they were kids," Lucia answers, though the question was directed at Theo. "My dear nephew is an accomplished violinist, and Nora was absolutely delighted when he offered to play at the ceremony."

"Aunt Lucia was gracious enough to invite me," Theo says. "I was honored to be a part of Nora's special day."

I move away, unnoticed, and slip outside. The wind is chilly, but I need some air.

Malcolm's only son publicly taking his opponent's side is a knife in his back—and Lucia's not beneath giving the cameras a show right in his presence. The whole thing made my skin crawl, but Theo played along without batting an eye.

Your friend has a silver tongue, Mr. Kashimura said. *He can talk his way out of anything—*

"Hey," comes Theo's voice. "You all right?"

I turn as he halts next to me. "Have you ever had acupuncture done before?"

Theo shakes his head. "What's that like?"

"First they stick a bunch of needles into your meridians. Then they attach a wire to each needle. The wire sends out electric pulses that go down the needle and right into your pressure point. And they leave the needles stuck into you for twenty minutes."

"Sounds uncomfortable."

"Nothing compared to how cringeworthy being trapped in the hall between your aunt and your dad was. I swear, I could *feel* the icicles forming on the ceiling."

"You know how theatrical Aunt Lucia can be." Theo sounds rueful. "And now you've seen firsthand what an ass Malcolm H. Somers is."

"Because he thinks I'm the guy who's trying to take advantage of his son!" I make a wide gesture. "What are we doing here, Theo? Am I still pretending to be your date? Or are we—"

I break off. I haven't worked up the nerve to finish the sentence.

"You tell me, Dylan." Theo's eyes meet mine. "What would you like us to be?"

I bite on my lip. Why is he forcing me to say the words out loud? "I think you know."

Before Theo can respond, Catherine pokes her head out. "Boys? What are you doing there? Dinner's starting."

As Catherine disappears inside, Theo looks at me. "Do you want to leave? It's your call."

I never wanted to be here to begin with. But if we bail, Malcolm will probably be smug, thinking I backed down because he struck a nerve. He'll have another reason to believe I'm guilty of what he imagines.

I sigh. "Leaving will make us look bad. Let's just get this over with."

We go back into the Great Hall and take our seats. I'm between Theo and Malia. Unlike the Hamptons, where the food was prepared to perfection, the grilled chicken is a little overdone. The telltale char marks on top would've earned a side-eye from Aunt

Jade, and the texture of the meat is dry instead of juicy. Anything cooked on the grill needs to be watched closely and flipped at the right time. The chef must've stepped away for a moment too long.

After the meal, Catherine wants to introduce Theo to some acquaintances. As Theo goes with her, Malia leans closer to me.

"I'm glad you're here tonight," she whispers. "So I don't have to avoid making small talk by pretending I'm checking the stock market when I'm actually playing *Pokémon*."

I gesture around us. "Do you ever get used to all of this? The glitz and glamor?"

"Definitely took some getting used to," Malia replies. "My family's well-off, but my parents still taught me to check bills before paying them and think twice before splurging on things I don't really need. But this is Cat's world: the paparazzi, the flashy cars, the excesses. Being with her means I'll have to be a part of the whole charade."

I grimace. "I think Theo's dad would do anything to make sure I never will."

Malia pats my knee. "Listen, it's shitty that you and Theo are caught in the middle of this mess between Malcolm and Lucia. But I can't help thinking of the Chinese phrase you shared at the wedding . . . remind me how it goes again?"

"Yǒu yuán qiān lǐ lái xiāng huì," I say. " 'We have the destiny to meet across a thousand miles.' "

Malia nods. "Theo's a great kid. His heart's in the right place. And it's clear, at least to me and Cat, that you've found a place there."

A shaky spiral of hopefulness rises within me. There are two possibilities: Theo and I are such good actors that we've fooled everyone, even his closest relatives who've known him since he was a baby. Or there's something real between us that we're both too afraid to acknowledge. We're on the precipice of . . . *something,* and I wonder what would've happened if Catherine hadn't interrupted earlier.

The host announces that the charity auction is about to begin, and Catherine and Theo return to our table. He puts a hand on my shoulder as he slides into the seat next to me.

"The Metropolitan Museum of Art is raising funds for Art from the Heart, a nonprofit organization that helps underprivileged youth pursue a career in visual and performing arts." The host gestures at a glass case onstage, which contains a medium-sized rock covered in splashes of paint. "We will be auctioning off this special work of art created by our budding young beneficiaries. Starting bid is five hundred thousand dollars."

I nearly choke but disguise it with a cough.

Malcolm raises his hand. "Seven hundred thousand."

"One million," Lucia counters.

"One point five," says Malcolm.

A murmur rises from the crowd. Theo can barely suppress an eye-roll.

"One point eight," says Lucia.

"Two point five," says Malcolm.

Catherine makes an exasperated noise and stands up.

"Three million," she announces, glowering at her two older siblings. "On behalf of the Somers family."

Surprisingly, Malcolm and Lucia don't counter, although their expressions are mutinous.

"Sold," the host declares. Everyone claps and rises in a standing ovation. "You have our deepest gratitude for your generosity, Mrs. Catherine Somers."

Catherine sits with a huff. "I'm now the owner of the world's most expensive paperweight."

Theo nudges me. "Hey. The speeches will be a bore. Let's sneak off and check out the exhibits."

I glance toward the museum entryway. "But the sign says the rest of the museum is closed."

Theo smirks. "That's never stopped me before."

We excuse ourselves and head to the restroom, but we slip off along another corridor instead. A flight of stairs brings us to the collection of Asian art on the second level.

Theo points at the Chinese calligraphy on display. "The curators regularly rotate the artwork because the silk and paper they're painted on is especially light sensitive."

We duck through a circular entrance flanked by two stone lions and find ourselves inside a re-created Ming Dynasty courtyard, complete with pine beams and tiled roofs with upturned eaves.

"This is my favorite." I walk past the rock formations and halt in front of the miniature pagoda. "I feel as if I'm on the set of a martial arts drama, like *Word of Honor.*"

Theo grins. "All that's missing are the cute Chinese actors in period costumes."

We go back to the first floor and wander through galleries filled with Egyptian artifacts before entering a spacious wing with a high ceiling. The lights are dimmed since the area is closed, but the illumination from Central Park slants through the transparent glass wall on one side. On a platform in the center is an Egyptian-style pavilion with two towering stone archways. It's surrounded by an expanse of reflective waters. A distance away, a pair of sphinxes stand guard like silent sentinels.

"The Temple of Dendur," Theo says. "Come on, let's go inside."

We pass under one of the archways and halt in front of the temple pillars. Above the entrance are images of the sun and a winged figure in flight, and the walls are covered in carvings of a king making offerings to numerous deities.

I've been here on a school visit, but everything seemed different in the daylight, with students laughing and running around. Now, the half-darkness cloaks the space with an air of mystery. For most of my life, I've stayed out of trouble and followed the rules like a good Asian kid—now, being where I'm not supposed to be is forbidden, exciting.

"Hello?" echoes a security guard's voice.

The excitement crashes into panic. Theo grabs my arm and pulls me inside the temple. We squeeze into a corner and hold still, hidden in the shadows.

The guard's footsteps draw closer to the temple entrance.

I forget to breathe. There's no space between Theo's body and mine. Suddenly, I don't care if the guard catches us. What's the worst that can happen? He tells us we're not supposed to be here, we apologize for losing our way and get escorted back to the Great Hall. Sounds a lot less dangerous than being backed against the wall by a boy I'm attracted to, with no ambiguity in the way my body is reacting to being so close to him.

I start to pull away, but Theo catches my wrist.

"Don't move," he whispers, his lips grazing my ear.

Heat blooms through me. This is pure torture. I desperately try to think of something else, *anything* but the scent of his after-shave and the tickle of his hair against my cheek.

"Status?" crackles another voice through the guard's walkie-talkie.

"Thought I heard something in the Temple exhibit," he re-plies. "A couple of rats probably got into the vents again."

Theo's shoulders shake silently, like he's trying not to laugh. I jab him in the ribs to make him stop, but that only makes him wriggle against me and burrow his face into my neck.

The cone of light from the guard's torch sweeps several feet away. "All clear. Heading back to my post."

"Roger that, over."

I exhale in relief as the guard retreats. I expect Theo to move back, but he doesn't.

"You smell good." His elbows are braced on either side of me, and his chin nudges into my shoulder. "I'm not sure why, but it reminds me of the Hamptons."

The shower gel. But I don't tell him, because our proxim-ity has rendered me incapable of breathing, much less speaking. From this close, Theo's lashes are dark, his eyes like the mirror waters around us. The warm flutter in my stomach whenever I'm alone with him coalesces into something sharper, more in-tense.

"Dylan . . ." He says my name in a way he's never done before.

I lean in and kiss him.

He doesn't move—I'm sure I've made the biggest mistake of my life, but then his mouth opens against mine, and my world spins out of orbit in the best way possible. There's no one else around, just the two of us inside a two-thousand-year-old Egyptian temple—no other reason for him to kiss me back except that he wants to.

When we pull apart, a soft breath escapes Theo's lips. He reaches up, holding my face between his palms.

"You know, that last night in the Hamptons . . . I really wanted to kiss you," he says. "But this was worth the wait."

His words send a flush of warmth rising all the way to the tips of my ears. This isn't our first kiss, but it sure feels that way.

"You sure?" I tease. "You didn't even look at me in the shower."

"Trust me, I looked." He sounds wry. "But I didn't make a move because I didn't want to pressure you into anything. You made it pretty clear you were my date only to return a favor."

"When we were watching TV in bed," I whisper, "I really wanted to kiss you too."

Theo smiles.

"Glad we got that cleared up." He takes my hand. "Come on. Let's get out of here."

We slip through the emergency exit and find ourselves in a secluded corner of Central Park. The air is cold, but Theo's hand around mine fills me with heady exhilaration.

I stop walking, and so does he. We're in the penumbra between two lamps—the light pools on either side of us, halting just short of the shadows around our feet.

"What about now?" I ask. "Is this real?"

Theo nods without hesitation. "I don't want to keep us a secret. Especially from my dad." He wraps his arms around me, pulling me close. "He can choose to cut me out of his life—but I won't let him decide who to cut out of mine."

I take a moment to realize this is what he's like with his guard down. I caught glimpses when we were alone in the Hamptons—

and although I was instantly attracted to the boy who never misses a beat and always has it together, *this* is the Theo I'm falling in love with.

I link my arms around his neck. Being around the same height has its advantages. "I've been meaning to ask—do you like my new haircut?"

Theo raises a brow. "Is that a trick question?"

"I'm serious." I gaze at him through half-lidded eyes. "Do you prefer my hair longer, the way it was before?"

He nuzzles my neck. "Your hairstyle isn't what I like most about you."

"Sure about that? Because I can honestly say your abs are your best quality."

He laughs. He strokes his fingers through my short hair, and as we kiss again, I can't help thinking, *I could really get used to this.*

Chapter 27

"Make sure you don't fill the cup to the top, or the machine won't be able to seal it," Tim tells Theo.

I suggested adding freshly prepared drinks to the menu, since they need less prep and have a higher profit margin. We're starting with two popular Singaporean drinks: chrysanthemum tea, boiled with longans and wolfberries, and chin chow, made with shredded black grass jelly and syrup. Cup covers don't do well in transit, and Aunt Jade ordered one of those cup-sealing machines that bubble tea shops use.

Tim read the manual, so he's the resident expert. And he's chosen Theo as his apprentice.

"Okay, this much?" Theo fills a cup of chin chow and shows it to Tim for approval.

"That's good. Leave enough space to add ice. And don't get any liquid onto the edge of the cup, or the sealing film won't stick." Tim hands him a dishcloth to wipe off the rim. "Now put the cup into the holder."

I lean against the counter, grinning. We've officially been

together for a day, and Theo's already being bossed around by my little cousin.

Theo puts the filled cup into the metal holder of the machine. Tim checks to make sure the cup is sitting properly in the tray before he gives the go-ahead. Theo presses a red button. The machine whirs, and the tray retracts. The top of the cup is stamped with a plastic film, and the tray comes out with the sealed drink.

Tim inspects the cup, turning it upside down to make sure there aren't any leaks. "Okay, great. If the film's not sealed on all sides, you have to tear it off and try again. Now make ten more and place them in the fridge."

Footsteps barrel down the stairs. Megan appears, dressed in a short black plaid skirt, knee-high socks, and a printed crop top.

She halts in front of us and twirls around. "Guess where I'm going?"

"Hmm, I'd say the Blackpink concert," Tim pipes up. "But are you sure you can climb the fence and run from security wearing that?"

"Very funny." Megan attempts to pinch her brother's arm, but he laughs and dodges. "You're just jealous that Theo's cousin had an extra ticket, which she offered to *me*."

From Theo's expression, I'm sure it wasn't a coincidence.

"She said she got floor seats," Theo says. "Second row in Section A."

Megan's eyes go wide. "Section A? Are you kidding me? Those seats are like, right in front of the stage!"

"I think Terri mentioned that, yeah."

Megan shrieks. "My friends are never going to believe this! Well, they'll have to when I live stream during the concert! Maybe they'll see Amy, a tiny speck in those nosebleed seats she refused to sell

202

me." She cackles. "I love your boyfriend, Dyl. Not in that way, of course. But who needs an actual boyfriend when we have yours?"

Terri's BMW pulls up on the street and gives a short honk.

"Be careful!" Aunt Jade calls through the serving window as Megan dashes out the door. "Don't lose your phone like you did at that Billie Eilish concert!"

Theo and I go outside as Megan jumps into the front passenger seat.

He braces a hand on the door. "Don't lose her, or her mom will kill me," he tells Terri. "And no climbing onto the stage, okay, chipmunk?"

She rolls her eyes. "I did that *one* time, and you'll never let me live it down."

Megan turns to Terri. "Is he always like this?"

"Nah, only when he's trying to impress his boyfriend." Terri grins at me. "Can you believe Theo tried to convince me you two were *pretending* to date at the wedding? I mean, who were you guys kidding, right?"

Theo and I exchange amused glances as Terri drives off.

"Thanks," I tell him. "You didn't have to do all this."

Theo smiles. "Like Terri said, plucking people out of the ocean is good karma."

We head back into the shop. I go to the kitchen to help Aunt Jade while Theo stays at the counter to make more drinks with the cup-sealing machine. After we prepare and dish out the last few orders, Aunt Jade tells me she'll handle cleaning up.

When I step out, Theo's packing the final batch of deliveries under Tim's watchful eye.

"Don't forget to double-check the order for special instructions," Tim tells him. "See this request? The customer doesn't want ice in their drink, so make sure you give them one without ice. And the next one wants extra chili sauce, so—"

"I add an extra packet of chili sauce," Theo says.

"Yeah. When you're done, staple the order slip onto the paper bag so Chung can easily read the address."

I saunter over. "What's his grade tonight, Tim? I'm guessing a B?" I halt next to Theo, putting my hand on his lower back where Tim can't see. "Maybe a B plus?"

"What are you talking about?" Theo surreptitiously leans into my touch. "I was an excellent student. Considering tonight's my first time on the job, I think I deserve an A."

"You picked up the steps pretty fast," Tim replies. "But you had to redo the seal on two drinks, so I'll give you an A minus."

Chung arrives on his motorcycle. As we bring the orders out and load them into the warmer bag, Chung glances at Theo. "Lei gor lam pung yow?"

I smile. "Yeah, he's my boyfriend."

Chung gives Theo a thumbs-up before zooming off. We go back inside. Tim usually takes Clover for her walk on weekends—she brings him her leash, wagging her tail.

As they head out, I turn to Theo. "Just because you're hanging out here doesn't mean you have to help out, you know."

"Are you kidding? I haven't felt this useful in a long time." Theo extends his hand. "I even have the battle wounds to show for it. See?"

There's a fresh graze across his knuckles. "Ouch. What did you do?"

"A piece of plastic jammed the machine, and I tried to pull it out. Dumb move. Don't worry, the cut isn't that bad."

I press my lips to the back of his hand. "Hmm, I was going to ask if you want me to take a closer look, but since it's not bad . . ."

An impish grin spreads across Theo's face. "You know what? My hand suddenly started hurting a lot. I need immediate medical attention. In your room. With the door locked."

"Clover's walk takes at least twenty minutes." I grab Theo's hand and lead him to the stairs. "If we don't waste more time, we can make the best of the next fifteen."

• • •

The takeout's closed on Monday, and Aunt Jade has a meeting at the bank in the afternoon. I tried to fish for some details about our financial situation at breakfast, but she was vague and changed the subject. A reminder of how badly we need this feature on *Off the Eaten Path*.

Megan and Tim aren't home yet, and I'm in the kitchen with Theo. The Mid-Autumn Festival is only four days away, and I'm going to make the entire mooncake from scratch. Theo's helping me in Aunt Jade's place.

Theo rubs his hands together. "Tell me what to do. I'm all yours."

"We'll start with the white chocolate truffle core." I point at a large bowl of chocolate chips. "I watched some YouTube tutorials and learned that truffles should be made with chips instead of bars. The stabilizers in the chips make the chocolate set more firmly. We'll scoop them into spheres with a melon baller and coat them with another layer of chocolate, which will help keep their shape inside the mooncake."

Compared to the mooncake skin and filling, creating the truffle core is easy. I add heavy cream to the white chocolate and melt the ingredients in the microwave at intervals, mixing until all the chocolate has melted.

When I lift the spoon away, Theo swipes the melted chocolate with his finger and dabs some onto my nose. I raise a brow. Is this war? Not a great move, since I'm the one with the spoon.

A moment later, Theo has smears of white chocolate on his forehead and cheeks. He holds his palms over his face, laughing. "Okay, you win! I surrender!"

I lower the spoon. "What will you offer as spoils of my victory?"

Theo lets his eyes travel up and down the space between us.

"I'm sure we can agree on something," he murmurs.

I step closer, backing him against the edge of the worktable. I anchor my hands on either side of him and lean in, kissing a smudge of chocolate near the corner of his mouth. "Mmm, I think I'll start here."

"Are you two planning on auditioning for the kind of baking show that airs on late-night cable TV?" comes Aunt Jade's voice.

We wheel apart as she walks in, looking smart in a tan blazer, pencil skirt, and heels.

"Hey, Aunt Jade," Theo says sheepishly.

"You're back early," I tell her. "How'd the meeting go?"

Aunt Jade leans in the doorway. "Good, actually. The manager put through my application for an installment plan, which'll help us meet our expenses. She's confident we'll get approved by next week." She snaps her fingers. "Oh, and your Gong Gong called when I was on my way out of the bank. He managed to contact one of Por Por's friends in Malaysia. Turns out, we've been missing one very important ingredient."

I perk up. "What is it?"

"Gula melaka."

"What's that?" Theo asks.

"A special kind of palm sugar made in Malaysia," she says. "The state of Malacca, to be exact, which is how it got its name. But there's one problem. We can't get the exact type of gula melaka here."

I frown. "Not even from any of the Asian specialty stores?"

"The sugar produced by each palm plantation has its own unique flavor, depending on the soil and the climate of the region," Aunt Jade replies. "Some taste smoky-sweet; others have notes of toffee and caramel and butterscotch. Por Por's friend would harvest the sugar by hand at their small family plantation in Malacca and bring her a few jars. This is the closest dupe I could find at the store."

Aunt Jade takes out a packet of unevenly shaped, dark brown blocks about the size of large ice cubes.

"But the label says gula jawa," Theo points out.

"This brand comes from Indonesia," Aunt Jade replies. "The crystals are made from the sap of the coconut palm as well, but they're called gula jawa—Javanese sugar."

I frown. "So the only way we can find the gula melaka Por Por used in her recipe is to hop on a plane and fly home to get it?"

"Pretty much. We'll make do with what we have. Gula jawa isn't the same, but at least it's closer to her original recipe than the cane sugar we've been using. I'll get changed, and we can start."

Aunt Jade disappears upstairs. Theo and I wipe the chocolate from our faces, and I cover the bowl of truffle with plastic wrap and put it inside the fridge. A wave of frustration crests through me. We've figured out the authentic ingredient we've been missing, but we're still no closer to perfecting this mooncake recipe.

Aunt Jade comes back, and we discuss the proportion of gula jawa to add to the lotus seed paste. I want the sweetness to be subtle, not overpowering.

"Did you know the Mid-Autumn Festival has been observed for more than three thousand years, but mooncakes only became an important part of the celebration much later?" Aunt Jade tells Theo as we skin the lotus seeds. "Six hundred years ago, in the Yuan Dynasty, China was ruled by the Mongols. . . . Wait, have you heard this bit of history before?"

"All I know is that Chinese people once used mooncakes to smuggle messages to one another during a rebellion," Theo replies.

"That's the one!" Aunt Jade seems pleased to have an audience. "Revolutionaries wanted to overthrow the regime, but they had to figure out how to communicate without their plans falling into the wrong hands. One of them came up with an idea: Mongols didn't eat mooncakes, so he asked permission to distribute them among the Chinese in honor of the Mongol emperor."

"With a message hidden inside telling everyone when to fight back?" Theo asks.

"The harvest moon is brightest on the fifteenth day of the eighth lunar month," Aunt Jade replies. "They launched a surprise uprising on that night and regained their freedom. Chinese families continued to make mooncakes to remember that victory."

"Does the salted yolk inside the mooncake represent the hidden message?" I once watched a TikTok by an Asian foodie reviewer talking about this. "Is that why some people say mooncakes were the inspiration for fortune cookies?"

"The message was more likely embossed onto the mooncakes using wooden molds," Aunt Jade says. "Mooncakes are usually given in boxes of four. Back then, each family went home, cut them into quarters, and rearranged the sixteen pieces to reveal the hidden message. Then they ate the mooncakes."

Theo chuckles. "Brilliant way to destroy the evidence."

When we taste the lotus seed paste mixed with gula jawa, Aunt Jade's eyes widen. "This is fantastic. The sugar makes all the difference."

She's right. The coconut palm sugar infuses the filling with a flavor that's hard to describe—like granulated honey and molasses, but with a hint of smokiness, like caramelized sugar. Excitement wells up inside me. I don't want to jinx anything, but with this secret ingredient, I might actually have a shot at winning the contest.

There's a loud knock on the front door. A man in a suit stands outside the shop.

Aunt Jade pokes her head through the serving window and points at the sign flipped to show we're closed. Instead of leaving, the man raps on the glass again.

Aunt Jade dusts off her hands and heads to the door. Theo and I go with her.

"Jade Wong?" The man gives her an envelope. "You've been served."

As the man walks away, Aunt Jade takes out the letter. My heart drops when I read the bold words at the top—*EVICTION NOTICE.*

"Our landlord is an asshole," I tell Theo, hoping to cover her embarrassment. "He's just using a scare tactic."

Aunt Jade rubs her forehead. "There must be a misunderstanding. I left him a voice mail about the installment plan I'm working out with the bank. Guess he didn't get the message. I'll call him later and get everything sorted." She lets out a shaky laugh. "Good thing he's not a loan shark collector in Singapore. They'll spray-paint OP—'owe money, pay money'—with your name and address on the wall of your block."

She puts the envelope under the counter.

"All right, boys, back to work," she says in a forced cheerful tone, heading to the kitchen. "These mooncakes won't make themselves!"

Theo gives me a concerned glance. I wave him off, but I can't help but wonder: Even if I can win this contest, will I be in time to save Wok Warriors?

Chapter 28

When I get back from school the next day, a silver Rolls-Royce is parked down the street. A bulky white dude in a suit and shades leans against the car. He crosses his arms and stares at me as I pass him.

I step into the takeout and stop in my tracks.

Malcolm Somers is sitting at the small table inside. A basket of xiao long bao and an almost-finished plate of egg fried rice is laid out in front of him.

Aunt Jade, who's at the counter, brightens. "Ah! This is Dylan, the nephew I was telling you about. He lives with us."

I'm speechless. Aunt Jade is terrible at recognizing people. Though I can't really blame her—Malcolm's photo in the tabloid was small, and today, he has ditched the suit in favor of a casual black golf shirt and gray pants.

"Hello, Dylan." Malcolm's smile is like a blade. He's in the same spot Theo sat the first time he came into our shop. "I've enjoyed chatting with your aunt. What a lovely little establishment she has here. Full of charm and character."

"This gentleman was intrigued by the photos on our wall,"

Aunt Jade tells me. "Turns out, he visits Hong Kong regularly on business, and he has dined in the same restaurants I worked in! Isn't it a small world?"

"Yes. Small world, indeed." Malcolm stands. "Thank you for the delicious meal, Jade, but I have to be on my way. I'd like to buy a copy of the *Times*—perhaps your nephew could point me in the direction of the nearest newsstand?" He shoots me a meaningful look. "My son—he's about your age—tells me no one reads print anymore, but I guess I'm old school."

A sheen of cold sweat has broken out on my forehead and neck. I can't wait to get him away from Aunt Jade. She waves goodbye as Malcolm and I step out.

I glance over my shoulder as we walk toward the Rolls-Royce. I'm convinced a couple of guys are going to jump out and beat me into an omelet. Or pull a bag over my head, bundle me into the trunk, and toss me into the river.

Malcolm stops walking. He turns to me.

"Your aunt has put her heart and soul into her business," he says, staring up at the takeout sign. "And those soup dumplings are indeed delicious. I would hate for Sunset Park to lose such a unique delicacy."

His tone reminds me of a snake hidden in tall grass. "What do you mean?"

"Well, someone brought to my attention that a good friend of Theo's had a bad experience with the food he ordered from your aunt's takeout. Something about spring onions he specifically didn't want?"

My mind stutters to a halt. How does he know about that incident?

"Adrian's father and I play golf every weekend," Malcolm adds, as if reading my thoughts. "Not sure if his boy's actually allergic or just hates spring onions . . . but we both know that if this gets out, the media won't care. Especially since the president recently signed a food allergy bill putting more responsibility on vendors to make sure their food doesn't make anyone sick."

I feel as if someone has opened a trapdoor inside my chest and my heart has fallen into my stomach. The New York City Department of Health takes food safety violations very seriously. We're already on the brink of getting evicted—any bad press, founded or not, could make the bank pull their funding, or worse, give our landlord a cause to terminate our lease. If Malcolm carries out his threat, even Lawrence Lim couldn't save us.

"What do you want from us?" I blurt out. "We can't afford to pay you—"

"Pay me?" Malcolm utters a derisive noise. "I would never take a cent from your family. In fact, I thought that was the reason you were clinging to my son. But the other night, at the Met, when Theo said you wouldn't keep the suit—I realized that I grossly underestimated you. You aren't after our wealth. No, you're far more enterprising."

I hope I don't appear as bewildered as I feel. I have no idea what he's talking about.

"Getting yourself on news feeds and tabloids is worth far more than a bespoke Kashimura suit and a free trip to the Hamptons," Malcolm continues. "Suddenly everyone's talking about scrappy young Dylan Tang—the boy from a working-class immigrant background who balances school with cooking and delivery runs for his aunt's humble takeout in Brooklyn. Masterful move. Everyone loves an underdog. Even money can't buy this sort of publicity." He steps forward, his eyes boring into mine. "You got

213

close to Theo because you wanted to use *our* family's name to elevate *yours*."

Everyone knows the most important thing to my dad is his reputation.

The five grand Theo gave us inadvertently helped Malcolm find our sore spot. And when Theo tried to convince him I wasn't after their money by saying I wouldn't accept the suit, Malcolm jumped to a more damaging conclusion. Now he thinks I'm a threat trying to profit off his reputation—and he's targeting not just me, but my aunt's business too.

Heat rises to my face. "Theo's not the kind of guy who lets himself get used by anyone. You'd know that if you actually cared about what's going on in his life—"

"You would do anything to help your family's reputation." Malcolm's expression is grim. "I assure you, I will do whatever is necessary to protect mine. Let me make myself clear: stay away from my son." He presses a rectangular envelope into my hand. "I believe this will give you excellent incentive to do so."

The driver opens the rear passenger door of his Rolls-Royce for him. I'm rooted to the sidewalk as they drive off and disappear around the corner.

I rip open the envelope with trepidation. There's probably a copy of the official complaint he intends to file with the health department, telling them how Wok Warriors carelessly ignored a customer's special dietary notes—

I pull out a cashier's check with my name on it. My jaw drops at the number of zeroes.

A hundred thousand dollars. More than I've ever had in my entire life. Offered to me by the father of the boy I've fallen for in exchange for never seeing him again. If I refuse, he'll find a way to force us out of business. Aunt Jade will have to close the shop, and we'll lose our home.

With this money, we could pay our landlord and avoid getting evicted. Aunt Jade won't have to worry about rent for a while. Tim could get a new violin—one made of higher quality spruce wood, which we've never been able to afford. Megan could buy a new phone. There might even be enough left for the four of us to go on vacation.

This piece of paper in my hand could save more than our takeout. It could turn our lives around. The decision should be obvious: choose my family over a boy I've only known for a few weeks. I shouldn't need to think twice. I shouldn't feel like I've gulped too much seawater and I'm going to throw up.

The door chimes as I enter the takeout. Aunt Jade's wiping the counter, although she stops when she sees me. "Dylan? Are you feeling all right? You look pale."

"The man you were talking to," I blurt out. "He's Malcolm Somers. Theo's dad."

Aunt Jade's eyes widen. "Oh my God. Was that him? He looks nothing like the photo in the paper!"

My tone is tight. "What did you tell him about us? About the takeout?"

"He asked how long we've been in business and what made me want to set up a Singaporean Chinese takeout in Brooklyn. He seemed like a nice man." Aunt Jade frowns. "What did he want to talk to you about?"

The check from Malcolm burns inside my pocket.

"Nothing important," I reply, heading up the stairs.

• • •

I zip the front of my jacket and stand under the lamppost at the opposite end of the street. From here, I can see customers going in and out of our shop. But I don't want to be close to home when I have this conversation with Theo. I don't want Aunt Jade and my cousins to know.

I stuff my hands into my pockets. Something stiff rustles inside one of them.

"Hey, you." Theo comes up from behind me. He wraps an arm around my waist and kisses my ear. "What's up? Why can't we meet at your aunt's—"

I shrug out of his embrace. The expression on my face makes his smile fade.

"Dylan?" He moves forward and reaches for my hand. "Is everything all right?"

I step back. "This isn't going to work out. I'm sorry."

"What? Where's this coming from?" Theo's eyes narrow. "Wait—my dad got to you, didn't he? What did he say?"

I take out the check and shove it into Theo's palm.

"This is what he thinks I'm worth." I can't keep the bitterness out of my voice. "This is how much he wants me gone from your life."

Theo goes very still, his gaze fixed on the check. "He sent this to you?"

"No. He delivered it by hand." I let out a humorless noise. "When I got back this afternoon, he was in the takeout. Eating our food and chatting with my aunt like he was just another customer. She didn't recognize him." The thought of Aunt Jade cooking for him still makes my stomach turn. "He thanked her for the delicious xiao long bao, asked me to step outside, and promised to ruin our business if I didn't stay the hell away from you."

"I can't believe he'd do something like this." Theo rakes a hand through his hair. I've never seen him so utterly blindsided. "I *told* him you didn't care about the money. And I made sure he knew through Bernard that you want to help your aunt open her own restaurant—"

Anger rushes through me. How could Theo tell his dad something so personal that I confided in him?

"Wow. Sharing my family's hopes and dreams with your dad was a terrific move. Now he thinks I'm with you not just for his money, but to get publicity for my aunt's business too." I exhale sharply. "Like you said, the one thing he cares about most is his reputation—and he's convinced I'm trying to profit off the Somers name."

"That's ridiculous." Theo paces, agitated. "He's out of his mind."

"He won't stop coming for me or my family as long as we're together," I tell him. "That's why we have to end this. There's too much at stake. Too much to lose."

"My dad tried to push us apart once. We didn't let him." Theo's expression is grim, determined. He really is more like Malcolm than he realizes. "We've come this far, Dylan. We can fight this. Together—"

"This is different," I interrupt. "You didn't want to keep us a secret from your dad—but what if he forces you to choose between me and your inheritance? What will you do if he threatens to cut you off and freeze your trust fund?"

Theo falters for the briefest of moments, but we both know the answer.

"I don't want it to be this way," I say. "You shouldn't have to choose between me and your future. I would never push you to make that choice."

A light rain begins to fall, dappling our hair. I imagine we look like a scene out of a Chinese drama—two lovers sharing a stolen moment under the eaves. But the reality is cold and damp and bereft, and my heart feels like a shriveled dead thing hanging inside my chest.

Theo pinches the bridge of his nose. "So we break up and never see each other again? We just let my dad win?"

"This isn't a game, Theo!" I burst out. "Our livelihood is on the line! Don't you get that? My aunt took me in after my mom died, when I had nowhere else to go. . . ." I force down the emotion rising in my chest. "I can't stand by and let your dad take away everything she worked so hard for."

Theo utters a hollow sound and holds out the check. "You're breaking up with me, like my dad wanted. Why don't you take the money to help your aunt?"

I push his hand away. "Because I want your dad to know he can't buy me off. Yeah, you can tell him that. This money will solve our problems, but accepting it will mean he's right about me. Some people will sell their dignity for a price, but I'm not one of them." I'm sure Aunt Jade would feel the same. "If the only way I can save our takeout is by winning the damn mooncake contest, that's what I'm going to do."

Theo's tone is plaintive. "Then let me help you."

He still cares about me even after I told him we can't be together. As much as I want him by my side, it's the one thing I can't have. "If your dad suspects we're still seeing each other and unleashes a smear campaign against Wok Warriors, even winning the contest won't help us."

"Then tell me what you want me to do." Theo takes my hand in both of his. "I'll do it. Please, Dylan. Don't give up on us."

He looks so wrung out—I wish I could pull him close and hold him tight. But the silence crystallizes between us, and the cold glow of the almost-full moon is nothing more than a pale echo of light. A beautiful illusion.

I let out a mirthless sound. "You know, Chinese sayings usually come in pairs. Yǒu yuán qiān lǐ lái xiāng huì is the first line. Not many people talk about the second half: wú yuán duì miàn bù xiāng féng."

Theo's forehead creases. "What does that mean?"

"If two people have the destiny to meet, not even a thousand miles can keep them apart." My composure threatens to crumble. I can't let him see I'm dying inside. "But if they don't, their paths won't cross even if they're right in front of each other."

Theo's voice is quiet. "Do you really believe that?"

I shake my head. "It doesn't matter."

I take out the bracelet with the glass vial. The hurt that flickers across Theo's face as I press it into his palm is almost more than I can bear.

I turn and walk away as fast as I can. Tears spring to my eyes, smudging the streetlights into starry blurs, like out-of-shape constellations. Like planets spinning away from each other.

When I reach the takeout, I glance back. Theo's still standing at the other end of the street. But he doesn't follow.

Chapter 29

feign a cold and stay home the next day. I'm too depressed to get out of bed. When Tim leaves for school, I bury my face in my pillow and let the tears flow freely. My heart feels like a xiao long bao that's been punctured, and all the soup inside has leaked out.

Aunt Jade comes up with a bowl of chicken soup and catches me red-eyed. She sits at the side of my bed. "Had a fight with Theo?"

"We broke up."

She sighs. "Whose idea was that?"

"Mine."

"Because of his dad? He said something awful to you yesterday, didn't he?"

"It doesn't matter." Repeating the last words I spoke to Theo sends a fresh pang through my chest. Aunt Jade doesn't need to know about the check I returned to him. "I hate to admit it, but his dad's right. We're too different. Things would never have worked out between us."

Aunt Jade puts an arm around me. "I'm sorry. I know he meant a lot to you."

I bite down on the inside of my cheek. Now I understand how

conflicted Chang'e must have been when she drank the elixir—the only way she could stop the evil student from becoming all-powerful. But she had to leave behind the one she loved and float to the moon, where they would be apart forever. What a terrible, impossible choice.

Aunt Jade has an appointment with the bank to discuss taking another temporary loan. After she leaves, I climb out of bed. She won't let an eviction notice stop her from fighting to keep us afloat. I need to stop feeling sorry for myself and do the same. If I want to win the contest, I don't need to make a good mooncake. I have to make a *perfect* one.

I wolf down a leftover sandwich and head to the subway. I ride to 74th Street and Broadway and change to the 7 train to Flushing, Queens.

The Chinatown in Flushing is similar to the one in Sunset Park, with shop signs in both English and Chinese. There's a mix of Korean and Thai places as well. People talk over one another in a cacophony of different dialects, which reminds me of how Mom and Aunt Jade used to chat and joke in Cantonese. Now the words are like a familiar song I haven't heard in a while, filling me with a strange, prickling nostalgia.

I check out a bunch of traditional herbal shops and specialty stores, but I can't find any selling gula melaka. A shopkeeper assures me gula jawa from Indonesia is just as good. But Lawrence Lim grew up in Malaysia, so he's familiar with the precise flavor of gula melaka from his home country. If the sugar tasted just a little different, he would know in a heartbeat.

As I wander past a vintage shop, an elegant handcrafted box in the shape of an antique Chinese apothecary cabinet catches my eye. Each drawer even has delicate gold ring handles. I've watched enough culinary shows to know presentation is an important metric in cooking contests—almost as crucial as the food itself.

I go inside the shop. Being incapable of passing a rack of T-shirts with funny slogans without buying one is my villain origin story, and along with the mooncake box, I get an indigo T-shirt that says MY THERAPIST HAS FUR AND PAWS.

A teenaged Asian girl is at the register, watching videos on her phone. Next to the counter is a small jewelry workshop with a handwritten sign: CUSTOMIZED RICE ART.

"Want one of these?" She waves at the glass vials fashioned into keychains, pendants, and bracelets. "My grandfather went out for a smoke, but I can get him. He'll write anything you want on a grain of rice. Even *the quick brown fox jumps over the lazy dog*." She grins. "Kidding. Maybe your name?"

A painful spasm goes through my chest. Now I understand why it's called heartbreak.

"No thanks," I reply. "Somebody already gave me one."

She shrugs, hands me my change, and goes back to her phone.

As I step onto the sidewalk, I try to be excited about my purchases—but the memory of Theo's devastated expression when I gave him back the bracelet is as stark as the circle of bare skin around my wrist.

. . .

On the eve of the Mid-Autumn Festival, a heavy downpour lashes against our living room windows. We closed the shop and locked up an hour ago, and I'm doing my calculus homework while Blackpink's latest hit blasts from Megan's phone. She's practicing the routine she and her friends have picked up from the dance video.

Tim comes out of our room, his violin in hand. "Meg, can you turn your music down?"

"Hey, check this out, Tim." Megan does a complicated move that ends in a chest pump and a body roll. "I'm in Lisa's role—"

"I don't care! My violin exam's in two days!"

Aunt Jade pokes her head out of her room. She's in her pajamas, a hairdryer in one hand and half of her damp hair clipped on top of her head. "Hey, what's going on out here?"

"I'm trying to practice, but everyone else is making as much noise as they possibly can," Tim retorts. Clover barks. "Stop it, Clover!"

A loud crash echoes from downstairs. We all freeze.

Megan shuts off the song on her phone. Tension ratchets. The break-in a few months ago is still vivid: coming downstairs to find broken glass all over the floor, the register jimmied open. Maybe the lightning shorted out our new alarm system—or someone found a way to disable it.

There's a sharp electric buzz, and the lights go out.

"What's going on?" Megan sounds panicked.

We maneuver in the dark with our phones, swearing as we bump into furniture. The wind howls through the tiny gaps in the frames, and a weird, eerie sound drifts from the level below.

Tim's voice is shaky. "Isn't this how horror movies start?"

"The storm must have cut the power," Aunt Jade says. "I'll head downstairs and reset the main breaker panel in the basement."

"Mom, no," Megan cuts in. "It's too dangerous—"

"I'll go with her," I tell Megan. "You two stay here. If we're not back in five minutes, don't call nine-one-one. . . ." I pull a blank zombie face in the glare of my phone screen. "Run."

She punches my arm. "NOT funny."

Clover barks as Aunt Jade and I slip through the gate. The thunderstorm stretches and warps the shadows, and the sound of gushing water grows louder as we carefully make our way downstairs, using our phones as flashlights.

When the darkened shop comes into view, we both stop in shock.

The sidewalk has become a swiftly flowing river. A huge branch fell against our front door, smashing it wide open. Torrents of water rush inside, flooding our shop—half a foot and rising steadily.

I start forward, but Aunt Jade grabs my arm.

"Wait!" She points at the wall socket close to the floor, submerged in water. "You might get electrocuted!"

"Don't worry, the circuit breaker has cut the power," I tell her.

She makes a muffled protest as I move in front of her and step into the water. Fortunately, I don't get fried.

The gale force winds blow the blinding rain almost horizontally through the broken doorway, lashing against our faces as we salvage whatever we can. Aunt Jade makes a beeline for the register. I hastily save the photo frames on the wall. Everything else can be replaced, but these memories can't. The wooden mooncake molds I bought from Auntie Chan are on the counter, and I grab them too.

We're drenched and shivering as we hurry upstairs. Tim and Megan are at the gate, anxiously waiting for us. They take the stack of photo frames from me. Aunt Jade's shoulders sag, and she can't hide the helplessness we all feel. But she pushes aside her wet hair and musters a brave face.

"What matters is we're all safe." She puts her arms around Tim and Megan. "We'll ride out the storm up here tonight and deal with the rest in the morning. Go on. It's late. Bundle up and try to get some sleep."

My cousins go back to their rooms. I sit on the couch and start wiping the photo frames. As I run the cloth over the glass of the picture of the five of us in Singapore last year, I gaze at Mom's face. Everything seems to be falling apart, and I don't know what to do. More than ever, I wish she were here to help put my life back together.

"Hey." Aunt Jade holds out a steaming mug. "Ginger tea. It's a little spicy, but nothing's better at getting the damp and the chill out of your body."

I put down the photo frame and wrap both hands around the mug, sipping slowly.

Aunt Jade sits next to me and nods at the picture. "If your mom were here with us right now, in this storm, what do you think she'd do?"

I consider this. "She'd be on the phone, running triage with animal welfare groups and volunteering to handle the SOS calls about stranded animals closest to us. And you'd be yelling that she's crazy to go out there in the flood."

Aunt Jade chuckles. "Sounds about right. Once your mom set her heart on something, nothing could stop her."

I stare at the bottom of the mug. "I wish I could be as strong as she was."

Aunt Jade gives me an odd smile.

"You remind me of her in so many ways. Even when you lied to me about going to the Hamptons as Theo's date, I knew you just didn't want me to feel bad about taking money from an outsider." I blink, surprised, and she waggles her brows. "Yes, I figured out from the start that the money came directly from Theo. He did much more than help you fill out the paperwork. Revolc Foundation, seriously? You're talking to the queen of word search puzzles. I saw Clover's name spelled backward in a heartbeat."

"Theo didn't want you to find out," I say sheepishly.

"That was sweet of him." She meets my gaze. "Of both of you."

The storm roars outside, battering our windows.

"Do we have flood insurance?" I ask.

Her weary expression is the answer.

"Wasn't expecting our shop to be destroyed by a flash flood in a non-flooding zone." Aunt Jade squeezes my hand. "Don't worry. We'll get through this. Everything's going to be okay."

"First thing when the rain stops, I'll go downstairs and board up the door," I tell her. "I don't want anyone stealing whatever's left of our stuff."

Aunt Jade shakes her head. "These are just things, Dylan. They can be fixed. Replaced. I'm more worried about you. Seeing how much you're hurting over what happened with Theo is a lot worse than a shattered shopfront."

A couple of tears escape from the corners of my eyes. I wipe them away, but I'm not ashamed of crying in front of Aunt Jade. The day Mom died, Aunt Jade was the one who stoically took care of everything. I went through the motions, still too numb to feel anything. I moved in with them that night. After I thought they had gone to sleep, she found me curled up in the corner of the bathroom, sobbing into my NO DRAMA, LLAMA T-shirt. She didn't say a word, just crawled next to me and hugged me as we cried together.

Now she puts her arm around me.

"When I decided to leave Meg and Tim's father, I called your mom from Hong Kong, bawling my eyes out," she says. "I told her I didn't have a clue what to do next. And you know what she told me? 'I don't either, but you shouldn't have to figure it out alone.' Hours later, I booked three one-way tickets to New York City for Meg, Tim, and myself."

I look at her. "Does heartbreak hurt this bad every time, or just the first?"

Aunt Jade's eyes mist over.

"Oh, sweetie," she says. "Giving your heart to someone is like learning to ride a bike. You'll skin your elbows and knees, but the pain will pass. You'll heal. And one day, the scars will be a memory, not of falling, but of getting up again."

I rub my eyes and sniffle. Here I am, crying on Aunt Jade's shoulder when her shop—everything she's worked so hard for over the past five years—is drowning one floor below us.

Aunt Jade nudges me fondly. "Remember the story of Hou Yi and Chang'e that Tim told over dinner the other night? Not many people know there's another version of the story that turns out completely different."

"What happened?"

"Hou Yi still shot down the nine suns and received the elixir, and the people made him king. But the hero worship and glory corrupted him, and he became a tyrant. Chang'e stole and drank the elixir to stop her cruel husband from being immortal. When he found out, he was so enraged that he fired arrows at her. But she escaped by floating to the moon, which became her refuge."

I manage a humorless laugh. "I can see why you chose to give Tim the version about undying love instead of attempted murder. But why are you telling me this now?"

"Because every story can have a different ending." Aunt Jade's expression is meaningful. "It all depends on which one you want to believe in."

Chapter 30

The storm's fury finally stops at dawn. I couldn't sleep the whole night. Aunt Jade and I put on heavy-duty boots to protect our feet. The floodwaters have receded to ankle depth, but the line of dirt on the walls shows how high the waters reached overnight. The stools are overturned, and the table is covered in dead leaves blown in by the wind.

"Guess the universe was fed up with my decorating skills." Aunt Jade lets out a strained chuckle. "I've been searching for a reason to replace the furniture."

My heart sinks as I pick up the mooncake box I bought from the vintage shop. The elegant wood is now stained and covered in muck. I managed to save the mooncake molds along with the photo frames, but I couldn't grab the ingredients I prepared for the contest. They're ruined as well.

The basement storeroom bore the full extent of damage. We can't even get halfway down the steps. Our freezer is floating in at least two feet of brackish, foul-smelling water. Nearly everything will have to be thrown away. Thousands of dollars of inventory down the drain, just like that.

I put my arm around Aunt Jade's shoulders. Her eyes are moist and she's shaking a little. I know it's not just from the chill of the morning air.

We make sure everything's safe before letting Megan and Tim come downstairs. Aunt Jade gets on the phone with our landlord, the power company, and the city council. We spend the entire morning cleaning up, scooping buckets of dirty water that never seem to end. Megan salvages her favorite Hello Kitty apron, and Tim carefully cleans the porcelain fortune cat with a cloth before setting it on a higher shelf. I put my ruined mooncake box into a garbage bag with the litter and debris that floated in.

As I carry two bags of trash to the curbside, a BMW pulls up. The window rolls down, and a young woman with strawberry-blond hair pokes her head out. "Dylan!"

I stop. "Terri? What are you doing here?"

"Meg told me the mooncake contest is today," she says. "Come on, I'll drive you there."

I blink. "But I don't have the ingredients. Everything got ruined in the flood."

"We can buy fresh supplies along the way." She waves at Megan and Aunt Jade, who come outside to greet her. "Hurry, it's almost two."

I hesitate. The other contestants are probably setting up in the studio as we speak. I'm already behind schedule. Snow-skin mooncakes take about three hours to make, maybe a little less. I still have a shot at finishing the mooncakes in time—but I don't want to leave my aunt and cousins to clean up this mess by themselves.

As if sensing my thoughts, Aunt Jade puts a hand on my arm.

"I have to stay behind to take care of things, but you should go ahead." She manages a grin. "We aren't going to let a little rain wash us out."

"Go on, Dyl," Megan chimes in. "We've got this—and so do you."

Suddenly, I'm more determined than ever to win the contest.

"Give me ten minutes," I tell Terri.

I hurry upstairs to wash up and get changed. Clover knocked over my laundry basket again, spilling my clean clothes onto the floor. I grab a white T-shirt and a fresh pair of blue jeans. I throw my stuff into my backpack, including the three wooden molds. Good thing I brought them upstairs, where they remained safe from the flood.

My eyes fall on the round-shaped mold with 念 on it. The one I bought to remember Mom. When Theo came to dinner, I stopped him from eating the mooncake embossed with that character. Now I'm not sure what *remembrance* means for us.

Clover appears with something in her mouth. She drops it at my feet.

Theo's white baseball cap. The one he was wearing when he came over and helped Tim with the drinks—after that, we went back to my room and made out.

A knot forms in my throat as I pick up Theo's cap. Clover eyes me solemnly.

I haven't heard from Theo since we broke up. I wish I could say that hope doesn't flutter in my stomach every time my phone lights up . . . but I would be lying. I miss him so much.

I put Theo's cap into my backpack and sling the bag over my shoulder. "Thanks, buddy."

Clover wags her tail, her tongue hanging out.

I head down to the kitchen. I have my wooden molds, and I can pick up fresh ingredients at the store, but I probably can't find another unique, decorative box to display the mooncakes on such short notice. I don't want to lose points because of poor presentation, so I'll have to improvise.

I rummage through the wall cabinets until I find a vintage tingkat—a circular, stainless steel bento container my grandparents used for takeout in the days before disposable boxes. Four different tiers keep the dishes, rice, and soup separated.

Aunt Jade comes up behind me. "Your Por Por gave that to your mom on her twelfth birthday. She loved her tingkat so much she refused to put food inside."

The emerald-colored enamel—painted with cranes in flight, wispy clouds, and rabbits leaping toward a full moon—looks both classic and chic.

I can't contain my excitement. "This is perfect for displaying the mooncakes."

Aunt Jade smiles. "Your mom would've loved that."

Tim, Megan, and Terri are waiting for us in the front of the shop.

"What time does the festival start?" Tim asks.

"It opens at six in the open-air plaza outside Lawrence Lim's studio in Midtown," I say. "The mooncake judging will be at seven."

"We'll be there," Megan says. "Rain, shine, flood, or total eclipse."

Aunt Jade hugs me tightly. "I'm sorry I can't help you at the contest. But you'll do great. I just know it."

I peck her on the cheek. "No way I could've done this without you, well . . . without you. Does that make sense?"

231

Aunt Jade beams. Her hair is matted, and her face is smudged with dirt—I've never felt so much love for her as I do now.

The Mid-Autumn Festival is a time for family. For reunion. Revolutionaries in the Yuan Dynasty made mooncakes because they were fighting for their families. I never imagined, centuries later, I'd be doing the same thing.

Wok Warriors survived the flash flood. I won't let Aunt Jade's hard work go to waste.

When I get into Terri's car, she grins. "Love your T-shirt, by the way."

I look down. I wasn't paying attention when I put it on, but it's EVERY BUNNY WAS KUNG FU FIGHTING.

Chapter 31

We stop at a grocery store to buy cooked glutinous rice flour, powdered sugar, wheat starch, shortening, groundnut oil, maltose, white chocolate chips, and the rest of the ingredients. Thankfully, the Asian specialty shop next to the store sells lotus seeds with their coats intact. They also have gula jawa, which I get along with a packet of dried butterfly pea flowers.

As we speed toward the Battery Tunnel, I glance at Terri. "How's Theo?"

Her expression sobers. Theo or Megan must've told her about the breakup. "He's okay. Listen, I hate how you guys had to go through that shit with his dad."

I force a shrug. "Two people shouldn't have to give up everything just to be together. We'd resent each other for what we've lost, which would've ended up pushing us apart anyway."

Terri's quiet for a moment.

"I'm not sure how much you know about rehab," she says. "But we can't bring cell phones, video games, playing cards . . . not even nail polish. Can you believe that? The strict rules are supposed to help us focus on recovery, but at times I felt like I was trapped in some kind of Zen prison."

I tread lightly. "How long were you there?"

"Two months. Theo visited me every weekend. We played Monopoly, my favorite board game—and he never tried to turn my obsession with collecting all the railroads into some psycho-analysis of why I blew up my life so spectacularly." Terri's tone turns pensive. "Everyone wanted me to get well—Nora would keep asking, 'Are you feeling better?' And my mom would be like, 'Is rehab working?' My dad would promise we'd go car shopping when I got out. But Theo was the only one who knew I didn't want to be reminded of the parts of me that had to be fixed. I needed to be reminded of the parts of me that didn't."

The clock on Terri's dashboard shows it's just past three when we arrive at Lawrence Lim's culinary studio in Midtown. I'm awed when the man himself steps out to welcome us. He shakes my hand.

"You must be Dylan Tang, our final contestant." He looks dapper in a jacket with no tie, and the dimple when he smiles is as charming in person as on TV. His brows climb when Terri gets out of the driver's seat. "Terri Leyland-Somers? To what do I owe this honor?"

Terri grins. "I did say I'd be back for seconds after tasting the delicious beef rendang you cooked at Bruno's soiree after the Grammys."

They know each other? Then again, I shouldn't be surprised—world-renowned chefs often rub shoulders with celebrities and wealthy socialite families who hire them to host private dinner parties. And Terri is certainly memorable.

Lawrence turns to me. "Mr. Wu, the contest organizer, was getting worried, but I assured him you'd show up."

"I'm so sorry I'm late," I tell him, still slightly breathless. "The storm last night flooded my aunt's takeout—she's supposed to be my sous-chef, but she had to stay behind to deal with the mess."

"So you'll be flying solo today?" Lawrence asks.

I nod. "I guess I'll have to."

We get the ingredients out of the car. Lawrence, ever the gentleman, helps Terri with the bags. Vendors are setting up their booths under two large festival tents in the open-air plaza outside the studio, and workers are getting the stage and video wall ready.

As we enter the spacious lobby and head toward the culinary studio, Lawrence speaks.

"Most cooking and baking contests are individual, but in real life, a chef is by no means greater than the sum of their helpers," he says. "Of course, we want to see the chef doing most of the work, and we'll keep an eye on that—but the unsung heroes are the ones who know exactly which spoon to pass without the chef needing to ask."

"Hey, since Dylan's aunt can't help him, maybe I can substitute?" Terri suggests. "Or is that not allowed?"

Lawrence halts outside a set of closed doors. "We try to be accommodating wherever we can. But I'm afraid I'll have to say no. The contest rules are clear: Dylan can only have one sous-chef."

I blink. What?

Lawrence opens the doors. A camerawoman mills around under the bright fluorescent lights, capturing footage of the seven pairs of contestants busy at their separate stations. And, standing alone at the stainless-steel worktable in the far corner, is Theo.

My heart slams into my rib cage.

"Hey, Dylan." Theo walks toward me. He has a jar filled with reddish-brown rock crystals in his hands. "I really like your T-shirt."

I open my mouth, but no words emerge. Terri and Lawrence are grinning. They were in on it too. The camerawoman circles around, lens pointed at me and Theo. I wonder if this is live on Lawrence's Instagram reel—he has twenty million followers.

"Your aunt called this morning and explained the situation with the flooding," Lawrence tells me. "Of course, we were sympathetic. She asked if someone else could assist you."

Despite everything, Aunt Jade not only remembered the contest, but also contacted the organizer without letting me know. I'm touched beyond words.

"I talked to Mr. Wu and my producer," Lawrence continues. "We unanimously agreed that these were extenuating circumstances, and you should be allowed to choose another sous-chef." He nods at Theo. "Your friend here appears to have gone through a great deal of effort to get a special ingredient."

Theo holds out the jar. "Your grandma assured me that this is the same gula melaka she used in her mooncake recipe."

I stare at him in disbelief. "Wait—you talked to my grandma?"

Theo nods. "Saw her too. You gave me the idea when you asked your aunt if the only way to get the gula melaka was to hop on a plane and fly to Singapore. So I did just that."

"Two eighteen-hour flights, back-to-back," Bernard adds, appearing from behind me. His tie is loosened around his neck, which he rubs with a grimace. "I'm getting too old for this."

"I have something else." Theo takes out a glass bottle filled with deep purple-blue flowers. "These are from the butterfly pea plant in your grandma's backyard. I know how much you want to make the recipe as close to the original as you can."

I can't believe Theo actually flew halfway across the globe to bring back the missing piece of my grandma's recipe. I want to throw my arms around Theo and hug him, but I'm frozen to the spot.

"Thank you," I whisper.

Theo smiles. "Let's make some mooncakes."

We get to work. The ovens and freezer fridges are shared, but each individual station is equipped with its own sink, tabletop induction stove, cookware, appliances, and baking tools.

"Let's start with the white chocolate truffle filling." I take out the chocolate chips. "We can speed up the setting process with the blast chiller."

While Theo microwaves and stirs the white chocolate, I boil the lotus seeds on the induction stove. When they're ready, Theo and I start rubbing off the coats and plucking out the tiny green shoots inside. Terri films us, navigating around the camera crew.

We take more than half an hour to finish the task. I boil the lotus seeds a second time and put them into the blender, while Theo goes to the freezer to check on the truffle filling.

"It's setting really well," he reports.

Social media teen chef Valerie Leung is at the station next to ours. Her grandma fusses over the mooncakes, chattering in Cantonese. Seems theirs are almost ready to go into the oven—the final step for baked mooncakes. Snow-skin ones don't need to be baked, but they have to be chilled before serving. We haven't even started on the mooncake skin—will we have enough time to get everything done?

The reddish-brown rock crystals of gula melaka turn into a thick syrup when they're melted in a pot. While I'm getting the wok ready to stir-fry the lotus seed paste, Theo accidentally touches the hot pot of syrup—he withdraws his hand with a sharp hiss.

I spin around. "Are you all right?"

"Yeah, I'm okay," he quickly says.

I still take his hand and examine it. The skin is reddened but not blistered.

"Be careful." I automatically press his fingertips to my lips. "I would feel awful if you got injured."

A flash goes off as a photographer snaps a candid shot. Theo blushes. Terri winks at Valerie and mouths, "Aren't they adorable?"

Lawrence makes his rounds, chatting with the other contestants about their cooking backgrounds and aspirations. I overhear some of them gushing about the favorite food spots they'd pick to be featured on *Off the Eaten Path* if they won.

When he comes over to us, he gestures at the lotus seed puree.

"I noticed you spent quite a lot of time removing the coats of the lotus seeds," he says. "Any reason you didn't get the ones that have already been skinned?"

"Those would definitely be easier," I reply. "But not better, since the lotus seeds would've lost their flavor. Removing the seed coats on the spot ensures the paste will retain its freshness and fragrance."

Lawrence nods approvingly. "That's a great technique."

I stir-fry the lotus seed puree with gula melaka syrup in the wok. When the paste thickens enough to be easily scraped from the sides, I put it into the blast chiller to speed-cool. Theo brings back the truffle core, which has set firm but not too dense. He scoops the spheres with a melon baller, and I coat them in another layer of white chocolate.

"Are we going to make the mooncake skin now?" Theo asks.

"Yeah. We'll need the cooked glutinous rice flour, wheat starch, sugar, and shortening."

I measure out the ingredients and mix them with ice-cold water. Theo steeps Por Por's butterfly pea flowers in a glass. I add the brilliant azure tea until the dough turns just the right shade of blue, making sure it stays bouncy and smooth like Aunt Jade instructed. Then I divide the dough into smaller lumps, which we roll into flattened discs.

The truffles have set well, but the lotus seed paste hasn't cooled as much as I hoped. There's no time to wait, though. We have to put everything together. The truffle core goes in the center, surrounded by a generous layer of lotus seed paste. I show Theo how to wrap the edges of the dough together to seal the filling before pressing the balls into the flour-dusted wooden molds.

At the stroke of six, when we have to put down our utensils, by some miracle, we have twenty mooncakes. Theo and I look at each other, matching smudges of flour and smiles of satisfaction on our faces.

Now for the moment of reckoning. I choose the least well-shaped mooncake, saving the nicest ones for the contest. As I cut it with a knife, I'm afraid the whole thing will disintegrate—but it doesn't.

Theo pops a slice into his mouth.

"How is it?" I ask.

He chews thoroughly. "I've eaten mooncakes before, but none tasted like this."

"What does that mean?"

Theo breaks into a grin. "It's freaking amazing."

I bite into the mooncake. He's right. The paste is smooth and velvety, and the gula melaka adds a delicious, smoky flavor. And the snow skin is so soft and silky it just melts in my mouth.

Mr. Wu tells us to bring the mooncakes outside, and we carefully arrange them in the tiers of Mom's tingkat container.

When we're done, Theo turns to me.

"I'm sorry my dad accused you of those terrible things," he says. "I gave him back the check. He knows you don't want his money. I also told him that if he doesn't stay the hell away from you and your aunt, the next breaking news story will be about how he tried to bribe a teenager and destroy a hardworking woman's business with his lies."

"I'm sorry too," I tell him. "For pushing you away that night. You wanted to help, but I didn't give you a chance. I wasn't thinking straight."

"You were just trying to protect your family," Theo replies. "And I wanted to help you do that. I asked your aunt not to tell you I was flying to Singapore to get the gula melaka in case I wasn't able to get back in time. I didn't want you to be disappointed."

"Disappointed?" I take his hands in mine. "You missed school, jumped on a plane, and flew halfway around the planet. Even if you came back empty-handed . . . what you did means the world to me."

A blush colors Theo's cheeks. He dips a hand into his pocket and pulls out the bracelet with the glass vial. He hesitates. "I have something that belongs to you."

I hold out my hand. He loops the bracelet around my wrist and secures the clasp.

"And I've got something of yours," I tell him. I reach into my backpack and take out his white baseball cap.

A flicker crosses Theo's eyes. "You brought it with you?"

I put the cap on my head before I peck him on the lips. "For good luck."

Chapter 32

By the time we step out of the studio, people are milling beneath the large tents in the spacious plaza, buying food and souvenirs from vendor booths. The trees are strung with fairy lights, and electric lanterns hang from wooden sticks tied to the lampposts. Mid-Autumn Festival events in the United States are usually held during the day, even though Mom and Aunt Jade told us that, back in Singapore, Chinatown comes alive for the celebrations only after the sun goes down. Lawrence probably would've done the same growing up in Malaysia—which may be the reason he decided to have evening festivities here in New York City.

A large video wall on the stage is playing behind-the-scenes reels of the contestants making mooncakes in the studio. Our mooncakes are exhibited on tables draped in red cloth. I write the description on an index card: *ONCE IN A BLUE MOONCAKE— butterfly pea flower snow skin with lotus seed paste and a white chocolate truffle core.*

We mingle with the other contestants and admire their mooncakes. Valerie and her grandma display their five-nut baked mooncakes in an old-fashioned bamboo box surrounded by a purple clay teapot and four ceramic teacups. Another pair—a high school junior who works at a pastry shop in Queens and his older cousin, who's a first-year student at the Culinary Institute of America—made yuzu-lychee-martini snow-skin mooncakes presented in a red faux leather box decorated with whiskey glasses. I didn't bring any props, but our mooncakes hold their own in Mom's elegant tingkat container.

"I'm starving." Terri appears and pulls us toward the vendor booths. "Let's grab a bite."

Vendors are selling traditional Mid-Autumn Festival foods: Peking duck, taro cakes, pumpkin, pomelos, osmanthus jelly . . . even river snails, which have been cooked in a brothy soup with lots of herbs. Theo and Terri try everything with relish.

"Seriously, this stuff's better than escargot," Terri says, slurping the soup. She glances over my shoulder and waves. "Hey, your aunt and cousins are here! And they brought your dog!"

Clover's trotting beside Tim, her tongue hanging out. None of them seem the least bit surprised to see Theo.

"You all knew?" I ask.

"He made me promise not to tell you," Aunt Jade replies. "You have no idea how hard it was not to let anything slip."

"I couldn't have met up with your grandparents without your aunt's help," Theo tells me.

"So, how'd the mooncakes turn out?" Megan asks.

"Fantastic!" Theo says. "You should've seen Dylan. He's a natural in the kitchen."

I smile. "I had a great sous-chef."

Mr. Wu's voice booms through the speakers, announcing that the contest judging is about to begin. We gather around the stage as he introduces the judges: himself, two popular bakery owners in Brooklyn, and of course, Lawrence Lim.

"Good evening, everyone!" Mr. Wu says. "Thank you for coming out for our most exciting mooncake contest yet. A special thanks to our celebrity guest, Lawrence Lim, for sponsoring the prize and taking time out of his busy schedule to judge these delicious treats. I'll now ask each of the contestants to come onto the stage and tell us more about the inspiration behind their creations."

I gulp. The entry form didn't say I'd have to stand up in front of a few hundred strangers and talk about my mooncake. I can't admit I'm hoping to win this to save our takeout. Aunt Jade's on the verge of losing her business and our home, and I'm not going to embarrass her in front of everyone.

Valerie goes first. She eloquently explains how her grandma taught her that the five nuts in her baked mooncake—peanuts, walnuts, sesame seeds, melon seeds, and almonds—represent the five virtues of ancient Chinese philosophy—benevolence, righteousness, propriety, wisdom, and fidelity.

I try not to freak out as the next two contestants are called. Maybe I can hide in the restroom until they've passed over my turn.

"And next we have Dylan Tang!" Mr. Wu says.

Damn, too late. Terri hoots, and Theo squeezes my hand in encouragement. My legs are a little wobbly as I climb onto the stage. Mr. Wu passes a mic to me.

"Dylan, tell us more about your blue snow-skin mooncake," Lawrence says. "What gives it the unique blue tint? And what made you decide to swap out the traditional duck egg yolk for a white chocolate truffle?"

"The blue is natural coloring from flowers of the butterfly pea plant." I hesitate before answering the second question. The cameras are rolling, and I don't want to get too maudlin. "Last year, my mom wanted us to join this contest together . . . but we never got the chance. My mom loved white chocolate, so I kept the traditional lotus seed paste filling but substituted a white chocolate truffle core. Reconstructing my grandma's lost mooncake recipe was one of the last things my mom wanted, and I came here to do that."

"What a meaningful tribute." Lawrence gestures to the camera crew, and a close-up of the mooncake with 念 appears on the video wall. "For those who don't read Chinese, this character is niàn—it means 'remembrance.'"

The crowd nods and claps.

"You also had an unexpected delivery of ingredients all the way from Singapore," Lawrence continues. "Can you tell us the story behind that?"

"Sure. My grandma's recipe called for gula melaka—a kind of palm sugar from Malaysia that isn't available here," I say. "Although we tried our best to find alternatives, it wasn't the same. But someone went . . . well, the extra ten thousand miles for me."

Lawrence smiles. "Must be someone special."

I look shyly at Theo. "Yes, he is."

The audience lets out an *aww*.

"I also couldn't have done this without my aunt Jade," I add, pointing to her in the crowd. She waves excitedly. "She works six days a week at our takeout, Wok Warriors—but no matter how busy she was, she still took the time to make mooncakes with me."

"So, what did you learn from this experience?" Lawrence asks.

I consider how to respond. Even though our lives are in chaos right now, we're all here, celebrating the Mid-Autumn Festival together. Nothing seems to be going our way, but we still have one another.

"Unlike other cakes, mooncakes were made during a time of turmoil," I say. "That's how this week has been for us. I was on the verge of dropping out of this contest. Then I remembered that the rebels in ancient China were in the middle of a revolution—making mooncakes probably wasn't high on their priority list, either. But they still found a way to turn the situation to their advantage. The mooncakes brought allies together and inspired people to rise up and fight for their loved ones. And that's how a war was won."

I find my family in the crowd. Tim waves, Megan gives me two thumbs-up, and Aunt Jade beams.

"I guess I learned that when everything seems impossible," I finish, "sometimes the best thing you can do is keep calm and make mooncakes."

The audience applauds as I step off the stage.

After all the contestants have taken their turns, the judges sample the mooncakes, jot down notes, and spend a few minutes deliberating before Lawrence moves forward, holding the mic.

"What we enjoyed most about these mooncakes isn't just how delicious they are, but the stories behind each one—the struggles, the setbacks, the solidarity," he says. "This same spirit brought people together and made mooncakes such a beloved part of the Mid-Autumn celebrations. We had a hard time choosing a winner and a runner-up. Now, please join me in congratulating our finalists—Valerie Leung and Dylan Tang!"

I'm stunned to hear my name. Did I actually make it to the top two?

"These two young chefs stood out for different but equally important reasons," Lawrence continues. "The five-nut baked mooncake is rich both in taste and the values it represents. This dessert tells the story of a seasoned baker passing down to her granddaughter, not just a recipe, but also a tradition. And the snow-skin mooncake truly lives up to its name—snowy soft on the outside, sweet and smooth on the inside. The flavor of gula melaka is so authentic that I feel like I'm back in my own Por Por's kitchen." He pauses. "And the winner is . . ."

Anticipation hums through me. Theo's hand closes around mine.

"ONCE IN A BLUE MOONCAKE!" Lawrence announces. "Let's put our hands together for Dylan and his sous-chef, Theo!"

Applause thunders in my ears, but I'm too overwhelmed to move.

Megan elbows me in the ribs. "Go on, get up there!"

Together, Theo and I make our way onto the stage. Lawrence congratulates us and presents me with a trophy.

"I have a question for the sous-chef," Lawrence says to Theo. "You went to great lengths to get ingredients from Dylan's grandparents. How do you feel about helping him win the contest?"

"I feel really lucky," Theo replies. "I was born here, but my mom was from Hong Kong. I never had an opportunity to reconnect with my family's Asian heritage . . . until I met Dylan." He looks at me. "Making mooncakes to remember your mom, letting me be a part of it—you gave me a chance to honor mine too."

I choke up a little.

"Anything else you want to say to him?" Lawrence asks.

Theo turns to me. His smile lights up the entire night.

"The first time I walked into your aunt's takeout, I knew I

wanted to be with you," he says. "You make me happy, Dylan. More than you know. I just hope I can do the same for you."

The audience *oohs*. My heart feels like a xiao long bao stuffed with too much filling.

I step forward, and the last thing I glimpse is the surprise in Theo's eyes as I press my lips to his. I almost can't believe this is real. Our impossibly different worlds have come together in the best way possible, and everything feels magical.

When we pull apart, everyone is clapping. Megan and Terri are jumping up and down, unable to contain their glee.

Mr. Wu invites everyone to try the mooncakes, which have been cut into small wedges so more people can sample them. Paper plates and wooden cocktail forks are on hand.

As we step off the stage, Aunt Jade is the first to reach us, pulling me into a crushing hug.

"I'm so proud of you, sweetie!" She embraces Theo. "And you—that was the craziest, most romantic thing ever."

Megan and Tim hug us. "That was epic!"

"Those mooncakes are freaking amazing," Terri says.

"Thanks for getting Dylan to the studio," Theo tells her. "I owe you one, chipmunk."

Terri waves him off. "Nah, let's call it even. I know you hate Monopoly."

"Congratulations, Dylan," Bernard says. "Your Por Por would be incredibly proud. In fact, I have a message from her for you."

He holds out his phone and plays a video. Theo appears on-screen, rubbing his eyes as he walks out of Changi Airport in Singapore. I grin. He's cute even when jetlagged.

Bernard, who's filming, speaks off-camera. "How are you feeling, Theo?"

"Tired but wired," Theo says. "I'm meeting Dylan's grandparents for the first time, and I'm kind of nervous because who knows what they'll think of me."

The video cuts to my grandparents' backyard. Theo doesn't know Bernard is filming him as he crouches in front of the butterfly pea plant with a pair of scissors in his hand.

"Auntie, I feel really bad about cutting up your plant," he calls out to Por Por. "How many flowers is enough?"

"Take as many as you need!" Por Por replies.

In the next scene, Por Por and Gong Gong's smiling faces fill the screen.

"Would you like to say a few words to your grandson to cheer him on?" Bernard asks.

"Por Por is so touched that you would go through all this effort to make my mooncakes," Por Por says. "Though I can't remember my recipe, in my heart I just know you will get it right."

"Gong Gong loves you very much and supports you all the way," Gong Gong adds. "Your mummy would've been so happy for you."

Tears spring to my eyes.

Por Por leans closer with a conspiratorial smile. "Gong Gong used to tell your mummy and Auntie Jade, 'Find a guy who would fly to the moon and back for you.' " She glances at Theo, who's in the garden snipping flowers, and giggles. "This is close enough."

Gong Gong looks at her. "I never told the girls that."

Por Por frowns. "Yes, you did!" Her expression softens. "I also wrote down in my diary how you cycled two hours from one end of the island to the other twice a week to see me."

Gong Gong chuckles. "My mother kept asking why I couldn't date a neighbor instead."

I laugh, wiping my eyes. The look of joy and love on my grandparents' faces is priceless.

Theo turns to Bernard. "While we were making mooncakes, you were busy putting together this video?"

Bernard nods. "I had strict orders from his Por Por to give him a surprise."

Aunt Jade raises a brow. "Hang on, you're the one who filmed my parents?"

Bernard beams. "You must be Dylan's aunt. Wit and charm clearly runs in your family."

She crosses her arms. "Didn't you just try to break up the boys a few days ago?"

Bernard appears contrite. "I hope you'll forgive my unfortunate lapse in judgment."

Before Aunt Jade can respond, a dry male voice cuts in. "Well, I hate to interrupt this delightful get-together . . . but I'd like a word with my son."

Chapter 33

Malcolm Somers is wearing a tailored suit, no tie. Aunt Jade and Megan glower at him. My stomach balls up with nerves. The temperature around us suddenly seems to have plummeted to below zero.

"Dad?" Theo's tone is tight. "What are you doing here?"

Malcolm's eyes lock with mine. "I had to see for myself what you would fly halfway across the world and back for on my dime."

"Who," Theo cuts in firmly, taking my hand in his. "*Who* I would fly halfway across the world and back for. And anything you have to say to me, you can say in front of Dylan."

Malcolm gazes around, taking in the festive atmosphere. Chinese instruments play cheerful music through the speakers, lanterns sway in the wind, and chatter and laughter from people lining up at the vendor booths fill the crisp night air.

Bernard offers Malcolm a paper plate with a slice of mooncake. "Perhaps you'd like to try Dylan's winning mooncake?"

Everyone is silent. Malcolm regards the mooncake with a critical eye before he stabs the slice with the wooden fork and takes a bite. He chews, and in this moment, he seems . . . more human than he's ever been.

"I know you think I'm not good enough for your son," I blurt out.

Malcolm turns to me, as do the others.

I take the plunge. "My family doesn't have much—we can only give Theo a fraction of the life he already has. But more than anything, I want him to be happy. To be part of a family. And if you can't find a spot for him in yours . . . there's always a place waiting for him in mine."

Malcolm arches a brow. I stand my ground. Theo's eyes are wide.

Malcolm turns to him. "You're sure this is what—who—you really want?"

"Since when do you care?" Theo whispers.

"Speak up, son."

This is the part where Malcolm cuts him off. Disowns him. I want to tell Theo not to provoke his dad any further . . . but this isn't my fight. All I can do is stand by his side.

Theo takes a deep breath.

"After Mom died, I felt as if I lost both of you." His voice emerges steadier and clearer than I expect. "I know now that you never wanted kids of your own . . . but back then, I was just a five-year-old who missed his mom and wondered why his dad was never home. I went to the wedding because I wanted you to know what being left alone by your own family feels like. If you have a problem with that, take it up with me. Leave Dylan and his family out of this—because the only thing they've done is make me feel more at home than you ever have."

Malcolm studies him with an intensity that would make anyone else squirm. "Do you remember who took you to buy your first violin?"

Theo's expression falters a little. "You did."

"Your mother took you to violin lessons, and she would film you practicing and send me the videos while I was away on business trips." Malcolm glances at Bernard. "After that, Bernard continued to do the same. Like any father, I wanted you to follow in my footsteps—go to law school, become a successful businessman, and one day prove yourself worthy of taking the reins of my companies." He shakes his head. "But I knew, even before you did, that I was going to be disappointed."

There's a long pause. I brace myself for the worst.

Malcolm continues speaking. "I'm told Julliard has a highly selective academic honors program for exceptional undergrads. Less than ten are chosen each year."

Theo can't hide his disbelief. "Are you serious?"

Malcolm extends his hand. "You'll apply this semester, and I expect to hear your name on that list."

Theo still looks stunned as he shakes hands with his dad. I'm pretty sure Malcolm hasn't hugged his son in the last decade, and he clearly has no plans to break that streak tonight. But at least the war between them is finally over. It ended with a truce, but somehow, it feels more like a victory.

"Happy belated birthday, son," Malcolm says.

As he walks off, I turn to Theo. "Hang on, when was your birthday?"

"Yesterday," Theo replies. "But I didn't exactly get one this year. I lost a day when I flew from New York to Singapore—when I got back, it was the day after."

"I'm sorry you missed your eighteenth birthday because of me," I tell him.

"It was worth it." A kaleidoscope of emotions wheels in Theo's eyes. "What you told my dad just now . . . you didn't give me a fraction of what I have, Dylan." His voice cracks a little. "You gave me a whole missing piece."

He kisses me. This time it's soft and sweet, and the touch of his lips lingers on mine even after he pulls back.

I gaze at the indulgent smiles on the faces around us: Terri, Bernard, Aunt Jade, Megan, and Tim. I'm still gripping the trophy in my hand—it's made of gold-plated plastic but feels heavier, like I'm carrying the weight of my family's hopes and dreams. Joining the contest and re-creating Por Por's secret recipe was one of Mom's last wishes—and winning a spot on *Off the Eaten Path* could give us the publicity we need to save Wok Warriors.

And we did it. *We* won.

Clover trots over to Theo and tugs at the cuff of his jeans. He reaches down and pets her affectionately. "You came all the way here to support your person?"

Clover raises her head and barks.

"She says she'll share me now," I tell him.

Theo drops to a knee in front of Clover. "Thanks, buddy. I promise to take care of him as well as you have." She wags her tail and licks his face. "I saw a stall selling dog treats shaped like mooncakes. Want to go over and check it out?"

Clover barks and pulls on her leash. As Theo and Tim allow Clover to lead them toward the vendor with the dog treats, Aunt Jade comes to my side. Even though I'm taller, she puts an arm around my shoulders.

"Your mom would've been so proud of you," she says.

I kiss her cheek. "You reminded me that I needed to believe every story could have a different ending."

She squeezes my arm. "And you reminded me the most important thing we have isn't money or a business—it's one another."

We watch Theo and Tim talking and laughing as they buy treats for Clover.

"You know," Aunt Jade says. "Your mom would've really liked Theo."

Happiness blooms inside my chest. "I think so too."

When Theo and Tim return, Clover has a dog treat mooncake in her mouth. Aunt Jade tells Bernard the yuzu-lychee-martini mooncake she's sampling needs way more gin. Terri and Megan bring us paper cups filled with oolong and pu'er tea.

"Mid-Autumn is a time for family." Aunt Jade raises her cup of tea. "For reunion."

We all toast to that.

As Mr. Wu comes over to congratulate us again, Megan asks, "Could you take a photo of us all together?"

Terri and Megan give him their phones, and we huddle close. I pick up Clover so she can be in the frame, and Theo puts his arm around me.

"Beautiful!" Mr. Wu tells us. "Say mooncakes!"

"MOONCAKES!" we chorus as the flash goes off.

As the girls take their phones back, Mr. Wu holds out an envelope. "A gentleman wanted me to give this to you on his behalf."

From one entrepreneur to another, reads the handwritten note on the front. *Congratulations.*

I take out the cashier's check in my name. My heart thuds. It's the same one Malcolm gave me outside the takeout, which I returned to Theo. From the expression on Theo's face, he recognizes it too.

I realize this is Malcolm's way of giving me something I never expected: his acceptance. He wants me to have this money—not as charity or a payoff, but as something I can accept with my head held high. And most of all, with Theo by my side.

Aunt Jade, Megan, and Tim gasp when they see the amount on the check.

"We can use this for repairs at the takeout," I tell her.

Theo speaks. "Actually, I have a better idea."

· · ·

We pile into two cars. Megan and Tim ride with Terri, and Bernard insists Aunt Jade come with us in his Audi. He opens the front passenger door for her with a bow.

"No worries, Bernard, I'll get the door myself." Theo smirks as we climb into the back seat with Clover.

We drive to Sunset Park. Theo directs Bernard to stop a few blocks from Eighth Avenue. Terri's BMW pulls up behind us, and she, Megan, and Tim get out. The seven of us gather on the sidewalk.

"What are we doing here?" Megan asks.

"The first time Dylan and I went out, he showed me this place." Theo gestures at a darkened two-story shop house with a For Rent sign. "He said it was the perfect location for Aunt Jade's dream restaurant. Bernard contacted the real estate agent, and she let us borrow the key to take a look around."

A jolt goes through me. Suddenly, everything falls into place.

I turn to Aunt Jade. "Instead of fixing up the takeout, why

don't we rent this new place instead? We can use the money to cover the deposit—"

"We could film the *Off the Eaten Path* episode here so people will know where to find us!" Megan adds.

Aunt Jade blinks. "Hang on, we're going to be on Lawrence Lim's show?"

I exchange grins with Megan. "Yeah, that's the mooncake contest prize—the winner gets to pick a food spot to feature on one of the episodes. We didn't say anything before because we didn't want to get your hopes up."

Aunt Jade still appears apprehensive. "A place like this would cost a lot of money. And I'm not sure our landlord will let us leave without paying for repairs after the flood damage—"

"Actually, if I may," Bernard interrupts with an apologetic wave. "I spoke to the agent about that. Your landlord's insurance will cover any structural damage from the flood. As a tenant, you'll only be responsible for your own belongings."

"We can get brand-new furniture and equipment." I can't suppress my enthusiasm. "We may even have enough to pay for renovations!"

"There's also a three-bedroom apartment on the second floor," Theo says. "With a separate private entrance as well as access through the main shop."

Tim's jaw drops. "You mean we're going to live upstairs?"

"The unit is unfurnished, so you guys can move most of your stuff over," Theo tells him. "It'll be like your old place, only a little bigger."

"This is freaking awesome!" Megan exclaims, pumping a fist in the air. "When are we moving in, Mom?"

Aunt Jade shakes her head. "I can't accept this, Dylan. You should save the money for your education—"

"I know Mom asked you to care for me after she was gone," I tell her. "But you did more than that. You treated me like your own." I look at my cousins. "All of you welcomed me with open arms. You were there for me when I felt alone. Now let me do my part for this family. Please."

Tears stream down Aunt Jade's face. Her dream of having her own restaurant is finally right in front of her, transformed into brick and mortar. Bernard doesn't miss a beat, offering her a pressed handkerchief.

She laughs sheepishly as she wipes her eyes. "I'm sorry to be such a mess, crying in front of an empty building . . . but I don't know what to say."

Theo takes out a bunch of keys and hands them to Aunt Jade. "Don't say anything until you've seen the place."

Aunt Jade unlocks the front doors, and we turn on the lights and venture inside. The main dining area is bare, but the space is large enough for at least twenty tables.

"We can put tables by the windows to make the most of the natural lighting," Aunt Jade says, spinning in a circle. "And on the other side, we can have booths with overhead lantern lamps. But I don't want the décor to be too posh. I want our restaurant to be accessible, so people with different budgets can come in and have a good meal."

Theo waves at a staircase leading to the floor above. "Come on, let's continue the tour upstairs."

Clover starts exploring the apartment as soon as we open the door.

"There are three bedrooms," Aunt Jade says. "Dylan should have his own, so—"

"I call dibs," Tim and Megan say in unison. They frown at each other.

"What? Since when do eleven-year-olds get a room?"

"You'll be off to college in a couple of years!"

"Actually," I interrupt. "I'm thinking your mom should have a room to herself."

Aunt Jade chuckles. "I'm certainly old enough."

Megan huffs. "Fine. We'll just put up a divider."

Clover barks and attacks Theo's shoelaces. He glances down at her, startled. "Whoa. Is she trying to tell me something?"

Tim laughs. "You're officially part of the family too."

I nudge Theo's shoulder with mine. "Hey, sorry I didn't get you anything for your birthday."

Theo reaches for my hand, and our fingers intertwine.

"Don't worry about it," he says. "Everything I could want is right here."

Epilogue

"Jade's Kitchen, nestled in a rustic shop house off Eighth Avenue, offers authentic, mouthwatering Singaporean Chinese cuisine that holds its own in the crowded Chinatown dining scene," Lawrence Lim says, standing in the middle of our restaurant. "With affordable prices, spices that aren't watered down, and generous portions that don't skimp on ingredients, owner and head chef Jade Wong is staying faithful to the mantra every Singaporean— and Malaysian—knows: 'cheap and good.' Trust us, this diamond won't stay hidden in the rough for long. Tables are limited, so make your reservation early."

"Cut!" calls the director. "That's a wrap!"

Everyone breaks out in applause and cheers. We've spent the whole day filming our *Off the Eaten Path* episode. The customers enjoying their meals stand up, clapping.

Aunt Jade beams, her eyes glistening. Our restaurant opened a month ago, and we're already getting rave reviews on the foodie scene. We're fully booked on weekends for the rest of December, and we're even hosting our first private party on New Year's Eve.

Yesterday evening, Theo invited his dad and stepmom for

dinner. When they showed up, Aunt Jade presented Malcolm with a legal document offering him a 5 percent stake in the restaurant as a token of our appreciation. He accepted, and they shook hands.

Aunt Jade's still in charge of everything in the kitchen, and I'm her apprentice. Recipes are the lifeblood of a restaurant, and they have to be kept within the family. We hired enough staff to handle everything else: hosts, servers, bussers, kitchen assistants, and dishwashers. Chung still handles our deliveries with two of his friends on motorbikes.

I won't lie—juggling senior year, family, dating, and cooking is no joke. Theo and I haven't gone on a proper date in weeks. But he never complains, and we make the best of the time we have together. I'm determined to see this through. All of it.

"Check this out, a food blogger who had lunch here last week posted about us, and it's trending." Tim reads the review off his phone. " 'We love how Jade's Kitchen doesn't lose the charm of its modest beginnings as the small, family-run takeout formerly known as Wok Warriors. If you drop by on evenings and weekends, you'll find a motley crew of teenagers—mostly comprising Chef Jade's relatives, including one who hopes to follow in her culinary path—making rounds and offering recommendations. You'll feel less like a patron in their restaurant and more like a guest in their home.' "

I laugh. "We're a motley crew now?"

"*Jade's Crew,*" Megan says proudly. "We should put that on badges."

Lawrence congratulates us again before he leaves. As the camera crew pack their gear, Aunt Jade and Bernard grab their coats.

"Going out to celebrate?" Megan asks.

Aunt Jade nods. She's still luminous thanks to the show's makeup artist. "Don't wait up for me, kiddos. I've got my keys."

Bernard's hand rests on the small of her back as they head out the door.

Tim goes upstairs, and Megan glances at the clock. "I'm off to Terri's. We're going to have a girls' night and watch the new rom-com that's streaming."

"I'm surprised you managed to pry her away from Lewis," Theo says.

"Yeah, those two are inseparable." Megan rolls her eyes. "But Lewis asked his teen brothers to come along and support our adoption drive next weekend. Can't wait to meet those cuties . . ." She catches my raised brow. "What? I'm talking about the puppies and kittens, of course!"

Theo laughs. Mom's birthday would've been next Sunday, and he helped me put together an adoption drive in her name at the animal clinic. I can't think of a better way to celebrate the day than helping pets find their forever homes.

As Megan leaves, I turn to Theo. "Seems like everyone has plans. Want to go for a romantic walk with me?"

He grins. "I thought you'd never ask."

We grab our jackets from the coat stand, which is next to our new wall of photo frames. The picture with Mom in Singapore is beside the one Mr. Wu took at the Mid-Autumn Festival—with all seven of us, including Clover.

There's also a picture of Theo with Por Por and Gong Gong, courtesy of Bernard. Theo is a head taller than both my grand-parents, and he has an arm around each of them. Por Por holds the jar of gula melaka, while Gong Gong has the bottle of freshly cut butterfly pea flowers.

"My Por Por asks about you every time Aunt Jade or I talk to her," I tell Theo. "She has this picture of you guys on her fridge, and she wrote your name down so she won't forget."

"We should plan to visit them sometime," Theo says. "Maybe next summer, if your aunt Jade can get some time off."

I used to dread the idea of going back to Singapore without Mom. I thought the trip would make her absence starker, more painful. But I know she would be so happy to see us now.

We step outside. Moonlight slants across the illuminated sign above the doors: JADE'S KITCHEN. The menu stand is in the shape of a pile of Zen rocks. Inside, lattice screens separate the booths, and minimalist rose-gold lanterns hang from the ceiling, filling the space with a cozy glow. On each table is a small potted jade plant with woody stems and oval leaves—a symbol of good luck.

Theo points to the sky. "Hey, look. A full moon."

A light snow has started to fall, and tiny snowflakes drift down and settle on Theo's hair. I pull his hood over his head and do the same for my own.

"Yǒu yuán qiān lǐ lái xiāng huì," I tell him.

Theo smiles. "We have the destiny to meet across a thousand miles." He wraps his hands around my waist, pulling me closer. "I'm glad we found our way to each other."

I lean in and kiss him. "Me too."

Acknowledgments

Like chefs, authors are no greater than the sum of their teams. I'm honored to have worked with some of the best in the publishing industry, who've put time, effort, and most of all, their hearts into bringing this book to readers.

Bria Ragin, my amazing editor, who championed this story every step of the way. In Chinese, 志同道合 (zhì tóng dào hé) can be translated "kindred spirit"—that's what she has been for me as a debut author.

Agent extraordinaire Jess Regel, owner of Helm Literary, who's not just my literary advocate but also a cheerleader, an optimist, and an anchor. Richie Kern of Paradigm Talent Agency, who's taking this book to places in the TV/film sphere I've only dreamed of.

I'm grateful for the support I've received at Penguin Random House: in particular, from Vice President and Senior Executive Editor Wendy Loggia; Senior Vice President and Publisher Beverly Horowitz; and President and Publisher of Random House Children's Books Barbara Marcus. Many others have put in valuable work behind the scenes: artist Myriam Strasbourg and designer Casey Moses, who created the brilliant cover; interior designer Ken Crossland; assistant editor Alison Romig; copyeditors Colleen Fellingham and Carrie Andrews; proofreader Tamar Schwartz; authenticity readers Ivan Leung and Adam Mongaya; and publicist Sarah Lawrenson.

Jason June, F.T. Lukens, Brian Zepka, Alison Cochrun, Adam Sass, Brian D. Kennedy, Caleb Roehrig, and Steven Salvatore, authors

I deeply admire, who generously read my book and shared their quote-worthy praise.

Venessa Kelley, whose gorgeous commissioned art captured Dylan and Theo perfectly as I imagined them. (Check out her amazing work on my website if you haven't seen it!)

Naomi Hughes, my Pitch Wars mentor, for her guidance and friendship; Sarvenaz Tash, one of the first to see this story and encourage me to keep going; Stephanie Willing, my Pitch Wars classmate, who I trust to whip everything I write into shape. My awesome critique partners: Jackie Khalilieh, Julia Foster, Richard C. Lin, and Kate Chenli, who read my revisions more times than they had to.

My talented writer friends: Vanessa Montalban, Gigi Griffis, Waka T. Brown, Kara HL Chen, Linda Cheng, Marith Zoli, Jessica Lewis, Cas Fick, Yvette Yun, Kevin Weinert, and Aashna Avachat. You have filled this otherwise solitary journey with so much joy and camaraderie.

My #FDAMstreetteam, for your unwavering enthusiasm; I cherish every post, retweet, and story share you've made for this book.

Finally, I would not be the person I am without my family and friends. Despite often being puzzled by the intricacies of publishing, they lovingly put up with the madness of having an author in their midst.

My husband, Fred—golden retriever to my Rottweiler, Pooh to my Eeyore, Zhou Zishu to my Wen Kexing. You are truly my better half.

My parents, who always supported my dream of seeing my name on a book cover. This one's for both of you.

Yilise Lin, Yingting Mok, Sze Min Lee, and Catherine Tan, for decades of friendship and encouragement.

And to two dear friends who prefer to remain anonymous, whose names are close to my heart.

I love you all to the moon(cake) and back!

About the Author

SHER LEE writes rom-coms and fantasy novels for teens. *Fake Dates and Mooncakes* is her debut. Like the main character, she has made mooncakes with her favorite aunt and has an abiding love for local street food (including an incredible weakness for xiao long bao).

She lives in Singapore with her husband and two adorable corgis, Spade and Clover.

sherleeauthor.com

📷 🐦